Haunted . . .

Haunted, Loren thought. The man haunts me. She sat up in her bunk and turned on the console, then pulled up the entertainment files. Old stories, she liked; the oldest, ones that took place on Earth.

A planet she had never seen. A planet no one she knew had ever seen.

The Consort probably knew Earthlings among the senior Crew . . . "Stop it," she whispered, and continued searching through her files.

Of course, everything was backward, just all wrong, here in the real world. Nothing like the stories. For it to be true romance, the Consort should have offered to carry the carryall today, not sent Loren on her way with a sharp word.

And she should be a stolen child of aristocracy—a princess in disguise, or hidden, through some astonishing mix-up of fortune. Awaiting discovery of her rightful place . . . and the hand of her price.

But no. Loren was already in her rightful place, and lucky to have it. Her workshift was not onerous, her teammates were decent and engaging, and Gramma Francesca was a benevolent work gang boss. She'd heard stories, knew how it could be.

So why did she feel as though her life was being wasted, one unendurable sliver at a time?

from "If This Were A Romance . . ."
by Shannon Page and Jay Lake

Also Available from DAW Books:

A Girl's Guide to Guns and Monsters, **edited by Martin H. Greenberg and Kerrie Hughes**

Here are thirteen tales of strong women, armed with weapons they are not afraid to use, as well as fists and feet of fury, from authors such as Tanya Huff, Mickey Zucker Reichert, Jane Lindskold, Kristine Kathryn Rusch, Nina Kiriki Hoffman, P. R. Frost, and others. These are urban and paranormal stories certain to appeal to all readers of this most popular genre. So sit back and enjoy as these empowered women take on all challenges with weapons, wit, and skill—and pity the poor monsters and bad guys who'll need rescuing from them!

The Dragon and the Stars, **edited by Derwin Mak and Eric Choi**

This unique anthology of science fiction and fantasy tales includes stories by authors of Chinese ancestry, who make their homes in places as varied as the United States, Canada, Singapore, Hong Kong, and the Philippines. The eighteen talented authors included here, such as Tony Pi, Derwin Mak, Eric Choi, Brenda W. Clough, Urania Fung and Ken Liu have drawn upon China's rich and venerable heritage as well as the traditions and cultures of their current homelands to create imaginative and fascinating stories. From the tale of a murder that can only be solved by spirit possession to a fortune cookie that offers an uncertain future ... from a man who believes his wife has become a Chinese dragon to an inventive army officer in the Ming conflict with Japan ... from a young woman's fateful encounter with a Chinatown shopkeeper to a Chinese rocket scientist caught in the perils of 1950s America ...

Cthulhu's Reign, **edited by Darrell Schweitzer**

Some of the darkest hints in all of H.P. Lovecraft's Cthulhu Mythos relate to what will happen *after* the Old Ones return and take over the Earth. What happens when the Stars Are Right, the sunken city of R'lyeh rises from beneath the waves, and Cthulhu is unleashed upon the world for the last time? What happens when the other Old Ones, long since banished from our universe, break through and descend from the stars? What would the reign of Cthulhu be like, on a totally transformed planet where mankind is no longer the master? It won't be simply the end of everything. It will be a time of new horrors and of utter strangeness. It will be a time when humans with a "taint" of unearthly blood in their ancestry may come into their own. It will be a time foreseen only by authors with the kind of finely honed imaginative visions as Ian Watson, Brian Stableford, Will Murray, Gregory Frost, Richard Lupoff, and the others of *Cthulhu's Reign*.

Steampunk'd, **edited by Jean Rabe and Martin H. Greenberg**

Science fiction is the literature of what if, and steampunk takes the what if along a particular time stream. What if steam power was the prime force in the Victorian era? How would that era change, and how would it change the future? From a Franco-British race for Kentucky coal to one woman's determination to let no man come between her and her inventions ... from "machine whisperers" to a Thomas Edison experiment gone awry, here are fourteen original tales of what might have been had steam powered the world in an earlier age, from Michael A. Stackpole, Donald J., Bingle, Robert Vardeman, Paul Genesse, Jody Lynn Nye, and others.

LOVE
& Rockets

Edited by
Martin H Greenberg
and Kerrie Hughes

DAW BOOKS, INC.
DONALD A. WOLLHEIM, FOUNDER
375 Hudson Street, New York, NY 10014

ELIZABETH R. WOLLHEIM
SHEILA E. GILBERT
PUBLISHERS
http://www.dawbooks.com

First Printing, December 2010

1   2   3   4   5   6   7   8   9

DAW TRADEMARK REGISTERED
U.S. PAT. AND TM. OFF. AND FOREIGN COUNTRIES
—MARCA REGISTRADA
HECHO EN U.S.A.

PRINTED IN THE U.S.A.

ACKNOWLEDGMENTS

CONTENTS

SFR—NOT JUST SCIENCE FICTION RESEARCH ANYMORE

Lois McMaster Bujold

Romance and science fiction as literary genres have both traditionally been hard to define. One senior practitioner of the SF form finally and famously defaulted to, "Science fiction is what I mean when I point to it." Romance, the older term, has passed through multiple meanings over the centuries, many of which still linger in formal academic discourse. But if one stands in a bookstore today and points to each, one will definitely find oneself pointing in two different directions, at two different populations of books and browsers. Yet in science, it's a truism that boundary conditions are always the most interesting, and that also tends to be true of literature. And the two sets of readers turn out to not be nearly as immiscible as had formerly been thought.

I have a science-fictional definition for romance stories: they are tales of the promulgation of human evolution through sexual selection. Since a recent theory among the evolutionary biologists is that human intelligence is itself a result of sexual selection, this isn't as much of a joke as it might appear. But many romance stories stop short of the reproduction part. So what's really going on, here?

The romances I've read, as constituted in the modern genre sense, actually seem to be stories of the power negotiation in a sexual relationship, in which the woman's agenda wins. The details of the agenda vary with the tastes of the writers and readers, but almost invariably a permanent pair-bond results with a hero capable of holding up his side. (In the case of same-sex romances, a permanent bond also results, and the "holding up his or her side" likewise persists.) The story is over when the deal has been proposed, tested—the "tested" part is where the plot goes—and sealed.

Many tales that feature sexual relationships are nonetheless not romances. *Romeo and Juliet*, most famously, is not a romance, but a didactic tragedy; *nobody* wins in that one, although the survivors are invited to learn a lesson. So love 'em and leave 'em tales or other tragic romances that nonetheless end in sterility and death (with or without lessons) fall outside the modern category. Romance, like tragedy, is defined by its ending.

A lot of people have the notion that all contests must be zero-sum games; if one wins, the other must lose. A satisfactory romance is the very opposite of a zero-sum game; unless both win, both lose. I sometimes wonder if the root of the more vociferous discomfort and negative response to romance by these readers is in the mistaken notion that if the woman has won, the man must have lost.

An extremely interesting counter-fantasy to ones in which the woman wins are the men's action-adventure tales, of which the most quintessential example is probably the James Bond series. His women notably don't win anything, but lose spectacularly. A romance with Mr. Bond is very much a zero-sum game, and marriage to him will result in the woman slumped over the dashboard of her car in the Swiss Alps with a line of bullet holes stitched across her back. James doesn't exactly win either—his life remains sterile—but also free of the dread domestication and adult responsibility, a lethal Peter Pan who never grows up or old. It's a perfectly reasonable vicarious reader-fantasy, and one which I've enjoyed myself in the past, but despite the inclusion of sex, it could never be classified as a romance.

(Comparison of K-selected and r-selected reproductive strategies versus women's romance and men's adventure, I leave as an exercise for the reader.)

Science fiction (and most fantasy) also have an added task on their literary plate: world-building. The world is very nearly another protagonist; by the end of the tale, readers rightly expect to have met it, explored it, and learned what makes it tick, just as they expect to have come to know the hero or heroine. The SF reader also expects to learn what is different about the world compared to our own—including especially new technologies, and their impact in the characters' lives, not to mention the plot. The novelties introduced should *make a difference*.

This leads to one of the most interesting tensions between romance and F&SF. Since sex was first invented in the primordial ooze, leading to the explosion of evolution, it has been deeply conserved, from the cellular level right up through the organism and its society, in the case of creatures complex enough to have societies, which most definitely includes humans. It wouldn't be so durable if it weren't so defended, despite all the change it fosters. There are deep reasons why romance tends to be a conservative genre, not in a political sense, but in terms of resisting destruction.

Science fiction (its co-genre fantasy is arguable, here) is all *about* change. So to my way of thinking, the ideal SF-romance crossover story would not be to drop the same-old-pattern down in front of a futuristic backdrop that might as well be plywood for all the difference it makes, but to actually explore what striking changes new technologies or other aspects of the world could make to the entire sexual negotiation. What new patterns of relationships might result? Who wins what, and how? It shouldn't be so hard; we've seen it in our own world, worked examples with the impact of birth control and other technologies that have partially liberated women, and with them, men, from the patterns of the past.

(Babies have their own implacable impact, of course; the whole point of the pair-bonding thing in the first place is to create a place for babies to thrive, in the interest of winning the genetic lottery by becoming grandparents. But that's usually past the end of the tale.)

The two genres—and here science fiction and fantasy count as one, romance as the other—also tend to have different focal planes. For any plot to stay central, nothing else in the book can be allowed to be more important. So romance books tend to carefully control the scope of any attending plot, so as not to overshadow its central concern, that of building a relationship between the key couple, one that will stand the test of time and be, in whatever sense, fruitful. This also explains some SF's addiction to various end-of-the-world plots, for surely nothing could be more important than *that*, which conveniently allow the book to dismiss all other possible concerns—social, personal, or other.

In fact, if romances are fantasies of love, and mysteries are fantasies of justice, I would now describe much SF as fantasies of political agency. All three genres also may embody themes of personal psychological empowerment, of course, though often very different in the details, as contrasted by the way the heroines "win" in romances, the way detectives "win" in mysteries, and the way, say, young male characters "win" in adventure tales. But certainly in the majority of F&SF books, to give the characters significance in the readers' eyes means to give them political actions, with "military" read here as a sub-set of political. So the two genres—Romance and SF—would also seem to be arm-wrestling about the relative importance of the personal and the political.

The two genres may also be doing different psychological work for their readers. With its young-adult-lit roots, SF runs heavily to coming-of-age tales, where the principal work at hand is separation from the family and growth to empowerment. The former is often handily accomplished by burning down the village or blowing up the planet and massacring everyone in sight in Chapter One, which, at a certain stage of one's life, is not so much a nightmare as a dream come true. Most all readers, if not young, have at least been young, and so can relate to the pattern. Romances may also start with burning down the village, if the heroine is young enough not to have already accomplished that separation, but they just as often start with the heroine already alone. The end-game of those tales is one of integration and the recreation of family, rather than empowerment as such. (The themes of later adulthood generally run to neither empowerment nor integration, but redemption.)

Add to that a decided streak of prudishness among some SF readers, and the amazement is that any writer can get the two genres to lie down and play nicely with each other at all. Trying to fit all these tasks into a short story length is a bravura exercise indeed.

Nonetheless, the writers in this volume are attempting just that. *<sfx David Attenborough whisper...>* Let's all be very quiet, here, and see if we are lucky enough to catch a glimpse of the peculiar and unique mating dance of these disparate species ...

SECOND SHIFT

Brenda Cooper

Kami closed her eyes and replayed Lance's tender whisper. "I love you."

Three words filled her. She listened again and again, memorizing the rise and fall of his voice. Glancing at the clock, she stripped the bud off her ear and pocketed it, afraid the temptation to hear him yet another time would take the tiniest bit of glow from the night.

Being this happy was as new as a dawn, as fresh as becoming an adult three years ago. Maybe it was even as good as being born in the first place. Her bones smiled.

Stupid. She knew it was stupid, knew Lance was a lifetime away from her and that every time she came on shift to be his company, his rocket companion, he was further away.

The HR girl who hired her had told her not to do this.

She liked the rebellion in it. It was only a small rebellion anyway, since her contract was good as long as Lance approved of her and the job existed.

Besides, she hadn't *done* it. Not really. Love happened, right? The long nights sitting alone and talking, or even listening to the silence of his sleeping breath had surprised her into love, delighted her in a way she hadn't expected.

Right on time, Sulieyan opened the door and started her morning routine. She plugged in an electric pot to heat water and opened the cupboard for tea. "Do you want a cup?"

Kami shook her head, hoping she didn't look as giddy as she felt.

"No? Anything I need to know? Was the night sweet?"

She always asked that way, but this morning Kami felt her cheeks grow hot. "Sure. He's asleep now."

Sulieyan smiled at the unnecessary observation. The monitors on the walls relentlessly reported whether Lance slept or woke, exercised, ate, or worked.

Kami picked up her empty lunchbag and gave the older woman a brief hug. "Gotta go."

An hour after she got home, she pulled on her running clothes and practically danced down the metal steps outside of her apartment complex. She jogged through the bright tunnel under the maglev tracks and emerged in the park, her feet springy with her mantra for the morning "*Lance Parker* loves me. Lance Parker *loves* me. Lance Parker loves *me*."

When she couldn't take another step, she sat on the little beach by the koi pond, running sand through her fingers and making a tiny house as if she and Lance would ever live in it. The tragedy and impossibility of it all sang in her, as if she were the star in a Saturday night film.

There were other pilots—men and women—doing solo trips to the moon and back. That's how the need for rocket companions came up in the first place. All the things about the flight and safety were handled by AI's, but computers weren't companions.

None of the other solos had been famous test pilots and race-jet drivers first, and none of them was set to go as far. The prize was the rocks themselves; towing them back to the station being built above the earth could make a lot of money—if it could be done on a shoestring.

The next night, Kami told Lance she loved him back. It was the first time she'd said the words. To seal them, she told him about the park and the koi pond and the little bite of fall in the air as she ran, about the one time a single gold leaf fell in front of her.

"Tell me what the air smelled like?" he asked.

His must be stale and metallic. "It smelled like water and sunshine and insects and the sand along the water. It smelled like the maglev when it sang by, and once of a wet dog that I almost tripped over." Because she couldn't think of anything else, she said, "It smelled like the promise of talking to you again."

She hadn't thought a smile was something you could hear.

"What are you doing today?"

"The air system filters need to be cleaned and changed. Fifty sit-ups and twenty pull-ups and a long trip round the world on the elliptical. And I'm working on a secret."

"A secret?"

His secret was a poem written to her. He sent it back with his day's records. Kami blushed when she realized the techs must have seen it. She posted it on the wall in her kitchen so she could read it every morning.

All the next year, she noticed smells and sounds in as many ways as she could, speaking descriptions into her wrist-recorder. The sun warm as a sleeping dog, the tiny perfection of the yellow in the center of a magenta azalea, the paper flutter of dogwood snow against her cheek. It became a game to come to Lance every night and give him a new description at the beginning of every shift.

Kami read about Lance with morning coffee after she left him to Sulieyan when they changed shifts. Tidbits. Things he said back to scientists and journalists and rock stars who wanted to know what it was like to be the first man heading to an asteroid.

She had meant this for a short job, a dalliance with the romance of rockets.

By her twenty-fifth year—her third with him—it grew harder to find Lance in the news. But not impossible. She followed others who followed him from around the world, little audible alarms that burred against her wrist to remind her he was real and alive. She followed his conversations and the conversations others had about him. The fact that the he was not entirely a forgotten hero touched her in each nerve.

She slept and ran and did laundry and surfed the nets, and came in late every day that she spent the night before with Lance. What work to be with your beloved?

She read him stories and he wrote her poems. She told him of beads of water on lacy spring-green leaves the size of her smallest fingernail and the brilliance of sun-struck snow on far mountains.

Noticing the world for him became habit, like green tea steeped for exactly three minutes and like running in the park and chanting his name as her feet hit the ground one after the other. When the distance built in a tiny time delay, she used the seconds to contemplate her next words.

Every morning, when she and Sulieyan shared cross-shift data over tea in the neglected break room, the older woman asked her about her plans for the day.

Kami said she would run through the park and she would find something beautiful. Tea with Sulieyan made a zen transition in her day and gave her someone else to talk to besides Lance.

On one of those mornings, Sulieyan said, "There is almost no rebellion in you anymore."

"I am in love."

"Are you?"

"Of course. I think of Lance all the time."

"Can you be in love with someone you can't touch?"

"Aren't your parents in India and hasn't it been five years since you touched them?"

Sulieyan nodded, and smiled, and sipped her tea. Kami couldn't really read her face so she decided Sulieyan agreed with her.

When she took the job, Kami had been told that travel to the asteroid belt was a story of slow ships and far-away places.

One September evening after she and Lance shared a meal together (using the valuable virt screen which he bargained for with free interviews when he could get them), he told her, "I never expected to get back. It's not like a government ship or anything, or the long arm of the taxpayer. They chose me because I was willing to sign papers that said no one would sue them, ever, if anything happened. The company may stay alive for the fifteen or twenty years it will take, they may not. They could get sold or go bankrupt or a key player could die and then where will all the publicity and money go? A faster ship could get built and pass me and come home before I even get to the belt."

"Why did you go?" she whispered, although she would never have known him if he hadn't. He was famous and she was a shift-girl at a two-bit rocket company with no real fame except for Lance and this trip.

"I was lonely, so I didn't care if I came back."

She held her breath.

"And now I'm not lonely any more, but I'm no more likely to get back."

She had known he might never come back, but the knowing felt deeper after he said it to her. Running was harder, and sometimes she stopped and bent nearly in two and heaved air sour with longing to hold him.

He almost never cried or seemed sad, except sometimes she heard those things in his smiling voice, pale as the whispers of wind against her cheek in the early morning on days she wanted to hold him so much she couldn't sleep through the afternoon heat. But some nights the loneliness piled up on him, so heavy she could see his shoulders struggle to bear it and his head bend under the weight. He would only talk about it a few times a year. Although she didn't ask him why, Kami thought it was for her, so she wouldn't feel his loneliness so hard that it drove her to stop coming to him every early evening with her dinner in a brown bag and a cup of hot chai clutched in her hand, and a bit of memory from her day on her tongue.

Once, in spring, when Kami looked forward to the first ornamental cherry blossoms against a blue sky, she patted Sulieyan on the shoulder and wished her good luck with the sleepy day shift, and walked away from work. It had been a tender night and she ached with emptiness. It was not yet morning, even though spears of light from the solar collectors beamed power down onto the city, a sign of coming true-dawn.

She liked this quiet time, the pad of her footsteps soft on the soft sidewalks, the first birds rustling and warming their throats, the cool nip that would fade early this time of year. Far away from her, Lance would be settling in to sleep through day shift, his way of choosing her.

A dark shadow separated from a dark wall and came toward her.

She clutched her backpack close.

"Kami," the voice said.

"Do I know you?"

He shook his head. "No. But you could."

He was getting close enough to reach for her. She took a few steps away, keeping some space between them. She started to stretch her calves, getting ready to run if she had to, watching him closely.

He stopped. "I didn't mean to startle you."

"You did."

"Not. I mean, I didn't mean it."

She shook her head and let herself relax a little bit. "Who are you?"

"I want to interview you."

She blinked stupidly at him. Her contract didn't let her do interviews, and Lance never talked about her to others. She and Lance were each other's secret. The company knew, of course. Techs that supported the connection. Sulieyan.

She liked being invisible.

"I'm Hart. I'm also Sulieyan's grandson."

Oh. "I'm probably too old for you."

It felt like an awkward thing for her to have said, but he laughed. "No. She started young. Why else would she still be working at dead end jobs?"

As if that was a bad thing. Kami said nothing.

"Grandma got pregnant when she was nineteen and had to drop out of vet school."

She should know more about Sulieyan than her patience and her way of making tea and that she never missed a shift. But Kami could think about that later. "Why do you want to interview me?"

"Because my grandmother said it might teach us both something about love."

Now he had startled her. Her voice shook. "We can have coffee together."

In the too-bright light of Morning Blend, Hart looked far less threatening than he had as a dark silhouette in a place she expected silence from. He remained dark on dark, dark hair and dark slightly-almond eyes over dark skin. He had a broad smile, and he looked both totally earnest and as uncomfortable as she felt.

After they'd ordered coffee and scones and sat down across from each other at a window table, he didn't seem to know how to begin.

"Who do you want to interview me for?" she asked.

He looked down. "I blog at Celebrity Love."

She couldn't stop herself from wrinkling up her nose.

He saw it, he laughed, brittle. "I'm trying a small column about relationships we don't usually see. I've done two of them, and I want to do a third. Grandma told me you have the best invisible relationship in the world."

"Why do I want to be interviewed for a place frequented by teenage crushes?" She took a sip of her coffee, savored the bitterness. "Why do you write for *them*?"

He shrugged. "What else do you do with an English degree?"

"Does it pay more than teaching?"

"No."

"So why?"

"It's writing. It's what I want to do, what I love. I'll get better jobs. But for now I have to do this one well."

"Shhhh . . . don't be defensive." She imagined him sitting at home working on novels. She didn't want to do the interview, but he was looking at her so expectantly, and she hadn't done anything different in a year. Maybe two. God. More. "What do you want to ask me?"

"Is it true? Grandma says you love a man you've

never met and never held and never will see, and she says you are so loyal it's got to be true love."

She'd thought of it as a miracle. Famous Ship's Captain loves a pretty little nobody. She looked into Hart's eyes and she didn't know how to answer him. She couldn't do an interview. "It's private."

"Do you love him?"

Whatever she said, Lance could see it someday. Strange things got sent to the ship, the choices made by people she didn't know. Being asked about her feelings made them seem as if they couldn't be real. She fought dizziness by putting her palms flat on the table and taking a deep breath. "I can't, I'm sorry." She'd gotten her coffee to go, maybe out of instinct, and he had a white porcelain cup in front of him. She grabbed her cup, taking her pastry naked into her hand and said, "Look— this isn't for the world. I'm sorry. Good luck."

Ten minutes later she shut her door behind her, sank to the floor, and finished her breakfast, spilling white crumbs on her chocolate brown carpet. Lance loved her. That's what she sang when she ran. And she loved him; she loved hearing his voice every time she worked, she loved laughing with him about small things, collecting the world for him and whispering of leaves and beetles and babies.

She changed everything about her routine except where she lived. She ran in a greenbelt with a long quiet path that was nearly always empty except for a few old women from nearby apartments walking dogs.

One Tuesday at midday, she stopped by a small bronze statue of a curious deer by a stream where no real deer ever came any more. She was running her hands across the nose, registering the feel of petting bronze, noticing that even though it was cold she felt like it might move under her fingers.

"Kami."

"You again."

Hart nodded.

"I can lodge a complaint and keep you away from me."

He spoke so softly he might have been trying not to spook a real deer. "I am your friend's grandson and I won't hurt you."

He was right. She wouldn't offend Sulieyan. There were many mornings she'd asked for something special for Lance, and known she could count on Sulieyan. "I won't give you an interview."

"May I run with you?"

For an answer she started off, curious to see what he would do. The path was wide enough for two, but she ran in the middle, keeping him behind her for the first mile. He kept up well. Only then did she move to the edge of the path. When he came up she spoke to him through the heartbeat of her runner's breath. "Tell me about your love life."

His breath was sharper and shorter than hers, and she could almost feel how his legs must be hot and the sweat must be slicking his back, but she didn't slow down. Finally he managed to gasp out, "I don't . . . have one."

"When did you last have a girlfriend?"

"Pretty." Pant, heave, pant. "Personal."

"You wanted to interview me."

"Not . . . any . . . more."

She slowed down to a fast walk, letting him catch up with her.

When he could talk more normally, he said, "I dated the same girl for all of our senior year in college, and my mother and grandmother started giving her little gifts for a household like kitchen towels."

She hadn't expected him to answer. "Did you love her?"

He nodded. "But I wasn't ready to settle for just one person. I didn't want to choose then for my whole life. Not then."

He must be thirty now. "No one else?"

"Yes. I told you the beginning of my love life. That was part one. Part two was a woman I fell in love with three years ago. Emily. A nurse. I loved her order and her brains and her compassion. After we had dated for a year I saved up for a special weekend and a moondust ring, and she turned me down."

A small laugh escaped Kami's throat. "Because she wasn't ready."

They ran while the sun dappling their skin as it penetrated the leaves above them. "Do you have friends?" she asked him.

"People I work with."

She out-raced him for a bit, lost in thought, and then let him catch up to her again.

They slowed down to pass an old woman clutching a tiny designer dog with purple ears close to her. The woman made soft mothering sounds in the dog's fur, and the dog stayed quietly settled in her arms, sniffing the air as Kami and Hart walked by, but otherwise only reacting to her owner.

Once they rounded the next gentle bend, Kami stated, "So you are more alone than that woman now."

"Dogs are what old people choose when their children and lovers have all gone on and only return for Christmas."

"You sound awfully bitter."

"Grandma says I'm like an old man."

Lance was probably ten years older than Hart, and he would never come back to Earth and she would never actually meet him. But he was more hopeful than Hart, who didn't need someone else to pet a bronze deer and report back. "Do you think she's right?"

"She told me you're an example of love. That love is steady and that it lasts as long as a life."

"That woman will love her dog as long as it's alive."

"But that isn't the same," he protested.

Maybe it was better than loving and leaving. She had never really done that. She'd drifted through dates when she was young, but no one had touched her heart before Lance. And she would not leave him for this man, either. At first she'd thought that was what Sulieyan wanted her to do, but now she was sure Sulieyan must have known Kami had been drifting like an un-tethered kite. "If you would like to run with me once a week or so, and if you will never print anything I say, I will meet you on Tuesday's. That will make your grandmother happy. But you must know I love someone else. I will not fall in love with you. But I will tell you a little of what I tell Lance and I can share how it is for me."

"And how will that help me?" He looked earnest, actually curious. "Other than I will get into shape."

"You will see that commitment exists." Her throat tightened. "And you will have company, which seems as uncommon for you as it is for me."

Just like she would not betray Sulieyan, he wouldn't betray Sulieyan. The old woman's love would bind them to good behavior.

He didn't answer her, but he followed her for the last mile. He would show up the next Tuesday and she would have company, and Sulieyan would worry less about her grandson. Perhaps it would be enough to keep Kami in this world while she loved a man who had left it.

That night, Kami ate her meal with Lance. She told him, "I touched a bronze deer and it felt so real I expected it to tremble under my hand."

He smiled, patient always. If she looked forward to meals with him, he must look forward to them even more. She had the park and the trail and the old women with purple-haired dogs and he had metal and electronics and propellant and stars. And now, maybe, she also had a friend besides Sulieyan. If she made her world bigger, she could help him keep his big enough. "I hope you make it home some day," she whispered. "You know that."

"I know that."

"I will love you until you do."

"And I you."

GATEWAY NIGHT

Nina Kiriki Hoffman

When you work as an ER nurse on a station at a skip node, where the Four Known Races touch the edges of each other's lives, and sometimes more than touch, you never know what you'll encounter on a festival night.

The first time I saw Kata Station, it was from the viewdeck of a node skipper, and it looked like a gleaming dark jewel. I was fresh off the home planet—had never skipped before—and even though I'd emped travelers a few times, I had never had the full sense surround, where I was seeing/thinking/living/feeling such a strange stretch of time. We dropped out of the node, a creamy green-streaked tunnel that lasted hours or a heartbeat, into light-pricked darkness. The nearest sun was only a little larger than the other stars. We were in a sea of darkness, and then, as we shot across no one's land toward the station, I saw the bubble on top gleam with reflected starshine. It was station night in the park, I found out later.

The Four Known Races each had their own quadrant of the station, sprawling collections of different-shaped structures, more like a scatter of seafoam than anything ordered and quartered, all topped with the park, which everyone shared. Each quadrant of parkland was landscaped like a favorite spot on one of the worlds its race came from.

As we closed on the station, I saw that one quadrant of park glowed faintly here and there, and another looked paler than the others.

Docks for skippers and in-system supply and tourist ships were at the outer edges of the station. Our skipper headed toward one of the docks in the Human Quadrant. I stayed on the viewdeck all the way to the dock, watching through the shield with five children and one indulgent grandparent. All the other passengers were seasoned travelers who couldn't be bothered to watch a station approach, but I had never seen anything more beautiful and terrifying, except the last sight of my home planet as I turned my back on it. Small minds, limited ambitions, I had thought, as its blue and white disk winked into nothing. And, I thought, home.

When we docked, I felt my heart drop. I gripped the edge of a chair as the sounds and shiver of the skipper connecting to the dock thunked through the ship. I was about to step into a new world, a place I would call home from now on. My old life and all its frustrations were behind me.

Six months later, I thought I knew my way around Kata. I had my nursing job in the Human Quadrant of the hospital, where I spent most of my waking hours. I had a tiny sleeping and storage compartment in the honeycomb of low-rent dwellings in the station's underside.

I spent my days off in the park, watching the other races and their replicated environments.

The Oerian, plant-animal hybrids, had the part of the park that lit up at night. They used small, colorful winged flyers as mobile components of their life cycle, and some phosphoresced in darkness; their glittering clouds illuminated the feathery leaves on their parent plants during station night. It always smelled delicious in the Oerian quadrant.

The paler quadrant of the park was the desert the Hallen preferred. The Hallen looked like big eight-legged lizards, only they were much more colorful than the lizards I had grown up with—no need for camouflage, I guess, and they rated each other on how colorful they were, so there was a lot of cosmetic coloring going on. All lizards on my home planet, Frillium, were poisonous, so I didn't feel relaxed around the Hallen.

The Human park had forest in some of it and a lake surrounded by tame plants in the rest. I didn't recognize any of the human plants. They were too green to suit me.

The Shurixit section had caves and crannies, sculpted rock, with a river wandering through it, the water green and smelling of copper. Forest grew on some of their cliffs, the trees bent-trunked as though they had knees and elbows, their leaves frilly and mobile.

I was very lonely.

Back home, the whole community gathered every sevennight to sing and share a potluck meal. I could sit in that circle and stare at my neighbors' faces and think, I don't like him. I don't like her, either. I remember all the times that boy called me a freak because I said aloud I'm not happy here. I wish he'd choke on his words.

I didn't really like any of them as individuals, but in aggregate, when we were singing, all our voices united in words and melody, I felt safe and at home.

I hadn't found any groups to belong to at Kata Station. The other nurses in the Human Quadrant of the hospital were guardedly friendly, when they weren't exhausted. I had met one of the Shurixit nurses, and we shared lunches at SpiceFire, a multispecies restaurant a corridor over from the hospital. Because of the explosive way Human-Shurixit chemistry interacted, we wore filters when we went where we might encounter each other. She asked me as many questions about my home planet as I asked her about hers, though I thought my answers disappointed her or upset her—it was hard to tell. Of the other three Known Races, Shurixit looked most like Humans, though the ones I met smelled strange, like heat and apples and lightning, and their faces didn't move the way ours did, or mean any of the same things.

Live Shurixit had two arms and two legs each, torsos a little longer and snakier than ours, heads and faces somewhat like ours, despite the patterned fur in multiple colors, and they were about our size. When the Shurixit died the first death, their bodies went through metamorphosis and entered another sort of life. I didn't know much about that yet, because the dead mostly stayed in the private areas of the Shurixit Quadrant. It was one of those things you weren't supposed to ask about.

That night, traffic was picking up in the ER. I took my lunch break at station midnight. I worked in the ER that served humans. Shurixit, Oeria, and Hallen all got treated in the same hospital, but in different places; our building was like the station in miniature, four quadrants with mixing along the edges. Not a lot of crossover on who treated whom; some doctors and nurses studied other races, but most found their own kind easiest to learn about and treat.

For my midnight lunch, I went to the hospital cafeteria, a big pale yellow room with a lot of small chrome tables and chairs bolted to the textured floor just in case there were gravity shifts. The walls were masked by live plants, which made the air smell better than most of the other rooms in the hospital. The servers had dark marks on their cheeks, arches flanked by dots, a glyph I didn't recognize, but there was a lot of that going around on Kata Station—graffiti in a lot of different alphabets/syllabaries, some of them only visible to people who saw in infrared.

I asked the server handing out flatbread, Tilla, what the marks meant.

"Ye gods and little sailfins, Fassi. Don't you know it's Gateway Night?"

"Enlighten me, Tilla." I had learned pretty quickly on Kata that my ideas about normal didn't match many other people's. Frillium was what other people called a single-node planet—no amenities for any race but humans, and precious little contact with anyone offplanet. Not many humans wanted to come there, and most who came didn't care to leave. They came there to get away from everything else.

Those of us born on Frillium had heard of greater pathways and other planets, and we had media access through the local node to a lot of entertainment and information the systemweb carried, but it all seemed like stories to me until I ventured out into the greater worlds.

My parents and their siblings told me to stop watching that webstuff and settle down and see how good the world was, but I didn't listen. My favorite story show when I was a child was about people who worked in a big hospital where the Four Known Races mingled. When I first came to Kata, I thought I would be living that kind of story show, but no. Still, it was different from home, and I learned how limited I had been.

Tilla told me, "Gateway Night is the consensus holiday, the only one shared by all Known Races. It celebrates us discovering each other. If you go to the Oeria quadrant tonight, they'll have free ria wine for everybody, and the Shurixit will give free bodymarks, and the Hallen give out bottles of scents favored by the other races."

"What do humans do?" I asked.

"Anybody who comes in here gets a free dessert of their choosing—guess I should have mentioned that to you—and other businesses offer other things. It's a good night to cruise the shopping strips. Everybody should have some kind of giveaway, and the clubs don't ask for a cover charge tonight, and everybody parties. If you go to the public parts of the other quadrants, it's like that, too, in their languages and cultures."

"Wah," I said. "Too bad I'm still on shift another four hours."

"Gateway Night lasts through tomorrow until station midnight," she said. She smiled. "Want a dessert?"

"Sure," I said.

Gateway Night had started at midnight, when I went for lunch. I saw the first effects after I got back to work. It started with blissed humans poisoned by too much ria wine, and that was simple to treat, if messy.

I had seen what happened to humans who took out their filters and interacted with Shurixit before, but never so many at a time, and never so extreme. One man who bore Shurixit bodymarks everywhere was lost in a haze of pleasure that had twisted him tight. He moaned without stopping, and reached for invisible things. The doctor gave him a relaxant, and a soberer that brought him out of his state, but his last sound was sadness as he straightened into a more human posture and finally drifted to sleep.

People came in with embedded Hallen scales that had to be removed. I didn't ask questions.

People came in with allergic reactions to a lot of different things, and most of these reactions I didn't recognize. Dr. Shalabi, who I was shadowing on this shift, had a lot of experience with Gateway Night, and I learned lots watching how she treated everything from dehydration to blue skin to swellings on various body parts I hadn't thought could get any bigger.

The dead Shurixit came in about half an hour before I went off shift. His skin was medium brown, like mine. He moved stiffly inside his Human overwrap, and walked as though he wasn't sure of the bounce shoes he wore.

Everybody else was busy, so I went to greet him. "I'm sorry, sir. Are you lost?" I asked, because even though dead Shurixit are hairless and sometimes their skins take on the same colors as ours, they don't look very human. This one was about my height—average for Human females, a little tall for Shurixit—and wore Human clothes, including a cap pulled low that shadowed his face, hid his ear frills, and concealed the three colored caste gems embedded in his forehead.

"I'm looking for my *thala*," he said.

"I'm sorry, sir. I don't know what that is. Could they maybe help you at the Shurixit ER?"

He touched my arm above my glove. I was wearing only the usual all-purpose nasal and mouth filters and gloves, because I hadn't expected to encounter anything that required full-body filters at work.

It was my first skin-to-skin contact with any Shurixit. Like others before me, I fell in love instantly. His eyes were an enchanting color, red with amber glints around the diamond-shaped pupils. He had a faint stippling of darker color across his nose and cheeks, I saw, as I leaned closer. I wanted to touch every streak and dot. I wanted to taste them. I wanted to offer my flesh to him to eat. I could imagine nothing finer than having him accept my gift of self.

"My *thala*," he repeated, and his voice sounded to me the way velvet felt, soft, deep, inviting a second stroke, a third. "That is my sister soul, *nalla*. I scent she has come in here."

"I am sorry, exalted one," I said, feeling my regret like a sour taste all through me. I so wished I could help him; I wanted to do anything that would make him happy. His pain was mine. He had called me *nalla*, underling, one of the few Shurixit words I knew, and that hurt me. I loved him, and I didn't want him to think of me in that way, but I had to accept it, because he was perfect. "I haven't seen a sister soul," I said. "I don't even know what one looks like."

"Useless *nalla*." He stalked past me. I couldn't help following, all my desires tied up in wishing he would touch or notice me again. I wanted to give him everything I owned.

One of the security bots emerged from its niche and said, "Apologies, honored sir, but you must not come in here."

The Shurixit brushed past it. When Shurixit die the first death, they lose all their hair and some of their body processes; they do not need to breathe with lungs except to speak or smell things, and they turn stony and strong and lose their silken mobility. The first dead usually follow treaty procedure and stay away from humans unless muffled in filters. We all depend on the treaties to save us from each other. The first dead are so strong it's hard to make them do anything they don't want to. But the hospital security bots can handle a lot of strength and force.

"Sir," said the bot, and three more emerged from nearby niches. They surrounded him. "Respectfully, we ask—"

His beautiful eyes gazed left and right, and he turned in a slow circle. He looked at me again, and his stance shifted from akimbo to upright. His triangular nostrils flared, and his chest shifted with breath. I saw the reverse chemistry hit him—slower from Human to Shurixit than the other direction, but inevitable. He had touched me, skin to skin, and some transfer had taken place, and now, he knew me.

He wanted me.

"Fassi," said Dr. Shalabi from behind me.

It was hard for me to shift my gaze away from the Shurixit, but I looked toward Dr. Shalabi.

"He touched you?" she said. "Or you touched him?"

"He touched me," I said.

She grasped my arm and pressed an infuser against it, thumbed the plunger. I felt the cold as the antivenom moved into my veins. A moment later, the unnatural love I felt for the Shruixit turned to nausea. I went to the supply wall, tapped for a vomit bag, and used it.

The Shurixit, with his surround of security bots, came toward me. Now I could look at him clearly, my eyes unclouded by love. It was as close to a Shurixit first dead as I had been, aside from his first touch. I wasn't in love with his features anymore, but he was interesting. His pupils were wide now, making the red, gold-flecked irises almost vanish into the circle of black surrounding them. The mobile lips that could elongate into a short tube or compact into plump, pleated bands that resembled human lips were a warm color that still invited touch, they looked so soft. His intense regard made heat rise in my face.

I turned away and slid my used vomit bag into the recycle slot.

"Give me you," said the Shurixit.

"Sir, excuse us," said the first security bot, "but you do not belong here, and in fact, you have violated several treaty provisions already. Excuse us, we mean you no harm, but we must escort you out." They hustled him away. He beat on their carapaces and tried to snap their mesh-skinned arms, but they were strong enough to stand up to him. He was hissing in Shurixit as the door shut behind him, and he stared back at me through the pressure glass. His cap had fallen off in the scuffle; one of the bots carried it. His head was smooth and brown, and his caste jewels were half-green, half-purple. I hadn't learned enough about caste jewels to know what that meant. My Shurixit nurse friend only had one caste jewel. It was red.

"You okay?" Dr. Shalabi asked me.

"Better," I said. I shuddered and pulled my pale blue nurse uniform jacket closer, as though I could warm myself with it, though I didn't really feel cold.

"Sorry about the Shurixit trauma, Fassi. It happens to most of us sooner or later. Get over it. We have a lot of work to do." The doctor gestured toward the treatment beds, which hosted more people who had figured out ways to mess themselves up on free party favors.

The shift was ultra busy until I got off, and I was totally exhausted. I didn't even notice the extra shadow that had lodged under the collar of my nurse's jacket until I went into the fresher to shower before heading home. That was when the shadow slipped out from under my collar and twisted in the air, a pale, dark, fluttering thing that light should have been able to chase away.

"Ye gods," I muttered. I had seen many strange things already today; a random loose shadow wasn't much compared to that. Still, it was annoying. I flapped my jacket at it, trying to drive it away. People talked about station ghosts and hitchhikers, little lifeforms that had attached themselves to one or another of the Four Known Races and arrived here by stealth. Kata Station was supposed to have excellent sanitation capabilities, but bugs got in anyway. There was always some kind of life figuring out a new way to adapt.

The shadow danced in front of me, and then darted toward my face. I held up my hands to block it, but it shot between my fingers and into my mouth and nose.

The next thing I knew, Dr. Shalabi was shaking me. "What happened, Fassi?" she asked.

"Shadow," I tried to say, but what came out of my mouth were several strange clicks and the word "Kista," which I didn't know.

"I hate Gateway Night," she said. "I'm supposed to be off now. Can you get up?"

I tried to roll over and push myself to my feet. I'd lost all coordination. My arms and legs flapped and flopped, but not in any direction I told them to go.

Dr. Shalabi sighed, scanned me with her diagnostick, clicked her tongue, and left the fresher. While she was gone, I stared up at the ceiling, where gentle light glowed in spirals, and then I looked toward the mirror wall and the sideshowers. I realized 1. I could move my head and focus my eyes. 2. I was naked. 3. I had bodymarks on my left leg, glyphs I couldn't read. They made dark red shapes against the brown of my thigh. I thought back to the shift I had just worked, and all those humans who had come in with bodymarks from the Shurixit celebration of Gateway Night. Dr. Shalabi had muttered over them, translating for me. They had said, "The Grace of Gates," or "Welcome Intruders," or "Welcome Strangers," or "Meet in Fear and Wonder." None of them had looked like this one.

I tried to sit up, and this time, after a host of misfiring signals and unintended motions, my body almost obeyed me. I managed to turn over and push myself up off the polished drainfloor. I stumbled over to the fresher controls and turned on the high pressure hot. Side showers sent cleaning particles blasting me from all directions except the mirror wall side. I turned and twisted, lifted arms that more and more responded to my control, stretched my legs. I turned my feet to the blast, and my back. I worked the cleansing beads through what there was of my hair.

"Coming in," the doctor said through the doortalker.

I hit the off button. The blast of cleansing ceased. The bodymark still showed on my thigh. Maybe it took special solvents to get it off.

Dr. Shalabi came into the fresher, accompanied by Dr. Maxta, the head of Emergency Medicine. He looked me up and down from not very far away. The hospital freshers weren't meant to hold more than two people at a time.

"Gateway Night. Fah," he said. "Why can't we get through one of these damned festivals without this kind of nonsense?"

"What happened to me?" I tried to ask, but all that came out of my mouth was a jumble of words I didn't understand.

Dr. Shalabi sighed. "It's a shame, Fassi. You're a good nurse, but you're useless to us now."

I shook my hands at her.

"Oh." She closed her eyes and swayed. We had both been on shift a long time. "Yes, I suppose you don't know what happened. It's one of the Second Deaths of the Shurixit, a *thala*—looks like it laid claim to you. I knew it was trouble when that First Death Man came in here."

"Gateway Night," said Dr. Maxta. "Just an excuse for bad behavior without consequences. They'll say it's a festival accident and no one will pay. Dr. Shalabi, I leave you to it. Nurse, put some clothing on." He left, shaking his head.

I looked for the clothes I'd been wearing when I stepped into the fresher, but didn't see them. I went to the closet slot and tapped it. A pole with uniforms on it extended from the wall, and I found one my size and shrugged into it. I wondered where my hospital ID had gone.

I shook my hands at Dr. Shalabi again, and she said, "The *thala*'s put its clan mark on you. Most of the Second Death ghosts don't re-embody, but every once in a while one gets the idea it would like to walk around in a body again, and it finds one. Mostly they re-embody in Humans, because we don't have the defenses live and

First Death Shurixit have. We haven't discovered a sure way to detach them once they settle in. I'm sorry no one noticed you hadn't clocked out sooner, Fassi. If the process is interrupted, the ghost sometimes dissolves without possessing a person, but you've been in here a while now; it is probably adequately integrated."

I said, "*Kumalli nelle kisna?*"

"No, there's nothing to be done now. We have a halfway house for people this has happened to. I'll send you there and they can explain it to you."

Oh, great. She could understand what I was saying, and I couldn't. "Can someone at least teach me the language?" I tried to say, but it came out as other words.

"No, I don't think you should go to the Shurixit Quadrant," she said. "Why would you want to?"

I couldn't tell her I wasn't even talking for myself. Or could I? I headed for the nearest report screen, which was not in the fresher. It was out in the ER. I got to it and looked back. The doctor followed.

I set my hands over the word pads and typed in: *I'm not the one talking!* I glanced back at her, and she came to see.

"Oh," she said. She cocked her head and studied me. *I don't even understand what I'm saying,* I typed.

"How can that be?"

I don't know, I typed. *I need to learn Shurixit.*

"Is there no crossover of understanding between you and the *thala*?"

I closed my eyes and listened in my head for a voice not my own. I had no sense of Other there at all. I looked at Dr. Shalabi and shook my head.

"I don't know enough about this kind of invasion," Dr. Shalabi said. "I don't know if every case is like yours. Let me ask a couple questions. Who are you?"

I pointed to my chest and lifted my eyebrows. She'd been calling me by name, even though I didn't have my ID. I was pretty sure she knew who I was.

"No. No. Not you, Fassi. The *thala*," she said. "If this works the way it has already, just talk, and she will answer, no?"

I opened my mouth, and words came out.

"You don't want to cooperate?" Dr. Shalabi asked.

I made my mouth move, but this time, there was no sound. I tried to force my voice out of my mouth. My throat hurt. No words.

"I need to send you to someone who knows how to deal with this, Fassi. I'm sorry."

Words burst out of me, fast and full of strange sounds I didn't know how to make.

"Not if you won't tell me who you are and what you want," Dr. Shalabi said.

What did I say? I typed.

Dr. Shalabi clicked her tongue, the way she did when she was irritated. "I'm not used to this," she said, "you being two people. She wants you to go to the Shurixit Quadrant and contact one of the elders, the First Dead."

If it's her brother, he's probably hanging around outside, I typed.

Words poured out of my mouth.

I didn't know what she was going on and on about, but I typed, *What, you didn't see him when he came in here and touched me with the madness? He was looking for you.*

Dr. Shalabi listened to what my mouth was saying, and told me, "He's not the one she was looking for. That's the one she's running from. She wanted protection from him. That's why she embodied."

I kept talking. She cocked her head and listened, but she was sagging against the wall. I was tired myself. "That one," she said, "has kept her in a soul cage, when her greatest desire has been to *intustikiya* with—I'm sorry, Fassi. I'm too tired to make sense." She reached into a pocket of her jacket and pulled out a prescription pad. She spoke into it, then said, "Go to the pharmacy. I authorized a translator for you. I have to go flop now."

"Thank you, Doctor," I said, only it came out as, "*Kreekree, alanka.*"

"You're welcome," she said. So I guess maybe the *thala* and I meant the same thing at the same time, for once. "It was a pleasure working with you." She left out the part about "before this happened."

I headed deeper into the hospital to the pharmacy, only I was stopped at the first door. I didn't have my ID. I couldn't explain it. The thala tried to tell them something, but it didn't get us any farther. I tried to ask myself what I had done with my clothes, where I had my ID pinned, but my other self wouldn't give me words.

I went back to the report screen and typed. I knew from before that my rider could read and understand the Standard I had learned before I came to Kata Station. *Clothes,* I typed. *ID. Where are they?*

I answered my own question in a language I couldn't understand.

Can you speak Standard? I typed.

"Ohnno," she said.

Can you say Dr. Maxta? I typed. Dr. Maxta at least knew what had happened to me, and might still be on shift.

"*Alanka Maxta,*" I said aloud.

"Say it louder. Ask—" I looked behind me and saw Mbanji Holari, a nurse who, I thought, liked me all right. "Ask that man for Dr. Maxta." I went to Mbanji and tugged on his sleeve.

"What is it, Fassi? You look terrible," he said.

"*Alanka Maxta,*" I said.

He frowned. He said something in Shurixit, and I answered him. I rolled my eyes, impatient with my own problems. Mbanji and my rider had a protracted conversation.

"That's all right," he said. "I can take you to the pharmacy." He reached for my hand. Without even thinking, I jerked it away.

"What's the matter?" he said.

I said something, and he laughed.

"No, Itana, that is Human-Human touch, and it is permitted. However, we can go without it." He turned and led me through the various security barriers into the bowels of the hospital and to the pharmacy, where he and the pharmacist had a conversation that sometimes included my rider, and I finally got my translator and installed it in my left ear.

"Know you me now?" I said aloud, or she said it

aloud in Shruixit, and it finally made some kind of sense to me. I had to think to figure out what my rider meant.

"Kind of," I tried to say, but she had total control of the mouth and throat.

"You okay now, Fassi?" said Mbanji.

I shook my head. If I wanted to talk to my rider or anyone else, I needed something with type pads. Or sign language.

"We go," said my rider. I found myself walking toward the exit. No, I thought. She's the rider. I'm not. She doesn't get to walk us around. I thought myself into the muscles of my legs. I tried to tighten them and stop us moving forward. It took me longer than I liked to halt us and topple us over.

"Don't do that," she said. She flopped around a bit, and managed to put a hand to our cheek. We'd come down face first. I tasted blood.

If you're going to take the body, give me back my mouth, I thought, but couldn't say.

I sat up, and she let me do it without interference. I went to the report screen. *You have to tell me what you want and why,* I typed.

She talked.

Gateway Night was still going strong when we took to the corridors. I heard laughter, singing, and music played on instruments I had never heard before. We passed tipsy groups that included Human and Hallen, Oeria (at least their flyers) and Shurixit, and various animals people had brought to the station as pets. I heard drinking songs I'd never heard before, with very bawdy lyrics—my translator worked on everyone's speech. So I finally realized the Hallen I passed every day on my escape from the hive to the upper regions were propositioning me and telling me how good I smelled. I also realized they said it to all the females of any species, even if they had female characteristics themselves, and they never reached for me.

My rider helped me not flinch when the Hallen approached. She rattled off compliments to them and wished that their eggs would be many-colored. They frilled their topscales and said I had learned manners since the day before.

We had crossed half the Human territory toward Shurixit when the First Dead man who had entered the ER earlier caught up with us.

"Itana. Itana. What have you done?" he wailed, and reached for us.

"Stop, Shringil!" We had donned the regular filters, plus a body sheath just for him, before we left the hospital. He grasped my arm above my gloves and I did not feel it. "I was never yours, and I am not yours now. Stop pursuing me."

"It is not you alone I want but your undead match," he said. He pawed at my arm, as if to break through the sheath of filter I wore.

"Stop," she cried, and then she called out in high Shurixit, and three strange Shurixit broke off their conversations with others nearby and came running. Each had only one caste jewel on his or her forehead, and their fur matched the color of their jewels: lilac, lavender, poppy, colors of flowers from a planet to which I had never been.

"I here denounce and abjure this one who was once my brother," my rider said, "and cast him into the third death. Witness it for me. Hear me and see me and swear me."

"We hear and see and swear," they said, and some strange current of air moved over us, so cold it raised goosebumps on my arms. I couldn't think how weather like that could happen in the corridors, which were maintained at a constant temperature just this side of comfortable for all Known Races. "Shringil Eftsolan, you have passed the third gate," they said, and he shrieked and fell to the ground and lay still.

I couldn't tell whether a First Dead had actually died again. It wasn't something they taught in med school, at least not the one I'd gone to on Frillium. I looked at the still form on the corridor floor and was only glad that his eyes were closed. I remembered the hopeless, overwhelming love he had forced on me with touch, and almost, I longed for that to happen again. In those few moments, I had had a purpose. I had had a home.

Itana spat on him, using my lips and my saliva. She stepped over him and walked on. I made us look. He did not move behind us.

We strode past the revelers, and she accepted a few sips of *ria* wine from some, a savor of scents from others, a cupcake here and a candystick there. She walked us into the center of the Shurixit Quadrant. Light came in nets and slices from above, fretted by narrow sword-shaped leaves of purple plants. A dank metallic taste rode the air. Slim rivers ran down the centers of their corridors, and cropfruit grew from niches in the walls, dangling orange and purple globes above the ground. She reached for one and raised it to my mouth. I managed to stop the gesture before it reached its end. I held out my other hand in front of us and shook it.

"Oh! I am sorry, Body," she said. "I forgot." She set the fruit on a nearby ledge.

Several Shurixit challenged us as we traveled. The rider spoke to them, and they looked to the ground and waved us on.

At last we came to an entrance in a rough, rocky wall that had a single blue gem above it. Itana stood in front of the entrance and sang.

> *Lost.*
> *We have lost.*
> *We are lost.*
> *We were reft.*
> *Cut like thread.*
> *Sliced in two.*
> *Death moved between us.*
> *Splice the rope.*
> *Reweave the thread.*
> *Bind the wound.*
> *Find me.*
> *Find me.*
> *Find.*

Several gray-striped Shurixit drifted from the entrance and listened as Itana sang. They looked at each other and then at me. One with two blue caste jewels in his forehead came to me and knelt. "Oh, my beloved, are you there? Are you there?" he sang, with a melody that echoed her song.

"Oh my beloved, I am here, I am here."

"Can we now be as one, be as one?"

"Be as one," she sang. She put my hand under his chin and tilted his face up. His eyes were pale green beneath the blue of his jewels.

"Will you be with me? Will you accept me?" she sang, and he responded, "It is my dream. I will be with you."

She knelt, too, and brought my face toward his. I tried to pull back. Skin to skin, Human to Shurixit, I'd already tried that once and look where it got me! But she didn't stop. She pressed my forehead against the stranger's.

His caste jewels burned with more than color. They pulsed and pierced into my forehead just while I was thinking, *Hey, I don't love this guy, even though he touched my unprotected skin.*

"Ow!" I cried, and then, "Oh!" A wind blew through my brain, picked up my rider, and carried her away.

I woke cradled in soft, furry grass, cupped in a depression in some rock inside a cave in the Shurixit Quadrant. "Hello?" I said.

My mouth. It worked again. I could speak my own language. I touched my cheeks, then pressed my forehead, where I felt a small hard bump.

"Hello." A male Shurixit came to stand over me. "How do you feel?"

I tapped the ear with the translator. I couldn't tell

whether he was speaking Standard or Shurixit. I guessed it didn't matter. "Better," I said, for the second time that day.

I sat up and looked around. The rock that held me had several depressions cushioned with grass in it, and the cavern we were in opened up, with a higher ceiling, just past the edge of it. A clear pool of water lay to one side of the cavern, and a pit with a fire ring sat in the other. The ceiling was sooted with smoke. It was hard to remember I was still on Kata Station.

I looked at the stranger and realized I knew him. He was the one my rider had sung to, only now he had a third caste jewel in his forehead, half green and half purple. I poked my forehead again and wished I had a mirror. I suspected the bump in my skin that itched so much was one of those jewels.

"Itana is gone, isn't she?" I asked.

"I am here now," he said, and patted his stomach, or where a stomach would be if he were a human.

"Good," I said. "I'm going home. You don't need me anymore, do you?" I checked the timeblock on the back of my hand. It was almost station midnight, and still the same day. Gateway Night.

"I'll show you the way," he said.

"Thank you."

We walked without touching through a maze of rocky corridors. "Memorize this pathway," he told me as we went. "You will always be welcome here."

"No offense, but I'm not sure I want to come back," I said.

"I know you," he said, and then he hugged me, stroked

his hand over my head. Still, I didn't fall into hopeless love with him. I kind of liked him, though. "You might never come back," he murmured, "but know you can."

"Okay," I said.

We came to the edge of the Shurixit Quadrant, and he stood in the corridor, watching as I headed toward the entrance to downunder, where my compartment was. He watched me until the corridor turned and we no longer had a line of sight.

Sleeping people lined the corridor, some wearing wreaths of butterflies, some entwined with others, some muttering to themselves. I ducked down into my compartment and studied my image in the mirror there. Sure enough, I had a blue-green jewel in my forehead now. I guessed I could scratch it out or remove it surgically. But I liked it.

THE WOMEN WHO ATE STONE SQUID

Jay Lake

I studied the virteo screen. The lander's sensors jibed with what we'd probed from orbit these last weeks. Partial pressure of O_2 a hair below 1.3 bars—perfectly breathable and not quite concentrated enough to induce oxygen toxicity. CO_2 just about absent, with about 79% inert gases. At least that last bit was Earth-normal, though the nitrogen component was slightly reduced in favor of helium, wherever *that* was coming from, and some NO_2. The air was maybe not so good for human tissue over extended exposures, with humidity like an old bone stored in high orbit. This planet's seabeds were as dry as Joan Carter's Mars, but local conditions had held stable since I'd grounded, oh, fourteen hours ago.

Carter was on my mind a lot. The rest of the crew-monkeys back up there in orbit had always said I was crazy, reading stuff from the Years Before. Even my sweetie, Dr. Sheldon, thought it was a bit much. But when we got here—Malick's World—even though I was a mere enlisted-grade localspace pilot, I was the only woman on the ship who had the least idea about alien ruins.

Everything I knew about lost civilizations I learned from Edgra Rice Burroughs, but that was still far more than the rest of my shipmates.

The comm squawked. I had it routed to the boards instead of my mastoid implant for the feel of the thing, like one of those old time astronauts—Hanna Reitsch or Laika the Sovcomm. "You all checked out yet, Ari?"

It was Captain Pellas, of course. On board the *Correct Thought Makes Correct Deed* her word was most literally law. As it should be. But procedure said that the commander of a vessel exploring an unsecured environment had final authority over her ship and crew, as officer on scene. Detached command, it was called. Well, though I didn't hold a commission in this sailor's navy—just a rating, me—I was commander and the entire crew of the *Sixth Virtue*, *Correct Thought*'s number two lander. And the only thing in space that trumped a captain's word-of-law was procedure.

Which meant that until I made orbit again my course of action was my own decision. What a strange feeling, in this woman's navy.

"Yes ma'am," I said. Obedience was an old habit, that and the fact she was my ride home. "All checked out, Captain."

"Then I suggest you get on with it."

"Yes ma'am."

Pellas had budgeted three ship-days to assess the first indisputable evidence of nonhuman intelligence ever encountered. I'd already used up most of one descending and doing environmental assays on my immediate surroundings. Time to step outside and play Joan Carter. "Maintaining comm silence during my first recondo, ma'am."

"We'll track you."

With three-centimeter software-adjusted optical resolution on *Correct Thought*'s main sensor suite, they certainly would track me. Combining that with my suit sensors, Pellas would know if I farted when I bent over.

I'd had the choice on descent of landing in the old seabed west of the developed shoreline, or atop the big pavers of the plaza that extended behind the docks into the middle of the city. There was no way to trust the stones of the plaza to take the lander's eighty-odd tons of mass, even accounting for the slightly sub-Terran gravity and the soft-load plates engineering had refitted on footpads to reduce ground pressure. On the other hand, the seabed was no more reliable . . . what showed up on sensors as solid ground could easily be a heavy clay crust over a slurry or a dust bowl.

I chose the plaza. For one, it captured my imagination. Even better, touching down in the city proper spared me the two-kilometer hike from the nearest sufficiently large and level bit of seabed, along with a three hundred-meter climb.

Now I was stepping out to a place where feet—perhaps—had once stepped that belonged to no human being at all.

First, I sealed my helmet and toggled the mike and

the cams. Then I locked *Sixth Virtue*'s boards to *Correct Thought*'s nav-comm signal in case I didn't make it back to the lander, recoded the hatch access password in case someone else made it back instead of me, and slapped the open key.

A line of shadow slipped by me with the raising of the hatch, and the light of a new world flooded my face.

Orange. Maybe orange-maroon. Appropriate, somehow.

Still framed by the thick coaming of the hatch, I looked across the plaza. My breath caught hard in my throat. A *new* world.

New, but older than time itself.

Late afternoon flooded the scene with that oddly-colored light, shadows falling at lazy angles. I could see an enormous building almost directly in front of me. Too-tall pillars rose from a curved row of bases to support a high roofed portico. The front facing of the portico was carved with a dense frieze of figures, crowding in their dozens along each meter. Wide, shallow steps swept from porch to plaza, while the building extended wings to each side. Instead of windows, there were sort of vertical slits, almost the inverse of the pillars, every few meters in the facing. Large buildings of varying but similar architecture loomed to each side.

We'd mapped this from orbit. I knew to the meter how wide this plaza was. But seeing it . . .

I stepped lightly down *Sixth Virtue*'s three-rung ladder. Set my foot on time itself. For some reason, I wished for a cutlass like Joan's.

"I can hear you breathing." It was the Captain, her voice nasty in my ears.

So much for comm silence. Lot of nerves up there in orbit. It was nice to know someone cared.

"Yes, ma'am." I smiled inside my helmet. "The Barsoomian banths ain't got me yet."

"Keep to the mission profile, Ari."

"Yes, ma'am."

Mission profile said enter one of the buildings without breaching existing barriers. In other words, an open door or window, nothing that could be shut behind me. Look around for portable artifacts, preferably something representing technology or information storage or, ideally, both. Then capture as many images as I reasonably could in a short amount of time, and back out to the lander.

1.3 bars of O_2. I could breathe here.

I pushed the traitor thought aside and concentrated on walking. Malick's World tugged at me with .91 standard gs. It was just enough to give me a sense of floating with each stride and make me have to watch my step. This was a nickel-iron rockball of a planet amazingly like Earth except for the absent hydrosphere. And how long had those oceans been gone, I wondered? After all, this world boasted the intact ruins of a seaport and a still-breathable atmosphere—even without oceans or jungles to maintain the oxygen cycle.

What did one do with a few trillion tons of missing seawater, anyway?

I was a little over two hundred meters from my initial target, the pillared building due north of the lander. As I approached, I looked up at the carvings once more. They were hard to see, dense, complex, fractal even, with enough curves and bends to make my eyes ache, and shadows rendered bloody in the orange-maroon light. The carvings showed something a lot like people fighting something a lot like squid. A giant pelagic wrestling match.

No, I corrected myself, death match. There were plenty of dismemberings, spearings-through-the-groin (or cephalopodian mantle), berserk necrophagic frenzies and whatnot portrayed up there.

It seemed a curious choice for public art.

I slowed my pace and panned my helmet cam back and forth across the frieze. Even if these buildings had been formed by some bizarre geological process—one theory which had made the rounds in force back on *Correct Thought*—geological process didn't spontaneously carve woman-eating squid. Squid-eating women?

Still, astonishing. My heart raced. This was how a species had seen itself, how it had thought about itself. Myth? Legend? History? Oh, Mother Burroughs, if only you were here now to see the Mars of your dreams.

At that thought, a crackle erupted in my helmet: "Why aren't you moving?"

I realized I *had* stopped. It was the sheer, boggling wonder of it all.

"It's a new world, Captain. These carvings are proof of it."

"What carvings?"

Oops.

"Check my cam feed, ma'am." I couldn't take my eyes off them. She couldn't even see them. Not good, that.

"I see a lot of rock, Ari."

"No ... ah ... squid?"

"No. I suggest you return to the lander now."

"Ah ..." I considered that one, quickly. I didn't *feel* delusional. But would I if I was? I was still breathing suit air, so there weren't environmental pathogens tweaking me. Could it be a virteo resolution problem or something? "Ma'am, I'm just going up on that porch to look through the doors."

"Get back to the lander."

"In a minute, Captain."

"Petty Officer Russdottir ... that's an order."

"Detached command, ma'am." I started walking again.

"It is my judgment that you are at risk of becoming unfit for command."

Eyes on the stone squid, I giggled. "Then Doctor Sheldon can examine me to certify that fact at her next convenience." Not that I minded being examined by Doctor Sheldon. As often as possible. I giggled some more. "As per procedures, ma'am."

The silence which followed told me how much trouble I'd be in once I returned to orbit, but ... would I ever have this kind of opportunity again? Not a chance, not by the Great Mother's shorts. High command would either seal this discovery over or flood it with doctoral nerds from high-credit universities like New Tübingen and Oxford-at-Secundus. Little old industrial-zone girls like me were never coming back here, except maybe as taxi drivers and cooks.

I didn't want to think about that any more, so I turned off my helmet audio. And hey, I was at the steps!

My helmet crackled back to life. Override from orbit. What the hell happened to my detached command, anyway?

It was Sheldon. "Ari," she said. "Sweetie. Please. I know you can hear me. Stop walking and think."

Up the steps. Too low, too long, maybe ten cents a riser but two meters on the tread. Somebody had wanted people to enter this building in an unsettled state of mind. Either that or they had really weird feet.

Tentacles.

No . . . I let that thought bleed from my head like oxygen from a jammed valve.

"Ari, dear. Listen. Something's going wrong. I don't want to lose you like this." Her breath caught. "Captain is putting together a rescue team, but you don't want to endanger your friends, do you?"

"Bullshit," I sang. Sheldon might be my lover, but she was commissioned and I wasn't. Her lies were always for the good of the ship. The whole reason for sending *me* in the number *two* lander was because we were both disposable. Gunny Heloise's expensive string of muscle-girls weren't going to do a combat drop to fish me out of the arms of some fucking stone squid.

Had I said all that aloud?

"Ari, please, you're leaving camera range . . ."

"Good!" I took a deep breath and popped my helmet free. There was a slight sucking noise as it came loose. I turned and hurled it back out into the plaza, where it bounced a little too slowly, with an odd ringing echo. Air density and composition a little off, I thought. Sound waves didn't propagate quite right.

Time to breathe the air of this world. *Joan Carter, I am here.* I released my breath, drew in a new one and let the smells and scents of another civilization flood into me on a river of oxygen.

Mostly it tasted like a granite plaza at night, though, oddly, there was an after-rain tang to the air.

Hand on the hilt of my cutlass, I stepped into the shadows looking for traces of the women who ate stone squid.

Inside was tall, horribly tall. The walls and ceiling were proportioned wrong. It was as if the same architect who'd designed those too-shallow steps had been turned on her plans sideways and stretched the building upward. That same damp granite smell tickled my nose, like must newly released from a long-forgotten freight canister.

Age and rot, even in this dry place.

My boots clicked against the worn flagstones as I walked on, accompanied only by echoes.

Pillars rose around me, covered with the same frantic, disturbing carvings that had decorated the portico outside. I walked toward one, touched the pillar with the point of my cutlass. It rang like honest stone, but when I tried to brush that bit of carving with my gloved hand, somehow it wasn't exactly where I had thought it should be.

"Not quite dead, are you?" I shouted.

They . . . whoever they were . . . had looked like me. Human enough for me to care. Like Joan with her Red Woman lovers on old Barsoom. The . . . squid . . . were everywhere. Detailed. Frightening. Real. Had it been the squid that drank the oceans dry?

Had it been the squid who built this city?

That thought scared me into walking again. This place must have been built by humans. *Must* have.

I bent to adjust my greaves, and my thoat-leather fighting harness. Nothing fit me quite right today. Like the very air itself, everything was subtly wrong. And where the hell were the monsters? At least these were squid, not something so seemingly human as the rykor-riding kaldanes that had taken Joan's daughter from her.

The injustice of the world boiled within me as I stalked between a pair of the overtall pillars, cutlass trembling in my hand. Something, someone, had consumed the women of this world, sisters to me at least as much as the Red Women had been sisters to Joan Carter. They had been drunk dry, to desiccate along with their oceans.

Then I found one of my world-sisters, of the stone squid-eating women, curled in a corner. She'd died here long ago. Her body was a husk wrapped in robes crumbling from dry rot. I could not tell what race she had been, she was so decayed, but I preferred to believe her a Red Woman rather than one of the degenerate Therns or First Born.

She had died here to warn me of the stone squid.

I heard a squawk: "Ari."

I whirled, cutlass ready, wishing I had my radium pistol. Had I left it behind on my airship? Some enemy must be clouding my mind. I was never this slow of thought.

"Sweetie, can you hear me?" It was a woman's voice, weak and quavering as women will be when confronted

with the sharp end. I circled again, but could not find
her. Magic, then, or some ancient machine sparked to
life in this temple.

She went on: "We've overridden your implant.
Sixth Virtue's relay is homed in on your carrier. Ari . . .
please . . . I know you're alive. You've got to come out of
that building, right now. Please, sweetie."

"No tears, woman," I shouted. Something was wrong
with my voice! It was high and thin, with a reedy qua-
ver. I had indeed been somehow ensorcelled. I knelt to
search my dead sister for help, parting her robes with a
muttered apology.

So much hair on that poor dead one's chest, I thought.
She must have struggled with an overactive testosterone
level. And her breasts . . . gone. Cancer?

Her?

What would a woman be doing here? He.

He?

Where had that word come from?

"Ari! Captain Pellas is authorizing a retrieval drop.
Listen carefully. Can you get a signal out to us?"

I ignored her.

Then his robes fell completely open. His clitoris, dry
as the rest of him, had grotesquely hypertrophied in life.
Inches long, perhaps. And his breasts . . . the poor dear
must have had a radical. Common enough in space.

Space?

His clit?

My free hand strayed to the lower skirt of my fighting
harness. Checking.

"Sweetie. They're launching immediately. Be down in

twenty-five minutes or so. Please, if you can hear me, sit tight."

I had an awful moment, my chest seizing cold and tight as my hand groped air between my thighs. Where was my ... my ...

Him? What the hell was a *him*? What the hell was I thinking? Animals were bedeviled with y-chromosome carriers. Humans, blessed by evolution and intelligence, had moved beyond that particular genetic disorder. *Everybody* knew it. There hadn't been a natural born male human since the days of Herad the Great—she'd put the last of the poor, damned mutants mercifully to death back the first of the Years Before.

"I'm ... I'm in some kind of trouble," I said aloud.

"We're coming, dear. Fast as we can."

A door opened before me. A four-armed warrior in battle harness loomed, cock swinging between his legs like an animal's. Then he was struck down from behind. A beautiful woman, of the Red race—a true princess of Helium, I realized—peered inward, bloody sword gripped firm. "Come," she called extending her free hand, "quickly."

"Hold on, sweetheart," the bodiless voice said within my ear.

I looked down at the corpse. Who could bear to live in a world of such horrible defectives, mutant in body, mind, and metabolism?

Throat harnesses jingled behind the princess. A cold wind chattered. All I had to do was step forward, into every world I'd ever dreamed of. Except for the ... *men*.

"Come."

"Stay with us."

The voice of dream called me on, the voice of love bade me stay. The voice of reason screamed somewhere deep inside me. Eyes clouding with tears, I hurled my cutlass at the princess. Somehow both startled and sorrowful, she withdrew, leaving me alone with an ancient male corpse. I huddled next to my dead sister—for even with a cock and a beard, she was still my sister—and waited for my rescue to arrive.

Far too soon, something slithered wet and huge upon the stone floor behind me, but I had already given away my weapons and returned bare-handed to the world my mothers had made. Instead I took the dead woman's hand and waited to see who would find me first.

WANTED

Anita Ensal

Evie hadn't figured on the comets. Until them, her plan had been working perfectly. Well, maybe not perfectly, but certainly she'd made a clean escape and had a chance of success.

But the shuttle wasn't reinforced like a miner's ship, wasn't nimble like a planet-runner, and wasn't equipped with a protective shield like the galaxy-class cruiser it had come from. It was supposed to go from the cruiser to a moon or space station. It hadn't been made for the asteroid belt and it certainly hadn't been made for comet showers.

The proof of this was that the shuttle was now damaged past any sort of repair Evie could hope to make. She was lucky she still had breathable air, but the water reclamation unit was damaged, she had little food, and she'd had to turn the grav-generator off.

She wasn't sure where she was, the shuttle's navigation system, like everything else about it, being rather too simple to tell her. But she was pretty positive she was many days' flight away from Asteroid Station C at full throttle, not to mention the Belt's orbit moved her farther away from Checkpoint Charley every minute. She was weeks away from Pallas Station, and a lifetime away from Ceres.

Not that she wanted to go to any of them. What she wanted to do was get away. Well, she'd done that really well.

She set the distress signal to maximum range and waited, staring at the millions of stars of which she had an unparalleled view. She'd never felt so alone in her life.

Days later, loneliness was the least of her worries. It was going to be a race to see whether she died of thirst or from freezing. The distress signal was still going, but almost nothing else on the shuttle was.

She'd managed to struggle into a spacesuit, but she wasn't sure she could attach the helmet properly. Besides, she wasn't sure what good it would do anyway. It wasn't like the oxygen tank in the suit would last her long enough to get anywhere, and there was nowhere to go. Just a lot of empty space and a million beautiful, cold, unhelpful stars.

She wanted to cry, but didn't want to dehydrate herself even more. So she counted the stars. It didn't help at all, but it did pass the time.

Evie was on star two-hundred-and-three when the radio crackled. "Distressed spacer, do you copy?" It was a man's voice, human, not robotic.

She sat there for a moment, disbelieving. Then she

lunged for the communicator. She managed to get the two-way working. "Yes." Her voice shook. "Yes, I copy."

"What's your status?" The man sounded calm and in control which was comforting.

"I got caught in a comet shower. My ship took a lot of hits. I can't get the engines to fire, I'm running on reserve generators, and . . . my water reclamation's shot."

"How long ago?"

"A week. I think."

"How many on board?"

"Just me. That's why I'm still alive."

There was a pause. "What happened to the ship you were on?"

"What do you mean?" Evie looked out and saw what she was pretty sure was an older mining ship. It didn't have either A-Class or Galaxy Mining markings, meaning it was probably an independent. Which might be good for her. Unless the miners on board were so happy to see a woman that freezing to death would seem like her better choice.

"You're in a shuttle, and one not capable of long-range flight. You couldn't have gotten here from Mars or any of the Lunars and certainly not from Earth."

Then again, maybe this was an ancient Galactic Police vessel. He was certainly asking law-like questions. "Could you interrogate me once you get me? I haven't had anything to eat or drink for several days and it's cold."

There was another pause. Evie got the impression whoever she was talking to was talking to someone else. "We're going to hook your ship." *We*. The someone else was confirmed. "Do you have a spacesuit?"

"Yes."

"Do you know how to seal it properly?"

"I . . . think so."

"Not something to take a chance with. What's your name?"

"Evie," she said slowly. He didn't react. "Who are you? Galactic Police?"

"No. I'm a miner. I'm Cal."

"Oh. Are they coming, the police?"

"No. Not unless they got your signal, which I doubt. We're a long way from any space station, let alone one of the giant rocks."

"Ah, okay then." Evie heaved a quiet sigh of relief. No police was good. And only the old-time miners called Ceres, Pallas, and the others 'giant rocks'. So he was probably a geezer, so unlikely to be interested in raping her as payment for rescue. "Can you talk me through getting the suit on right, Cal?"

"Are your airlocks working?"

"I think so."

"Then wait there, have your suit and anything you need to take with you ready. I'm going to hook your ship, then come help you get suited up."

"Thank you." She hoped she sounded grateful. Because she was.

The ship sent cables across but a robot did the hooking. Evie hadn't seen a model like this one in active service—the conglomerates wouldn't use something this old due to repair costs.

It was an adaptable model. When it left the mining ship it looked humanoid, but it turned crab-like to scramble down the cables and run all over the outside of her shuttle. She waved to it when it looked in at her. It waved an appendage back.

She expected the robot to come get her, but it went back up to the ship and a spacesuit-clad figure exited shortly after. She assumed this was Cal. He crawled across carefully. She lost sight of him once he was on the shuttle.

A new voice came over the communicator. "Hello, Miss Evie." It was definitely robotic. "I'm Mule. Cal is at your airlock. Can you activate it, please?"

"Yes." She pulled the lever and shortly heard the clomping of magnetic shoes.

Evie stood and turned around. There was someone in a spacesuit, all right. He had his helmet on, so it was hard to see what he looked like, but he was tall—she only came to the middle of his chest.

"Are you Cal?" He nodded. Helmet or no, she saw he was gaping. "What is it?" she asked nervously.

"You're beautiful!" He shook his head and blushed bright red. "And a baby."

"I'm twenty-five. But, thanks for the compliment, I think."

"Sorry about my outburst." He sounded embarrassed. "You aren't what I expected."

"Clearly. I appreciate your coming." Her voice shook and so did she. She tried to control it.

"Let's get your helmet on," Cal said gently. He sounded back under control.

"I have my things packed." Evie pointed to the suitcase and lockbox she'd tied together and hooked to the captain's chair. Unfortunately, she caught her foot against the box and lost her balance. He caught her as she gasped and stumbled.

"Gotcha," he said as he righted her. "There's food and water on my ship. We'll get your things over there with us, don't worry."

It was a good thing he'd come, because she could barely manage to get the helmet on with her hands in the suit and she had no idea how to lock it. "How do you do this all the time?" she asked as he took it from her and got it situated.

"You get used to it." He glanced at her belongings. "You work for A-Class Mining?"

Evie cursed in her head. The lockbox had the A-Class logo on it. "Not exactly."

"Huh." He didn't say anything else about it, but she had the feeling his suspicions were raised. Cal found some rope and tied it around his waist, then around hers. He hooked her belongings to the rope around her waist, turned the distress signal off, and then led her through the ship. He put his helmet against hers. "Is there anything else you need that's on board?"

"No."

"Then follow me, don't fight me, and don't untie the rope connecting us."

"No worries there."

They reached the airlock and, once the outer hatch was opened, he felt around for what turned out to be his lifeline. He hooked it on, never letting go of her hand. He pulled them out and crawled them along the ship to the main cable. She did what he did. They reached the cable and he put her hand on it, indicating she should climb across first.

She nodded and started across. Cal stayed right behind her; there was just enough play in the rope connecting them that they didn't pull on each other.

Finally they were in the belly of his ship and Cal closed the doors. Evie felt the pressure come back as the inner door opened and Cal helped her through it.

She was alive and presumably safe. The tears she'd held back all this time cascaded down her cheeks.

Cal unlocked her helmet and took it off, then did the same with his. They were both still in their spacesuits, but he put his arms around her. "It's okay. You're safe now."

She didn't stop crying, but put her arms around him. Cal patted her back while she sobbed. "I thought I was going to die," she said finally.

"I know. But you're not." He let her go. "Let's get out of these suits and get you some food and water."

She nodded. "That sounds like a brilliant plan."

It turned out that Cal and Mule were the entire crew of the *Gold Rush*. Mule made her a light but filling meal while Cal monitored her water intake. He didn't let her eat or drink too much too fast, so she didn't get sick.

She'd been wrong about Cal's age. He was using old equipment, but he wasn't old himself. She figured he was about thirty-five. He was also ruggedly handsome, with longish dark brown hair and bright, dark blue eyes. He was as tall as she'd thought in the shuttle, and he was broad and well-muscled, too.

He wasn't like most of the miners she'd met, and not just because of his looks. They were usually crude and uneducated—asteroid mining wasn't considered the best career in the solar system. But Cal didn't speak like most miners and he also seemed gentlemanly and old-fashioned.

"Do you need anything more to eat or drink?" he asked. "And are you still cold?"

He'd put her into a sweater of his which was like a short dress on her, and wrapped her in a blanket as well. Between these, the food, and drink, Evie felt almost normal. She shook her head. "I feel better than I have in a long time."

"Good. Now," he said gently, "tell me what you're doing out here."

"I got lost."

Cal sighed. "Don't lie to me, please."

"I'm not. I was trying to get away and I thought I could hide in the Belt."

He nodded. "What did you do?"

"Nothing illegal."

Cal snorted. "Right. Look, tell me this—did you kill anyone?"

She felt shocked. "No. Do I look like a murderer?"

"No. You look like a beautiful young woman." He said this without blushing, which was sort of a disappointment. "But beautiful young women don't appear in short-range shuttles in the middle of the Belt by accident."

"Well, it surely wasn't by design."

He chuckled. "Fine. Hurt anyone?"

She rolled her eyes. "Call it a victimless crime, since you're so sure I'm a criminal." She didn't know whether to be angry, flattered, or relieved. She settled for annoyed.

He shrugged. "Fine. I'll take your word on it." She didn't believe he was going to let it go forever, just for now. "Let's get you settled."

"Settled where?" Evie prepared herself for the "what you need to do to thank me for rescuing me" explanation. At least he was handsome.

"In your cabin." He led her to a hallway with a series of doors and opened one. Evie looked around. Her suitcase and lockbox were in here, but the room didn't look lived in. "Where do you sleep?"

"In my cabin, which is not your cabin."

"You're not . . . expecting anything for rescuing me?"

His eyes narrowed and she got the impression she'd insulted him. "Just that you'll do your share of the work until we're back at a space station."

"We're not heading back to Ceres or Pallas?"

"I'm a miner. I need to mine. In fact, I left a claim to come get you. I have to mine that before we consider where we go next."

"Okay." So, no forced companionship. Cal really was a gentleman. This was a relief. And, in a way, a little bit of a disappointment. "I'm a fast learner. I'm sure I can help." She knew she could help, but it wasn't a good idea to let him know that.

"Good. Get unpacked. I need to determine if we drag your shuttle or leave it."

"Leave it," she said quickly. "It's not going to be worth repairing."

He gave her a long look. "How would you recommend we log it with Ceres Central?"

She knew it was a test, and she also knew he clearly thought she was a criminal. But better that than what she really was. "Log it as large debris. There's nothing worth salvaging on it."

"I had a feeling that's what you were going to suggest." Cal sighed. "I can't salvage anything from it, you're not willing to tell me the truth about what you're doing out here, and I don't feel like fighting with you or having a visit from the Galactic Police. Large debris it is."

"Good choice. Really."

"I'm sure." He shook his head. "I'll give you a tour of Goldie after you're unpacked."

"Goldie?"

"It's my nickname for the *Gold Rush*. She likes it."

"I'm sure she does." He'd given his ship a nickname. And the robot was called Mule. Space did funny things to people's minds. Space or loneliness.

Cal nodded to her and left, closing the door behind him.

Evie looked around. It was the smallest room she'd ever been expected to live in, but it was more than big enough. And she was alive and, against all the odds, on a ship where she might not be found. The plan was back to working.

It didn't take her too long to unpack. Evie shoved the lockbox under the bed, put her clothes into the dresser, her toiletries in the bathroom, and was pretty much done.

She wandered out. Goldie was what was commonly called a family-miner, meaning you could crew up to a dozen if people were bunking double. For one man and a robot, it was a lot of space.

Space Cal wasn't exactly filling up. She didn't know where he was, so she gave herself her own tour. There were seven bedrooms, which didn't skew with other ships she'd seen. She opened all the doors, but only two of the rooms seemed lived in. One was clearly the captain's quarters, and not just because it said it on the door. This was obviously where Cal spent a lot of time and had his things, such as they were.

The other bedroom appeared to be a child's, but there was no child on the ship. She considered this. Goldie was old, and so was Mule, and a lot of miners willed their ships to their children. She studied the room.

One big bed, raised high up, under a domed ceiling. The bed looked like it was slept in, which was odd, because the bed in the captain's cabin had also looked slept in. There were pictures of different ships taped to the walls, several drawings of the solar system, and lots of drawings of houses and spaceships. She was pretty sure the same person had done all the drawings.

The houses were interesting. They were clearly on the surface, not underground, and they didn't resemble Earth or Martian houses. They were asteroid houses, under domes, placed on what looked like floating rocks. Each house had a spaceship nearby with the letters 'GR' printed on it somewhere. From what she could tell, the artist wanted his own home, on his own asteroid, with his spaceship handy. She could relate to the desire.

"What are you doing in here?"

Evie spun around to see Cal standing in the doorway. He didn't look happy.

"I was . . . looking for you."

He took her elbow and moved her out of the room, shutting the door firmly behind them. "You can usually find me or Mule on the bridge, in the galley, or in the rec room."

"No idea where those are from here."

"Let's rectify that right now then." Cal's expression said he knew she was lying.

She sighed. "Brilliant plan."

The tour didn't take too long. Afterward, Cal suggested Evie get some rest. She didn't argue. She hadn't slept much for what seemed like a very long time.

She was awoken by someone gently shaking her. "We're at our claim," Cal said when her eyes opened. "I'd like you in your spacesuit, we need to go out."

"You mean you don't want to leave me alone on the ship while you and Mule are on the rock, right?"

He smiled. "You didn't strike me as stupid."

"No, I'm not. I don't suppose we can shower or take a bath?"

"Not today. Since you're here and we have a good water supply, while we're mining we can bathe twice a week. Once a week otherwise. If needed."

"Do I need it?" She could easily believe she stank.

He chuckled. "No."

Back into the spacesuit. Cal showed her how to lock her helmet alone, but he still helped her with it. He had her practice sealing his helmet, too, but he locked it again himself before they left the ship.

Evie had a lifeline, just like Cal and Mule did. The robot went first, then Cal. He turned and helped her across to the rock.

"Thanks." She looked around. "It's not very big, is it?"

"It's a kilometer in diameter and it's got good nickel readings all the way through." Cal sounded defensive.

"I'm sorry," she said quickly. "I'm not familiar with . . . independent mining."

"Huh."

He showed her how the equipment worked, and she decided she'd better shut up and pay attention. It was harder to pretend to be learning what each thing was than she'd have expected. But it wouldn't do for him to realize she was very familiar with mining, because then he might make connections she didn't want him to.

They started drilling and this was very different. Evie knew what everything was for and what it did, but she'd never used the equipment herself—it had been considered unacceptable work for her. But Cal didn't seem to share that idea. He had to help her with the drill at first, but she got better at it quickly. And it was kind of fun.

After an hour Cal felt confident enough to let her drill alone while he drilled another patch a little ways away. The plan was to cut the top crust off in sections to send through the ship's extraction system. They had to be careful not to destroy the actual nickel, which was harder than it looked. After the initial drilling, they used lasers to make the cuts.

Once the pieces were free, they manhandled them to the ship. Mule and Cal could do this alone, but Evie had trouble and lost her chunk. It floated out of her reach.

Cal tossed his chunk to Mule, then jumped off the rock. Evie gasped. He caught the floating chunk just before his lifeline played out. Mule hauled him back.

"I'm so sorry," Evie said, waiting for his reaction.

"It happens. We'll cut smaller chunks for you or I'll help you."

"You're not . . . mad?"

He looked at her. "Are you experienced with this kind of work?"

"You know I'm not."

"Did you do it on purpose?"

"Of course not!"

"Then why would I be angry with you?" Evie stared at him. "Are you all right?" he asked. "Did you get hurt?"

"No, I'm fine. Just . . . relieved, I guess." And confused, but she didn't want to tell him that.

"Let's get back to work. Lunch break's soon." He turned back to his laser. Evie's throat felt tight, but she did what he wanted . . . she went back to work, determined to do better.

Days went by. Evie got better with the equipment, more confident in the spacesuit, and more comfortable with the ship and the routine. It was a different routine from what she'd ever experienced, but in many ways it was more satisfying. There was always something to show for the effort.

They ran on Earth standard. They were up at six in the morning, ate, helped each other into their suits, then went out to work with Mule, who, when they mined, never took a rest break. Lunch break at eleven, dinner break at four, supper break at nine. Done for the day after supper.

They finally ored-out the rock and, according to Mule, ended up with a good load of nickel. Cal seemed happier than she'd seen him so far. "We did good work. You too," he said to her with a smile.

"How much will you get for it?" she asked him.

He shrugged. "Depends on the trade rate where we go to barter."

Fear hit her. "We're going into a port?"

"Sometime, yes. We'll have to restock."

"Oh." Evie fought down the panic and tried for a positive. "Did I help you finish faster?" If she was useful, maybe he wouldn't want to get rid of her so quickly.

"No. You slowed us down by at least four days."

He said it casually, and without any nasty inflection, but it hurt and she didn't know why. "Oh." She looked down. "I'm sorry."

"It's okay. You're learning. It's not a problem."

She nodded wordlessly, still looking at the floor. She'd been kind of proud of herself, but clearly it was an inaccurate assessment. She'd slowed him down, and why would he want to keep dead weight around?

"Why don't you take the first bath?" Cal said. "You'll feel better."

She went to her room and had a quiet little cry. Then bathed like he'd told her to. She tried not to feel completely alone again, but didn't manage it. She was with him, but she wasn't a part of his crew, and clearly never would be.

Weeks went by. Evie researched the ship's logs, usually when Cal wasn't aware she was doing it, so she knew a lot about him by now. His parents had been miners in this ship, they'd sent him to Titan to go to school, but he'd come back to mine and had never left the Belt since. He had no family left, just Mule and Goldie.

She was sure he liked her and that her being with him made him less lonely. But he pulled back any time it seemed like they moved toward the remotest kind of intimacy, and he never asked if she wanted to stay with him. She wished he would, even if it might mean she had to tell him the truth.

So Evie went for the next best thing, to be useful as a crew member. She was good at everything now, though the stronger machinery was a little beyond her. She could fly the ship, though Cal didn't like her to—he seemed to think she was too reckless or too slow, depending. Mule let her prepare meals and Cal even let her do some navigation and rock spotting. Though he didn't always listen to her, which drove her crazy. Like now.

"Why are you ignoring those rocks?" she asked for the tenth time.

"They're small," he replied for the tenth time. "It's a lot of work to check them and they're likely to have little to nothing that's worthwhile in them."

"You said we're using more water because of me. Even if they only have a little water, that would be a help, right?" They hadn't made port yet, which had been good in most ways. But she'd almost died once from lack of water and didn't want to do so again. "I mean, you haven't let us bathe for three weeks." She heard the panic in her own voice and clamped down on it.

Cal realized what was bothering her. "We're not going to run out of water."

"You can't be sure."

"Of course I'm sure!"

"You haven't had anyone but you on this ship for years. I looked at the logs. When your parents were alive you had triple the amount of water on board than we do right now."

"There were three people. And what were you doing going through my logs?"

"Learning. And, fine, three is more than two. But that means we should have double the water that we do."

"My reclamators work more efficiently than the ones we had when I was young. Besides, I don't know what you're worried about. You're off the ship when we make port."

It felt like he'd slapped her. Evie's throat went tight and her eyes filled with tears "Oh."

Cal looked uncomfortable. "Well, aren't you?"

She turned away. "Sure. That's what you want. I just thought . . ." She shook herself. "Never mind."

"Evie, I'm—"

"Used to being alone. I know." She held herself. It wouldn't do to cry in front of him. "It's okay. Sorry I was worried about nothing. Do whatever you want, it's your ship and everything." She walked off, hoping to get to her cabin before she lost control.

"Evie, wait—"

She ran for her cabin, closed and locked the door, then threw herself on her bed. She buried her face in the pillow and sobbed.

There was a quiet knocking on her door a while later. "It's me. Can I please come in?"

Evie got up, wiped her face, and opened the door. "Sorry."

Cal shook his head. "No. I'm sorry I hurt your feelings. I didn't mean to."

She couldn't look at him again. "It's okay."

"No, it's not. Look, I want to show you how to net."

Despite herself, Evie looked up. "Net?"

Cal looked embarrassed. "It's how we gather in a lot of small, likely useless rocks, what we call 'fish'."

"Ah. Sounds interesting." She debated saying anything else and chose not to. She could recognize a peace offering when one was handed to her.

It took a week, but they finished clearing out the cluster. Water reclamation didn't require a lot of effort on her part, so Evie spent the time searching for another rock. She found one, two kilometers in diameter and they headed there immediately. Cal felt it was iron-rich, which was good news.

"We got lots of water from that cluster," Evie remarked as Mule radioed the information to Ceres Central and logged their latest claim. "It'll give us enough so we can mine this new claim without worry, I think."

She saw Cal look at her out of the corner of his eye. She tried not to look smug. She refused to say 'I told you so', though she desperately wanted to.

He sighed. "Fine. You were right."

She grinned. "Did it hurt?"

"Did what hurt?"

"Admitting that someone else might have a good point?"

"I'm not like that."

She snorted. "Right. How many times did I have to say we should mine the cluster? A dozen?"

"Ten." He rolled his eyes. "Everything with you is dramatic."

"I'm a girl."

"True."

"And you're a man. I'm clear on the differences."

Cal blushed, which Evie found fascinating. "What does the log tell you?" He busied himself with something on the instrument panel.

"That we're okay as long as we don't decide to shower every day."

Cal laughed. "Do we have enough water for baths?"

"Yes. Easily. *Now*."

He grinned. "Ladies first."

"Saying I smell more than you?"

"Doubt that's possible."

She patted his cheek. "You smell male. It's not a bad scent."

He got a funny look on his face, but he didn't say

anything. She headed for her cabin, wondering if she should have suggested they save water by bathing together. Evie had the impression Cal would blush all over his body if she said that. It was certainly something that would be worth discovering.

Evie got dressed, then listened at Cal's door. She heard water running, so she knew he was bathing. She went to the rec room to wait for him.

She'd put on a short skirt and a tight, short-sleeved top. Her arms and legs were bare and she didn't have shoes on. No time like the present to give it a shot. From what she could tell, they'd have to make port the moment they were done mining this claim. And when they did, unless Cal's mind was changed somehow, she was going to be handed over to the authorities—and she knew what would happen to her then.

Cal came in. His hair was still wet and tousled. It made her want to run her fingers through it. He saw her and stopped dead, his mouth open. She grinned at his expression. "Sometimes a girl likes to get dressed up."

"Even when there's nowhere to go?" His voice sounded strangled.

She stood up and shrugged. "There's always somewhere if you know where to look." She held his gaze. He looked panicked and trapped. Evie sighed to herself, trying not to let her disappointment show. Despite her hopes, he wasn't interested and had no idea of how to tell her so. "If you want me to change clothes, I will."

He shook his head and took her hand. "Come with me."

Evie knew she looked surprised and he hesitated. She squeezed his hand and he relaxed a little. "Where are we going?"

"My old room. Not for any improper reason," he added hastily. "I just want to show you something."

Her lips quirked but she stopped herself from smiling or laughing. "I could take that as an improper suggestion." She sighed. "But I know you don't mean it that way, Cal. Lead on."

He took her to the room she'd seen on her first day on Goldie, the one with the domed ceiling, high bed, and all the pictures in it.

"This is where I grew up, I guess," he said when they got inside, confirming her suspicions. He crawled up the step ladder and onto his bunk. "Come on." He reached his hand down.

Evie laughed. "Brilliant plan." She took his hand and climbed up.

Cal lay back. "Lie down, and watch."

Evie lay next to him. "Big bed."

"Yeah, my parents spoiled me."

"No, they didn't," she said softly. "Believe me, I've met plenty of people who were spoiled." Far too many, really. "Some of them turn into loathsome adults. You're not like that."

He looked at her for a long moment. "Neither are you," he said finally. "Now, watch." He pressed a button and the steel plating drew back.

Evie gasped and grabbed his arm. "What's happening?"

"This was the observation deck, originally. My father

refurbished it as my bedroom because I liked it here so much. Don't worry, the glass is thick and well insulated. I check every month."

Evie couldn't help it, she still clutched his arm.

Cal put his hand over hers. "It's okay," he said gently. "I won't let anything hurt you. The plates go back quickly and there're patch kits everywhere, including right here at the head of the bed."

She took a deep breath and relaxed. They lay there, staring at the stars together. The view was amazing. Evie could see more stars this way than she ever had before.

"When I was . . . in the shuttle waiting to . . . die I looked at all the stars," she admitted finally.

"Did that make you feel better?"

"No. It's very beautiful but so . . . vast and . . . uncaring. It made me feel lost and alone."

"I don't see them that way," Cal said softly.

"I counted them, to keep from thinking about dying. Have you ever done that?"

Cal chuckled. "I used to try. It was how I'd fall asleep. Some people count sheep, I counted my stars. The most I ever got to was about two hundred. Most of the times I'd lose my place and have to start over."

My stars. He thought of them as his. "You worried about skipping some?"

"Every star is another sun, and that means it's got the potential to have someone lying there, counting our sun while they try to fall asleep. I wouldn't want to miss them, any more than I want them to miss me."

Evie turned on her side and looked at him. "It doesn't make you feel lonely?"

"No. It makes me feel . . . connected. To everyone and everything." Cal swallowed. "That's why I sleep in here at least half the time. With my stars, I'm never really alone."

Evie's throat was tight again and so was her chest. She wanted to tell him she understood loneliness and that it was worse when you were surrounded by thousands of people who didn't really know you or care about you. She wanted to tell him she didn't feel like that with him, the few times he let her in. She wanted to tell him what she was hiding from and why.

She put her hand on his cheek. She opened her mouth to try to say something, anything, that would make him want her to stay. But instead she kissed him.

She knew she'd surprised him, but Evie hadn't given it a lot of thought. She'd just finally done what she'd wanted to for a long time. And now she didn't want to talk, she wanted to keep on kissing him.

He kissed her back, gently at first, but she slid her hand into his hair and suddenly his arms were around her and he wasn't being tentative any more. Her arms tightened around him while his hands ran over her body. Evie moaned softly as Cal rolled on top of her.

He pulled away. "Are you . . . okay with this?"

She stroked his hair. "Make love to me under your stars, Cal. Please."

He smiled, bent, and kissed her. And this time he didn't pull away or hesitate.

They lay there together, hours later, still under the stars. They didn't seem remote any more; they seemed warm and comforting, like the universe was watching over them. Evie kissed Cal's chest while he stroked her arm. She'd never felt like this before, ever. It took a while to come up with the right word: contentment.

"Why don't you want to be part of a conglomerate?" she asked.

"I don't like to take orders from other people." He kissed her head. "A man's only supposed to take orders from his wife."

"Your father tell you that?"

"Yes. He meant it, too."

Evie sighed and snuggled closer. "I could stay here forever."

"You can if you want to."

She looked at his face. "Really? You're not going to leave me at the first port?"

"No, not if you don't want me to."

"Why not?"

He swallowed. "Because—"

Something caught her eye. Evie jerked and froze. "Cal? I don't think we're alone."

There was a Galactic Police cruiser hovering above them.

They had time to get dressed before the cruiser attached to them. "Give them what they want. I'm sure it's in that lockbox."

"Cal, it's not like that."

His mouth was a straight line. "I'm sure I'm about to find out exactly what it's like." His eyes flashed. "You knew they were on their way, didn't you? That's why you . . . not because you . . ." He turned away and stalked off to the airlock.

Evie wanted to cry, to run after him and explain, but it was too late. She heard voices.

Mule joined her. "I'm sorry. I should have warned you they were nearby."

"You knew?" She felt betrayed, for no good reason. She hadn't trusted them and now that was going to cause her to lose what she'd discovered she really wanted.

"I've existed much longer than Cal and I'm not swayed by beauty or loneliness, in any direction. I made logical inquiries and gathered data I didn't share with Cal."

"You brought them here?"

"No. But I gave you as long as I could. They would have found you the moment we docked at a port." He put a metal hand on her shoulder. "I understand what you're running from, and why."

"You'd be the only one, then."

Footsteps came closer and there he was, surrounded by Galactic Police—the owner of the A-Class Mining conglomerate, also known as the richest man in the Belt. He looked older, more haggard, and Evie felt guilt hit her. "I'm sorry. I had to. You wouldn't listen."

He shook his head. "We'll talk about this at home, Evelyn."

Cal looked back and forth between them and she saw realization dawn. "Your father is Howard Akers?" Evie nodded miserably. "You stole from your own father?" Cal sounded horrified.

"Stole?" Daddy bellowed at Cal. "She didn't steal

anything. It's *my* damn cruiser, so if she wrecked its shuttle, well, so what?" He glared at Evie. "Young Leonard's willing to take you back."

Evie groaned. "Can't you understand? I don't want to marry him!"

"Nothing wrong with the boy. Rich, smart, successful, reasonably good-looking. Comes from an excellent Earth family, too."

Evie lost it. It didn't matter who was here. It didn't matter what Cal heard any more. Daddy never listened to her, he probably wouldn't now. But she couldn't stop herself. "I hated Earth! I hated Mars! I hated the Lunars!"

"Nonsense. I sent you to the best schools, on the finest holidays, gave you anything you wanted. What every girl dreams of."

"You sent me away!" she sobbed. "I'm a Belt girl, I like it *here*. And no one likes us *there*. You're someone here, Daddy, but we're considered rich trash on the planets. The new nouveau riche. You think Leonard loves *me*? He loves your money and I'm a convenient way to get it, without him ever having to dirty himself by coming within a million miles of the Belt. And all the others you shoved me at were the same. No one loves me for *me*." She looked at Cal. He looked shocked and furious, more angry than she'd ever seen. "No one."

Evie turned and ran for the nearest room, which happened to be the one she and Cal had just left. She beat them there, slammed the door shut and locked it. They'd get her out soon and this time Daddy would lock her up until she was married to someone who treated her like pretty, expensive trash.

She raced up the ladder, lay back on the bed, and let the tears flow. The cruiser blocked the stars. Now that she knew how Cal thought of them, it would be worse. She'd never see *his* stars, never see him, again. She wouldn't even get to say good-bye.

It was worse to have had a glimpse of what she could have had and have it taken away. She lay there, sobbing, until she cried herself to sleep.

Something woke her up. Evie opened her eyes and stared at the sky. Something was missing, there was nothing but Cal's stars. The cruiser was gone.

She turned in time to see him climbing the ladder. "What happened?"

He lay down next to her. "They've left. You'll meet up with your father when we dock at Pallas Station. It'll give him time to calm down and think things through. He doesn't want you miserable."

"Oh. It's not typical for Daddy to lose quietly."

Cal chuckled. "I wouldn't call it quiet. But, once he was done shouting and threatening, and once Mule verified that I'd had no idea who you were, I reminded him of a certain Belt law."

"Which one?"

"The one that says as long as no crime is accused, a miner's ship and any of his claims are his sovereign property. Including all equipment, robots, relatives, and crew members living on-ship or working a claim. Meaning no one can take any of my crew without their consent or my permission."

"I'm a crew member?"

"Per the logs you've so accurately kept and the work you've put in, you're due a third share of everything we've mined since we found you. It should be enough for you to get wherever you were running to."

Her throat was tight. "I don't want to go there anymore."

Cal rolled onto his side and looked at her. "Where do you want to go?"

"Nowhere." She gulped. "Unless you're there, too."

"Not worried I want to keep you around for your money?"

She shrugged. "Won't have any. It's all in Daddy's control."

Cal grinned. "So he told me. Right after he told me that he didn't care that he could tell you were in love with me." His expression softened. "Is he right?"

Evie stroked his hair. "Well, he has known me all my life."

"What's in the lockbox? Your father checked it but wouldn't take it."

"You didn't look?" He shook his head. "My valuables. Pictures, mostly. Of him and my mother and me. From when I was young and we had a little house on Ceres."

"You want that again?"

Evie smiled. "As long as there's a place for Goldie to park there."

Cal's eyes shown, like all of his stars reflecting back at her. "Sounds like a brilliant plan."

AN OFFER YOU COULDN'T REFUSE

Sylvia Kelso with Lillian Stewart Carl

The fuse popped and the big aerial shell flew hissing up exactly two hundred feet, then burst with a satisfying *Crump!* Darryl almost felt the *Aaaahh* from the crowd behind the safety fence. A perfect Chrysanthemum, he thought, as the great globe expanded in a deluge of brilliant blue meteors. And this time I didn't just get to carry in the shell-boxes and haul the rails around. This time I was the one trusted to bed the mortar, to set and connect the shell itself.

Beside him his boss's fingers had already keyed another sequence. Three Palms flowered in the Chrysanthemum's wake, vivid magenta plumes fanning round the smoke trails that symbolized their trunks. Behind them, on the ground, white and emerald fire burst from the first of the seven Cakes. *A bit too fast,* he protested silently, as he always did. *Let them savor the last one a bit ...* But he knew his boss's eye was set on the height of pyrotechnic ambition: New Year's Eve, running the Sydney fireworks display.

Picture the Bridge, Darryl thought, its famous bow ablaze from end to end with sparkles, blazes, shooting stars, jets, and serpentines of light . . . Two rockets shot roaring through the Palm dust and burst high overhead, showering down a double wave of first red and then fierce emerald, and beyond the firing enclosure the crowd went Aaah again. Might be worth the effort, he conceded, if what you wanted from life was to make people sound like that.

Another Cake erupted in blue and crimson showers. Three Peonies followed, bursting into brilliant gold amid a shower of sparks, while a salvo of flares bloomed overhead in silent, searing white. The click of keys faded as Darryl sank with the crowd into the salvos of color and fire, the crackling, hissing crump and thump, the exhilarating stink of gunpowder that infused it all.

Then the last fusillade subsided; the exclamations stopped. The smoke began to drift away. At his side Darryl's boss said, "OK, Mr. Tomasetti. You can start disconnecting now."

"Right, Dora." Twelve months, he grumbled internally, since sugar went belly up and I had to quit the cane-farm and leave Inverside; six months since the Centerlink employment woman slotted me in here. There can't be ten years between us. And you've been "Dora" to me for weeks, but whatever I say, I'm still "Mr. Tomasetti" to you.

He moved warily out into the mortar-infested, lead-entangled, smoke-wreathed park. The distant football lights were on, but here it seemed dark as natural night. Experience identified the blot of the big firing desk. He found his pocket torch and located the main switch.

Thought I knew the Chinese, Darryl's mind ran on as his fingers yanked plugs. More clannish than the Italians, and God knows Inverside famiglie were tighter than the Mafia. But four or five generations and some Chinese're still old-style: make a good living running restaurants, sell fireworks to these round-eyes, but no fraternizing. No mixed marriages. No half-breed kids. Even if you go native enough to have a daughter with Dora for a first name and Yee for a last—or would that be the other way about?

His refractory mind's eye presented an image of his ex-wife: tall, broad, and exuberant, North Italian fair. And then of his boss: five feet four to his gangling six-one, delicately boned as a sparrow, silk-straight hair blacker than his south Italian curls, exquisite features, and the classic epicanthic fold above those almond eyes . . . Could be, he grumbled, as he traced the first rail-lead to its socket, those Chinese grandmas know what they're on about.

With the nearest Cakes disconnected and their mortars packed, he gathered up an armload and headed for the gate. The steady ebb of headlights said most of the crowd had gone, but just outside the fence the field-lights backlit one motionless shape.

"Yeah, mate?" Darryl worked the padlock, edged through, and swung the gate to at his back. "Help you with anything?"

The shape moved closer. Appeared to be·Male, by the shoulders, half a head below Darryl's height. Very well cut hair, to judge by the silhouette, and—was that actually a coat? In Ibisville, on a hot Australia Day evening in January?

"Yes, please." The voice was as quiet, polite, and precise as an ABC news anchor's, and a strange prickle went down Darryl's neck. "I wish to speak with Miss Dora Yee."

Bloke wears a coat and talks like he's straight from the Abe's head office. A bit out of place, but why's he prickling my neck? It's just an ordinary voice. Except that undertone, like the sound down on a half-bad mike. That sort of whistle—crackle? Whine?

"If you will ask her to come here?"

She won't like that "Miss" and I don't like you. The judgement came faster than reason, faster even than the training of his job. "You'll be hauling gear and helping out in the workshop," Philip Yee had said at the interview. "And watching out for Dora on site. For setup and firing, she's the best we have, but sometimes people want to come round. They can be a bit odd. And for a woman . . ." He had lifted his well-shirted shoulders in a tiny shrug they both understood: Just being a woman can bring her more trouble than a man. You're along as muscle, in both senses of the word.

"I'll put this lot in the van." Darryl tried for noncommittal, if not polite. "Then I'll ask if she can spare a moment. What was your name again?"

The featureless head inclined. The precise, disturbing voice replied, "Miss Yee knows my name."

Arrogant so-and-so. Darryl clumped to the van, fuming under his breath. He flashed the remote, and the side-door amid the painted coils of fire-breathing dragon unlocked. Who does he think he is? "Miss Yee knows my name." Firebug? No. Seems sane enough. I just don't like the feel of him.

He shoved the mortars into their chest and locked it. Locked the van for good measure and thumped back to the gate, past the waiting shape. As he clicked open the padlock he growled, "I'll see what she says."

"He says I know his name?"

"Yeah. Would that be right?"

Darryl's boss was reserved, formal, always impeccably polite, efficient as the computers she controlled, and usually as quick. The long pause made Darryl want to step closer. Perhaps between her and the gate.

"I can tell him to go . . ."

"No."

"Dora . . ?"

"No," she said again. She came away from the console. "I'll speak to him. Mr. Tomasetti, could you stow the computer gear?"

She *never* lets me touch the comp. She always puts her electronic stuff away herself. She means to keep me out of it. If I disobey she'll fry *my* circuits. But . . . Darryl stood in the half-dark staring after the small figure walking away, stiff-backed as a soldier going into battle. Blast it, Dora, I know you hate coddling, but—!

Half an hour and three miles later, when the light turned red at the big riverside intersection, Darryl finally dared break the hush in the van's front.

"Ah—what did that guy want?"

He felt the air bristle.

"Sorry, not my business, but he seemed odd to me."

I couldn't hear a word even when I sneaked in tackling range, and you hardly talked two minutes, but I could read the body-speak. And if I'm just the gofer, he let the silence add, it's my job to be a trouble-sniffer as well as muscle. The whole firm understands that.

"And how—um—how did he know your name?"

He knew better than to expect an answer like, "One look at the van, with 'Yee's Fire-Sights' in the psyche-delic colors I strong-armed my Dad into using for pro-motion, would tell him that." But again, the silence was extraordinarily, unnervingly long.

"He's an agent," Dora said.

"For a job? A big job? Then why's he shimmying around sites in the dark instead of ringing the office like anybody else?"

"It's . . ."

And it isn't like Dora to stop in mid-sentence. His stomach sank. Is this not an agent at all? Is this some-thing else? Some-one else?

"It's—an unusual job."

But it is a job. His stomach settled. Just a job, and by the sound, not a job she likes.

"They want a low quote?"

"No." Another pause. "They're willing to deal. To meet almost any price we name."

"*Any* price? This isn't illegal, is it? They want the gun-powder for pirates? They're gonna sell flares to terror-ists?"

"No." But she didn't sound irritated, or even af-fronted. Not, he thought, that he would have known if she was.

"Well, Jeez, Dora, what's it about, then? And why's he asking *you*?"

The light finally changed. As the traffic creaked forward Dora let the words out, more reluctantly than she would have let him key through an entire firework display.

"It's a deal with the firm. But the thing they want most is mine."

When Darryl reached home the Messages light was blinking on his phone. He dumped his protective coat and levered old-fashioned wooden louver windows open, then pressed *Read* as he switched on the ceiling fan.

"Dad," said his son's voice, "I'm short four hundred bucks for the iMax bill this quarter, I just hadda watch the tennis live ... I'll pay it back in February, I promise. Thanks, Dad ..."

Idiot, Darryl grouched, and hit *Next*. His daughter said, "Dad, I've got summer school in Brisbane this week, can I leave the cat with you again? You know the food she likes. I'll bring her round tomorrow. Thanks, Dad ..."

Darryl scowled, sighed, and pressed *Next* again. His wife said crisply, "Darryl, will you just talk to Roberts for once? You can't make that place pay any more. You know you'll never go back. And we'll all get something out of the land-price. Roberts can arrange an auction. Phone me tomorrow night."

Then it's gone for good, Darryl told the peeling rafters. *The farm Granddad knocked out of the scrub, the*

*farm Dad built up to a showplace. The farm I couldn't
save.* He went into the kitchen, the best-renovated room
in his downstairs half of the old Queenslander. As he
filled the electric jug his rebellious mind added, *But
I can cope with bills and cats and thieving lawyers. If
Dora'd just come clean, I bet I could handle the bloke
that's monstering her as well.*

Fire-Sights had a small job next evening, a twenty-first
birthday party in Ibisville's most expensive suburb, high
on the side of Fortress Hill. The worst part, in Darryl's
opinion, had been trying to trench mortar beds in almost bare native rock, while the owner's wife fended
him off her orchids and the owner decreed repeatedly
that no fallout must reach the neighbors—"we can't afford damages!" And Darryl bit his tongue on, *So why'd
you order fireworks?* and kept muttering, "Be okay. The
boss set it up. Unless you gave her bad measurements,
everything's jake. She doesn't make mistakes."

Except when it came to shutting me up, he fumed,
finally navigating the van back down the narrow twist of
street, while the noise of young male jollification echoed
behind them, and Dora beside him sat wordless as a
tomb. *Whoinhell does he think he is, that bloke, coming after her to a private function, hanging about at the
top of the drive, cutting me off like a front-row forward
to jabber at her . . . And the confounded party making so much noise I couldn't get a word except "offer"
and "terms and conditions." Or that last bit, after she
snapped him off:* "The family thinks otherwise."

But I got the way she went absolutely rigid then. And

the tone of that, "Excuse me," before she dodged like a veteran winger, and then—then she had the nerve to call, "Mr. Tomasetti, let's go!"

So I couldn't even stop to deck the bastard, let alone dig out the story, or get him off her back for good.

Darryl learned the family's thoughts next morning. He was in the workshop, lackadaisically checking leads on a voltmeter, when he saw Dora vanish into the block across the yard. Weekly schedule-meeting, he thought. Philip Yee's office. But as he passed, headed to Dora's own office for the next work-list, the voices inside carried even through a closed door and air-conditioning.

"I said No, and I mean No!"

A male rumble where Darryl, frozen on one foot, caught, "... from the start ... University ... supported you ... computers, no matter what your mother said ... married ... years back ... biggest deal we ever ... owe the family ... !"

"I won scholarships to Uni, and you know it. You wanted me to do IT for the firm. I did it. I don't owe you ..." Dora's voice began rising. "... make deals for the firm and good luck with it ... but not ... deal for me!"

The door knob grated and blinds rattled. Darryl had just time to whisk back before Dora slammed the door resoundingly and swept away.

"Ah, boss?"

He had knocked, and stuck his head in first for good measure. She was behind her battery of keyboards and monitors, shuffling papers that would be lucky to survive. Her face was rigid, but when her head flew up he very nearly recoiled.

"Oh—Mr. Tomasetti. The work-list . . ." She's gritting her teeth, he thought, and that final waver almost undid him. He pushed the door wide enough to step through and said brusquely, "The work-list can wait."

"But I haven't done it yet—"

"Whatever you do's OK with me."

Another door slammed. A truck pulled in. Voices rumored while they stared at each other, both of them realizing, understanding, accepting all that had been said.

Then Dora looked down at the papers in her hands. Squared them, as precisely as usual, set them down, and glanced by reflex at her main monitor, and then Darryl said, "What is it with that deal, anyhow?"

Their eyes met. He held his breath. Then her shoulders slowly loosened, and she started to speak.

"The client's from overseas. It's confidential where. They're bidding for a very big display, they're worried the opposition might, I don't know, spy, outbid them, maybe even try sabotage—We've said we'll plan the project, and we put in a shadow quote, but they want us to do the set-up as well. And send a technician. They still won't say where, but they keep saying, money's no object. Make the quote whatever you like. Just guarantee the personnel."

"And that's you."

Their eyes met again, acknowledging their just-altered status. No longer employer and casual worker, but a leader given personal allegiance. And in return, offering confidentiality.

"What else is it they want?"

Her hand twitched on the monitor rim. Darryl shut the door and said, "Something of yours, you said the other night. So not just being there. Something you've made—something you've . . . done?"

"Mr. Tomasetti." She looked thoroughly surprised. "That's very . . . Yes, something I've done. With the—um—programming—um—"

Her visible attempt to dumb it down was too much.

"Look, I know I'm just a broken-down cane-farmer, only fit to pay kids' bills and mind the cat and run round gofering, too old to get the half of this. But just once, can I be Darryl the Dumbo while I try?"

"Oh!" He had startled her again, but this time into her very first spontaneous laugh. "Mr . . . Darryl. You are *not* dumb. You've learnt the job faster than anyone else. And you notice things. Okay. I've been messing with the algorithms. For the setup software, I've, um, worked out a new choice path, so you can trip several fuses simultaneously."

"But don't we do that now?"

"Not quite. This system still uses sequential firing. We've made it faster and faster as computers improved, but it's still sequential, it will be even if they get it down to nanoseconds. But this—" her eyes gleamed, "—this is different. Eventually, this'll need a whole new way of programming. I'll maybe have to figure out an entire language. We can't even use it with this system, it's too different."

"Then why do they want it? How'd they know about it, anyway?'

"My father." Dora's nostrils pinched. "I told him something. Just a bit. Of course he blabbed it, trying to sew up the deal, my daughter's a computer wizard, she's got this wonderful idea . . ."

"So that's all they know?" He had begun to relax when he saw Dora's face change. Her eyes flew to the monitor and her hand dropped automatically to the mouse.

"You told somebody else." Of course she would, his ever-reserved boss was only human. There would be some specialist, some other young IT genius, who would really understand. A sudden pain went through him, in the vicinity of what he vaguely considered his heart.

"E-mail," Dora said. "They could hack our server and monitor the traffic. My traffic. If they're as paranoid as they seem, they'd do that the minute they started checking us out. And when Dad spilt the beans . . . We have ordinary encryption, but somebody serious . . ." She jerked the mouse. Two clicks and a snatch of Microsoft melody and the screen turned blue. Preparing, even Darryl knew, to shut down. "But that'll only get them into the desktop." She was breathing visibly faster. "That's why they're still chasing it, me, the firm. The new stuff's on my palmtop, that's never been connected. And I never let it out of my reach."

"Jeez." Darryl felt his own heart speed up. "This thing. This could be more than a new way of doing fireworks, couldn't it? This could be something really—" his son's slang returned to him, "—really out there. Couldn't it?"

The face Dora turned on him spoke for itself. He swallowed involuntarily and wilder thoughts flew past him, international deals, big money, battling corporations the size of Microsoft. Burglary, mayhem, kidnapping. Security, new locks, maybe a watchman at the office. As for Dora herself—Jesus, where in Ibisville do I turn up the likes of a personal bodyguard?

Time stuck. Then a nanosecond showed him the rest of the hypothesis. If we hire anyone they'll know we're onto them. Dora has to have someone, but she's already got all she can have.

The bodyguard has to be me.

Dora tolerated his popping in and out of her office almost hourly. Working late before the next night's job, she accepted his offer of a visit to McDonalds for them both, and even took the hamburger with an absent smile. But she objected strenuously when, the job over, he insisted on following her to her unit, locking the van, and escorting her upstairs.

"There was nothing tonight," she was protesting as they turned the last corner. "They've probably given up. They won't—" She stopped in mid-step and Darryl shot past her to the top of the stairs.

The block corridor was dimly lit after eleven PM, and the interloper had again positioned himself against the light. Darryl heard that unmistakeable voice ask, "Miss Yee?" and his own fuses popped.

"She said, No, mate. And when women round here say, No, they mean, No!" He felt Dora climb the last step and nudged her behind him. "Now why don't you just get out?"

The silhouette did not move. Blocky sod, even allowing for the suit. Korean, maybe? That'd go with the English. And the local ignorance. Darryl balled his fists to step forward and the silhouette spoke.

"Who is this man?"

Dora's hand shut suddenly and fiercely in the back of Darryl's shirt. She wormed up beside him and said rapidly, "Darryl, this is—Major. Major, this is Mr. Tomasetti. He works for us."

"Major, huh? You military?" Darryl ignored the twitch at his sleeve.

There was a pause. Just before Darryl broke it, the silhouette said, "*Mister* Major." The head turned slightly. The peculiar voice asked, "This is your mate?"

"My—No!" Dora very nearly yelped. "Darryl's just looking out for me . . ."

Mate, Darryl translated belatedly, doesn't mean friend this time. It means—damn!

"I'm her minder!" He nearly shouted too. No, if he's Korean, "minder" won't translate. "Her guardian—I'm watching out for her." If that hasn't queered my pitch with her for good . . . And now I know I want a pitch, blast you . . . "Anyway, it's time you left."

Whatever his tone added, Dora let him edge her away from the stairs. Her hand tugged him on down the corridor, and they stood watching, as the figure slowly approached the steps, began descending, and disappeared.

Dora stood in the centre of her unit, motionless, mute, while Darryl flicked on lights, checked windows, prowled the rooms from end to end. As he came back to her she whispered, just audible, "He knows where I live."

Darryl put a hand on her shoulder, unable to help

himself. He felt her shaking, and furiously suppressed the impulse to pull her into his arms.

"He's gone now. It's okay."

Ever so slightly, her head shook.

"We can call the cops. He's a bloody stalker . . ."

"The cops!" It went up to a sort of squeak. "What can they do? Issue a restraining order? For that they have to know his address."

"But doesn't the firm . . ."

"He—they won't give us one. They always phone us. We don't call them. And the number's blanked. I wanted to hack it, but Dad said, No. Not polite. It'll upset them. Risk the deal."

"The *deal!* Listen, I can talk to him tomorrow morning. Make him—"

She looked at him, and the words died on his lips.

"What is it, do you think," she was speaking very deliberately, "that Dad wants most?"

The deal. Come hell or high water, and if that includes his daughter, includes letting the client put pressure on his daughter . . .

"I can stay here tonight."

Their eyes held, silently following the statement's back-trail: In case he comes back. As silently, the future opened before Darryl's eyes. Tonight. And tomorrow night?

He very nearly reached out again. He did notice, too vividly, the way Dora's hands almost moved, and stilled. Before she set her lips, and shook her head.

"I'm inside now. I've got good locks. Go home, Darryl. You need the sleep."

Her face silenced his protests. She's got her old man on her back as well as this ... stalker ... She's had enough tonight already. Don't make it worse.

She went to open the door. But as he came up, she rose suddenly on tiptoe and a butterfly brushed his cheek.

"Thank you," she whispered. "Very much."

Darryl went downstairs with his head worried silly and his heart cavorting somewhere up in the stratosphere.

Fire-Sights had three days of uneasy peace, enlivened by another mighty quàrrel from which Dora emerged raging so visibly that Darryl dared not even try to comfort her. He stuck to driving home after her each evening, checking the unit, and in daytime, keeping her nearly always in sight. Except for the quarrel she was fraught and silent, giving him an occasional fragile smile, and burying herself in the work for their next big job: Saturday night, the season's launch for the Ibisville football team.

The display had been laid out at one end of the stadium. It was very late before they had everything pulled down and packed, and again, almost all of the crowd had gone. As he carried the last load of rails and leads out the stadium back gate, Darryl looked across empty acres of an ill-lit concrete parking lot and felt a tingling nervous sense of *déjà vu*.

Dora's shoes tapped behind him. She had the palm-top in her pocket, the laptop under her arm. He pushed the gate wider for her and went ahead across the twenty feet to the van. As he turned, the shadows under the stadium wall moved.

Darryl had one startled glimpse of dark shapes, mis-shapen heads, caught the glint of metal and felt a searing shot of adrenaline before Dora screamed, "Run!"

Darryl's body took charge. He ran, faster than he ever moved in his life, straight back to her.

Ten feet from the van his feet stuck. His limbs stuck. He kicked and fought like a fly in amber and with every muscle flex the invisible bonds tightened until they were crushing his chest, cutting off his wind, strangling him.

Darkness filled with spangles over what was left of his eyesight. Somewhere a voice was shrieking like a fire siren, "Let him go, you bastards, you *dingoes*! Let him *go*!"

A sudden blur, then his eyes cleared. The restraints had stopped tightening. He could, very carefully, breathe.

He orbited his gaze madly: Dora, frozen just outside the gate, a small shadow in the dusk. The shapes around him, bigger than he was, ominously blocky and solid, with projections that did not match human form.

Battle gear, his frenziedly racing brain called back from TV News pictures. They're soldiers or something, they've got armor and helmets and weapons and . . .

Beyond them, in front of him, stood another, famil-iarly suited, less blocky shape.

"You heard me," Dora was saying. Her voice quiv-ered a note too high, but it was adamant with pure rage. "You let him go! Or I don't go anywhere!"

Darryl's heart stood still. He wanted to call out but his voice was silenced too. Frenzied, despairing, he tried to make his eyes cry. *Don't promise just to save me! I don't matter! Don't do it! Don't go anywhere!*

"Does this mean that you will go?"

It was Major's familiar distorted voice he heard. Dora answered, with a steel ring he had never heard before.

"Only if I have answers first. Who are you? Where do you come from? What are you doing here?"

Silence. Into it, Dora bit off the next words.

"Or I can smash this palmtop, here and now. And whatever you do to me, I'll never be able to put the algorithm together again."

Another pause where Darryl's heart choked in his throat. *Don't dare him,* he wanted to bawl, *who knows what he—they—can do to you? Look what they've done to me. Dora, don't!*

"You will know soon enough."

"I'll know first." Dora jerked her chin up. Her face was a blur but he could guess how it looked. Good luck, mate, he thought, crazily amused, on arguing with her now.

Major turned slowly half away from her, toward Darryl. "Even for his sake?"

Dora laughed at him, wildly as a banshee. "Oh, sure! As if you won't do something—kill him, mind-wipe him—anyway!"

The pause this time, Darryl realized suddenly, through the choke of his own fear, might have been faintly bemused.

Then Major took one pace back, lifted a wrist toward his face, and overhead the sky took fire.

They slid silently down out of the blaze, one, two, three, grounding lightly as bubbles and as airily, one somewhere behind him, one to either side, and Darryl's insides liquefied with pure molten fear.

Oh God, oh, God, his mind gasped, whipped back through childhood memories, it wasn't just a movie after all, it's not the big saucer with the lights and music but there are aliens. Back in '14, there was talk of contact, signals out of space. We all forgot it when nothing happened. But they're real. They're here.

The bubbles stood motionless on mundane concrete, silvered, sleekly rounded pods, bigger than a ship container, taller than Darryl's head. No lights or portholes like Spielberg's. I can't even see engines. Just a faint haze reflecting from the mirror sides, a tremble round them like heating in the air.

It was the most terrifying moment of his life, and he could not tear his eyes away. Until beyond Major he heard Dora catch her breath on something like a choke. And then bring out the words with ferocious bravado.

"Oh, very impressive. So what *are* you? ETs? Alien life forms? Green snakes with three mouths and tentacles, I suppose?"

Major drew him—her—itself? up. "We are a carbon-based, oxygen breathing life-form." It actually sounded affronted. "As bi-symmetrical as you."

"But this isn't what you look like, is it?"

The pause might have been embarrassment.

"Your planet has considerably higher gravity. We find it—uncomfortable. Mostly, we prefer to appear as—simulae."

"Images?"

"You would say, holograms."

No wonder he—she? it? always stood against the light; no wonder the voice sounded weird. Sweat was clammy on Darryl from toe to armpit, but his brain had refueled on terror, and suddenly the words burst out of him too.

"Where? Where'd you come from? Where?"

Where's Dora going—oh God, what can stop her? Where's she going to?

Major's figure turned very slightly toward him. After another moment's consideration, the voice replied.

"My correct—names—as you understand them, would be Major. Ursor Major."

The pause was expectant. Darryl gaped, lost. But Dora gave one short gasp and exclaimed aloud.

"*Ursa* Major! Oh—oh!" She clapped both hands over her mouth and tried to stop the spurt of laughter. "Oh, *God*, that is the most awful joke!"

Shut up, Darryl tried to telegraph, *Dora, shut up!* But despite what could have been called bridling, Major—Ursor Major, he corrected himself bewilderedly—made no other response.

"And you came all the way from the star, the constellation—all the way *here*? To this system? This planet? This country? This *town*?" She was battling more hysteria. "Or are there more of you? Are you all over earth, the solar system, do you . . . What in heaven's name *for*?"

When the voice came this time, Major sounded almost humanly resigned.

"There are no more of us. We have not landed elsewhere. The rules of—" the voice crackled unintelligibly as a thoroughly ruined mike, "forbid mass intervention in native groups. And this is an obscure satellite of a very small star, in a seldom-travelled galactic arm." *Talks like a book,* Darryl thought, amazed, *when he—she? gets going.* "That was precisely why we came."

"But for *what*?"

Major's arms moved. For the first time the body language was utterly unhuman, somewhere between a telescoping and a ripple in their lower halves. Dora waited. At last, the words came.

"We were seeking—art."

Dora's laughter almost did become hysterical. In terror Darryl tried to hitch himself closer and the restraints let him shuffle a couple of feet before she got control of herself.

"You wanted *what*?!"

"We wished—we require an artistic form. An exotic, utterly unusual, spectacular artistic form, never seen before. It was—it may still be—our" *crackle, sputter,* "for the," *splutter, Crack!* "at which, we must prevail among the other," *fizz, crackle!* "or lose the—perhaps your word is, throne."

Dora's jaw sagged. Darryl's feelings got the better of him and before he knew it he had exploded in turn.

"If you mean fireworks, there must be a million other bloody 'art shows' round the world, New Year's Eve in New York, in Sydney, the Melbourne Ekka, America, any Fourth of July . . . Better than ours are! Bigger than ours are! Why'd you have to pick on *us*?"

Major's figure swiveled toward him. The voice answered almost at once, expressionless. "Because in such a remote area, there would be less concern if an—inhabitant—disappeared."

Darryl's voice dried in his throat.

"There are still plenty of other places!" Dora snapped. "With better pyrotechs than me!"

"But not," Major answered softly, "one who understands alternate space."

The pit fell out of Darryl's stomach and kept falling into emptiness. They understand what she did. They really understand it. Oh, Mary, Mother of God—the old prayer came more than naturally—now they'll never let her go.

Night hung round them, laced with city lights, but none of the sounds that should have accompanied them. No bird calls from the park, no rev-up of distant traffic, no passing jets. We're alone, Darryl thought. They've already taken us into another world.

He shut his eyes. Then they flew open and fastened on Dora as on his last hope of life.

And Dora was staring back at Major as she had at Darryl, a bare four days ago. As if actually seeing him for the first time.

Then she came a pace forward. Very softly, she said, "You know."

Major's head inclined. She took another step. Her voice began lifting, but no longer in fear.

"You know what I did. You understand it. You *know*."

"Some of us know. Not all. To have another who knows—and not one of us—would be a gift beyond price."

Dora's lips parted and held. She stared.

"An artist," Major spoke almost as softly as she had, "such an artist, using such a form as yours, would be honored as never elsewhere. An artist who also saw alternate space, who could transmit that vision—such a one might claim any honor, privilege—materials, facilities, possessions, wealth, as you understand it. Any of such that is imaginable. Every slightest, greatest desire."

She's going to go. Darryl's heart turned to ice in his chest. She wouldn't go for coercion, and she won't go for the bribes, but for the understanding . . . to work with people who know what she really does, where she's coming from, where her head might take her . . .

She's going to leave.

"Dora, don't!" It burst out of him again, beyond control. "You can't do it! Not go off with these, these—you can't leave here, Ibisville, the firm—your *family* . . ."

"My *family?*"

Dora whipped round on him. Her chest rose and fell. Then she took four fast paces and they were nose-to-nose. "Let me tell you about my family. Great Grandfather came here for Gold Mountain, in the 1870s, he dug his mine and carried his gold out in two baskets, all the way to Ibisville. Then he was rich enough to marry, back home. But the gold haunted him, so he brought back his wife and her brother, the apprentice of a firework maker. They sold crackers and skyrockets to the stupid diggers until they had a business, land, money. My grandfather inherited, then my father. But always—always! this was Gold Mountain. A trading place, an outpost. The Family, the real family, was in China. At Home.

"And now my father wants to show off to that Family,

to make some great coup, because he still thinks China's the same China, and one day he can go *home* . . ."

"But you're his daughter!" The venom had shocked Darryl into speech. "The backbone of the business! You'll inherit the firm—"

"Hah!" Dora almost spat at him. "The one who inherits will be Charlie—my brother—the eldest son! He's off in Macao, pretending to study accounting and running wild with his rich cousins. But one day, he'll come home. And then my father will hand over the company without a second thought. And Charlie won't understand either. There'll be another client someday and he'll sell off me and the algorithm, just the same!"

"B-but—your mother—surely she wouldn't let them—"

This time it was the bitterest of laughs. "My mother wanted me to marry a cousin and make us truly rich. She thinks computers are unwomanly. Now that I'm over thirty, she tries not to see me. Her friends all know better, when they're boasting about their kids, than to mention *me*."

Darryl's tongue had frozen. All he could think, looking into the too bright glitter of her eyes, fury just stemming tears, was, *And I thought* my *lot were rough.*

"So you see," she sounded almost shaky, "why I might find it—easier—even better—" she swallowed, "—to leave."

Reality recoiled on Darryl like a blast from a deep-freeze. "For God's sake, you can't want to go that far—leave, yes, but— They're aliens! You'll be all alone!"

She looked up at him, fighting suddenly for control.

Not at what he had said, he realized. At the concern in his voice. The human warmth.

Then she wiped the back of a hand over her eyes, and tried valiantly not to sniff. Her voice hardly wavered when she spoke.

"I'm used to it."

The inflection pierced him like a lance. He found he was struggling in his now passive bonds. "No—Jeezus, not like that! Dora, not *alone*!"

She went to retort and stopped. The half-withdrawal of her body's reply stopped too. Suddenly her face changed. Understanding, excitement rose there, something even wilder, that might have been hope.

Then she stepped suddenly forward and said, "Then you come too."

"What?"

"You understand why I'm going. You aren't that scared of them. You mightn't know the math but you see things—you think. And you don't—discount me. Don't think I'm—I'm some kind of—"

"No," Darryl said. He looked full in her face and said the words with absolute sincerity. "*I* think you're bloody wonderful."

"Oh ..." Her eyes actually might have gone misty. Then she smiled up at him, tremulous and starry-eyed as a teenager. "That's good. Because actually ... I think you're pretty wonderful too."

"Oh, Dora." He yanked one arm out of the invisible cocoon. She reached for him, the bonds suddenly undid and he had her in his arms, Dora hugging him furiously while he tried to reach her face for the first kiss.

When they let go, both breathless, Major loomed suddenly at Dora's elbow. "*Now*," the unhuman voice almost sounded long-suffering, "you are ready to leave?"

Dora looked round. Drew in a long breath. Then she picked up the laptop, dropped in the heat of stress, and glanced up at him—her? it? "We're ready," she said.

Major signaled. The silent pods opened, door sections swinging up and out and ramps extending like the reality of every science fiction film Darryl had ever seen, and for a moment pure wonder stole his breath.

Something tugged on his hand. Dora looked up at him, suddenly uncertain, deadly serious.

"Darryl—you sure?" She glanced at the pods. "Those things—and the way they stopped you, before. They could do anything to us. Ursa Major—you know, we probably aren't coming back?"

"Yeah," he said, following her eyes, feeling the fear rise. And fall again. "I reckoned that."

"But what about *your* family?"

Darryl looked down at her, recalling the messages on his phone. Then he said to Major, "Hang on a minute, mate. Gotta make a call." He dragged the cellphone from his pocket and dialed the number he knew by heart.

"Bianca? This is Darryl. Get Roberts to make a voice-test, so he can swear this isn't under duress. Then tell him to sell the farm. Split the money with the kids. Tell Alys to find another cat-feeder, and Joe, when the farm money's gone, he'll have to pay his own bills. I won't be around." He felt himself smile down at Dora, unable to help it. "No, haven't got time to explain. But someone's just made me an offer I couldn't refuse."

Acknowledgements

Many thanks to Ian Riedel of Fireworx Brisbane, who patiently answered a cascade of queries about pyrotechnic terms and procedures. Any errors in pyrotechnic matters are my doing.

Thanks also to Cat Johnson for advice on football terms, and a homage to James Tiptree Jr., for this story's foremother, "The Women Men Don't See." Thanks even more to Lillian Stewart Carl, whose part in this story was fundamental.

IN THE NIGHT

Steven H Silver

The communications department was the eye in the calm of the storm as *The Pride of Pavo* prepared for orbital insertion around Oshun. Communication Sub-Officer Lolanyo Oum was completely removed from the typical pre-insertion, organized chaos that reigned supreme on the ship as he made contact with Oshun's navcom officer.

"*The Pride of Pavo* requesting orbital slot." He tried to keep his voice calm, but knew that he failed. In many ways, Oshun was like any of the fifteen other worlds the *Pavo* had visited since it was last here, but Lolanyo knew there was a difference. Oshun was the home of the sexiest voice in the galaxy. With luck, the voice would be on duty and respond to provide him with the coordinates to feed to the ship.

"*The Pride of Pavo* requesting orbital slot," he repeated.

Lolanyo double-checked the distance to the space

station and the frequency. Assured he was broadcasting properly, he was about to repeat his request when Oshun Control responded.

"Oshun Control to The Pride of Pavo, *insertion data is being provided on B-band."*

Lolanyo's heart leapt. It was her. He didn't know what she looked like, nor her name, but he had fallen in love with her voice—which called to mind the soothing, mellifluous tones of an oboe—on the three previous trips to Oshun, and this time he was ready to act.

The Communications Shed on the space station Oshun formed a safe cocoon for Dianthe Secca. The small room kept her separated from the physicality of other humans while allowing her safe, limited communication with people thousands, if not millions of kilometers away.

"The Pride of Pavo *requesting orbital slot,"* the voice of the spacer commie came faintly over her com. She could almost hear each of the million kilometers the message had to cross from the ship to the station. The *Pavo* came to the station about once every six months. She called its record up on her computer and sent them information over the B-band.

"Thanks, Oshun. We're looking forward to seeing you." It was just a friendly greeting, but it made Dianthe tense up. All too often, the men who traveled between the stars seemed to want to meet her. Spaceships generally had an almost equal mix of men and women on the crew, but after traveling for months on end with each other, anyone would seek out variety. Dianthe had no desire to be that variety.

A sudden klaxon sounded and she jerked her eyes back to the computer. Another ship had come through the wormhole on the *Pavo*'s tail. According to the data scrolling across the screen, the new ship and the *Pavo* were too close to be safely traveling at near-relativistic speeds.

"Oshun Control to *The Pride of Pavo*, take evasive action. Mystery ship at 420 plus 8. Set heading 156 and minus 21!

"Oshun Control to mystery ship," the computer displayed its name, taken from its guidance beacon, "Oshun Control to *Zubarah*! Take evasive action. *The Pride of Pavo* at 156 minus 8. Set heading 420 plus 21!" She pressed the button to have her instructions repeated.

Six seconds later, she received her first acknowledgement. "Pavo *confirms new heading of 156 and minus 21.*"

She waited, but there was no acknowledgement from *Zubarah*. She kept an eye on the data scrolling on her screen, watching *The Pride of Pavo* making its course correction while *Zubarah* continued on its set course. She tried to imagine the klaxons on both ships and wondered what was happening on *Zubarah;* there was no response to either her directions or what must be happening.

Suddenly, the data showed the ship pulling away and almost simultaneously a voice with a thick Mindeni accent. "Zubarah *to Oshun. We acknowledge orders and are changing course.*"

The scrolling data showed the two ships moving apart. At their closest approach, they were less than

1,000 kilometers apart. A near collision that the Captain of *Zubarah* would have to answer for once he docked.

Dianthe turned her attention to the next ship arrival and finished off her shift without any further incidents.

Several hours later, leaving the ComShed, she was still jumpy from the close encounter. Without her job to occupy her thoughts, she found herself quivering with nerves.

One of the advantages to living on a space station was that, although the population was mostly human, there were enough aliens around that she could ignore human culture. She had discovered a Nardak rumination center that catered almost exclusively to an alien clientele. It would be crowded, but when Dianthe was among aliens, she was still separate from her own kind and could imagine a solitude that was otherwise lacking.

A bat-like Tseekahn led her to a rumination pit where she could lay on a strange, jelly-like substance that would support her weight. Nutrients and relaxicants would infuse into her skin through the jelly. In fact, as she lay down, she could feel the tension disappear from her bare arms and neck, replaced with a deep warmth.

The moments of panic when the second ship had appeared vanished. The thousands of humans on the station could just as easily have been on the planet below. She was alone on a soft, warm bed. Aromas from the Nardak homeworld filled the air, ashy smells mixed with the tang of ozone. An atonal, bichronial tune played softly. When Dianthe had first heard the Nardaki music, she didn't think she could stay in the room longer than a few minutes, let alone relax to it. It seemed to work with the relaxicants, though, and while she wouldn't listen to it in normal circumstances, it seemed right in the rumination center.

Soon it was as if she was alone. The rest of the station vanished from her thoughts.

"May I join you?"

Dianthe opened her eyes to see a young officer standing above her and looking out of place with his neatly pressed uniform and, more importantly, his human features. For a moment she wondered how the alien clientele of the rumination center looked at her, but that passed as she realized she was simply annoyed that anyone would interrupt her when she thought she had found solitude.

"If I wanted human company, I would have gone to a bar. I wouldn't be here." she closed her eyes, focusing on the Nardak scents.

"But you are Lieutenant Dianthe Secca. I was told you might be here."

The rumination center was a strange, almost psychedelic experience. A thin, moss-carpeted path wound between pits filled with variously colored slimes. Lolanyo had stopped at the front desk and asked the attendant if a human was using the facilities. The bat-like Tseekahn pipped through its translator, indicating there was one relaxing in the back. Lolanyo wound his way through until he saw her lying in a pit of pink goo.

She wasn't what Lolanyo would consider pretty. She

had a nose a little too broad for her face and her hair was a washed-out rust color. But she had that voice, and at the very least, he wanted to thank her for helping avert disaster when the *Pavo* dropped into norm-space.

"May I join you?" he asked, unsure of the niceties of the situation. Should he even be talking to her in a rumination center?

She opened her eyes and glanced up at him, closing her eyes dismissively. "And I've already told you, if I wanted human company, I would have gone to a bar." Even her terse tone couldn't hide the quality of her voice and in spite of himself, Lolanyo could feel his heart quicken.

"But you are Lieutenant Dianthe Secca," he pressed on. "I'm Lolonyo Oum. From *The Pride of Pavo*. I wanted to thank you for your quick action earlier today." He could feel the words burbling out of him, staccato, nervous.

"You've thanked me. And set back my relaxation."

He nodded. "Well, anyway. Thanks for spotting the other ship. It was nice . . ." he realized she wasn't listening, had dismissed him.

On his way out of the center, Lolanyo stopped once more to talk to the attendant.

The kid was gone and Dianthe listened to the music and allowed the smells to overwhelm her.

The rumination center allowed her to drift away from her daily concerns. Ships coming and going were her co-workers' concerns. The crowds that were between her and her apartment were imaginary, easily ignored. Oshun's walls were closed down to just the walls of the pit in which she lay, the music soothing her despite its utter alienness.

And despite herself, Dianthe found herself thinking of the earnest young officer who had disturbed her. Nobody had ever searched her out before, at least not successfully. Every commie she had ever spoken to had been at a distance of millions of kilometers. He had intruded and introduced himself to her, but she had no recollection of what his name was, merely that he was from *The Pride of Pavo*. Or possibly the *Zubarah*. One of the ships involved in the incident. She had no idea what he looked like. Slight of build? Perhaps. She would never see him again.

Normally, she would have been annoyed at the interruption and the fact that she was dwelling on it, but the jelly was giving her a steady supply of relaxicants and she found she couldn't muster the anger she knew she should.

She realized she was herself impressed with the anonymous commie's diligence. Eventually, she rose from the jelly and stopped at the front desk, only to find that the commie had paid for her session. Enough of the relaxicants were still in her bloodstream that she couldn't get angry and she left to seek the comforting vacancy of her own apartment.

Lolanyo saw the lift doors begin to close and he ran for them, calling. He managed to catch his foot between the doors and as they reopened, he slid in. There was only one person in the lift.

"We meet again, Lieutenant," he said, immediately cursing himself for how stupid he must sound.

"I'm sorry," Dianthe answered. "Have we met?"

"A little while ago. In the relaxation place. Lolanyo Oum. From *The Pride of Pavo*."

An awkward silence filled the car. It was eventually broken by Dianthe.

"You had no right," she started before taking a breath, "Thank you for paying for my session. It was very generous."

"You're welcome. It was the least I could do after this morning."

Silence again as Dianthe made a concerted effort to examine the buttons on the wall in front of her. Lolanyo looked up at the floor display while trying to catch glimpses of Dianthe out of the corner of his eye and trying to think of a way to start a conversation. Anything just to hear her voice.

Suddenly, the silence was made even more complete as the lift shuddered to a halt between floors and the lights dimmed.

Dianthe began pushing random buttons to no avail. She tapped on the lift's com unit.

"Is there anyone there? We're stuck in the elevator."

She was greeted by silence and pulled a com unit from her belt.

"Damn! No signal." She said without even trying to call out.

Lolanyo began banging on the lift doors, shouting through them. He noticed that Dianthe simply sat on the floor in one corner of the lift.

"What are you doing?"

"They'll realize we're stuck eventually and get us out. The com unit isn't working and I don't have a signal. Yelling isn't going to help if we're between decks. The only other option would be to climb through the access hatch," she pointed to the trap door in the lift's ceiling. "And I'm not about to do something that risky."

She reached into her pouch and pulled out a sharp needle.

"What's that for?"

"Embroidery," she responded. "We're going to be here for a while. I can do that or I can talk to you." She continued to pull cloth and thread from her pouch.

Lolanyo was amazed. No matter what she said, no matter how harsh her tone or how dismissive her words, her voice had an uncanny ability to make his heart skip.

He turned back to the door and began to pound on it, yelling for help.

After a few moments, Dianthe spoke up. "Could you stop that? It won't do any good."

"It seems my only other choice is to watch you knit, which doesn't strike me as any more interesting or productive on my part."

"I'm embroidering, not knitting." Dianthe lapsed back into silence.

"Why?"

"Sorry?"

"Why are you embroidering?"

"It beats pounding on the door and yelling my head off."

Lolanyo thought about it for a moment. "Has anyone ever told you that you have a beautiful voice?"

Dianthe looked up. "That's changing the subject a little."

"No, really. A lot of other commies have mentioned that they look forward to arriving at Oshun because they enjoy hearing your greeting."

Dianthe scoffed. "That's just change. You've all been hearing the same voices, seeing the same faces, since the last port. Anyone would sound good welcoming you to a station."

Now it was Lolanyo's turn to scoff. "You've never heard 'Gravel Gryta' at Beowulf." Lolanyo dropped his voice, put in a heavy rasp, and said, "You're clear for approach on vector alpha three-nine." He sounded like an old woman who had spent too much time living hard and Dianthe couldn't suppress a snort of laughter.

"So, why are you doing embroidery?"

Dianthe completed a couple more stitches. "I bet it seems old-fashioned."

"I thought it was all done by machine," Lolanyo admitted.

"The commercial embroidery is. If you see it on a shirt or napkin, or whatever, you're looking at something the robots have made. But this, I learned it from my aunt. She lives on Gedrosia and is really active in recreating ancient terrestrial art. She does needlepoint, calligraphy, and so on. I stayed with her one summer when I was growing up and she tried to get me interested in different crafts. Embroidery is the one that stuck with me. I can do it while sitting in the ComShed and it gives me something to do while waiting for your ships to come in."

Lolanyo found himself drifting as she spoke. For all her voice was beautiful when Dianthe gave instructions or even when she was telling him to get lost, when she spoke about something she cared about, and she clearly cared about embroidery, her voice took on an even more magical quality.

Lolanyo realized that she had finished talking. "I hike." Even as the words were coming out of his mouth, he realized he should probably have kept quiet.

As he said the words, the commie turned from her to look up at the numbers, as if they would magically begin counting down again. Dianthe put her embroidery down on her lap and looked up at him, seeing him for the first time.

"Being a com officer on an interstellar spaceship seems a rather odd profession for someone who enjoys the outdoors." It just seemed so random and incongruous.

He glanced down at her. "I come from Greyfox." Seeing her blank look, he explained, "It is a small moon orbiting Redtail, which has been almost completely tamed. The parts of the moon that aren't urbanized have been turned to tame farmland. When I was young, my father took me to Orbis, another moon orbiting Redtail. Orbis is untamed. Small mining towns built into mountain passes. It seemed to be everything Greyfox wasn't. Of course, now I know that Orbis has its own cities, but then, it was amazing and different."

Despite herself, Dianthe found herself listening to

this young man. Lennie, or something like that. She looked over his uniform to see if he had a name tag and only found his last name, "Oum."

". . . only way I'd be able to hike in as many different places as I wanted to was to get off Greyfox. I left home and signed onto the first starship that would take me. I've been on the *Pavo* ever since.

"But when I get leave, not on a space station like Oshun, but on a real world, I take off for the hills or the forest . . . anywhere wide-open nature can replace the claustrophobic nature of the *Pavo*."

He looked around at the tiny confines of the elevator car. Both of them burst out laughing.

"But those wide open spaces are exhilarating. On Ontal, there's this lake, kilometers from anything, high up in the mountains, one of the most secluded places I've ever been. The lake has a large mollusk population that gives it this deep purple hue. It's like looking at a pool of ink. You're standing there, the only person for kilometers enjoying this wonder. You have to see it to believe it.

"So you know how I got here," he said. "How did you make it from your aunt's place on Gedrosia to the space station?"

Dianthe looked at him. He had been listening to what she had said. In her experience that was a rarity. If she wasn't giving instructions that people's lives depended on from the ComShed, she might as well not speak. Although from what Lennie said, perhaps that wasn't entirely true.

"As you might have noticed, I'm not the most outgoing per . . ."

With a loud clang, the lift started moving again. Dianthe quickly packed her embroidery away and stood up. When the door opened, she slipped out without another word, leaving the spacer in the elevator. She could feel her face redden as she made her way to her apartment, not believing that she had opened herself up to him at all. Telling a stranger about her time with Aunt Lydia . . . it was just wrong, an invasion.

Dianthe's apartment was typical of all the residential cubes on Oshun. It was essentially an efficiency. The furniture—a bed, table, a couple of chairs—all folded out of the walls with a small kitchenette in one corner of the room. The community bathrooms were down the hall. As she entered the apartment the lights came on and a chair and side-table sprouted from the wall. She walked over to the kitchen nook and tossed a dinner package into the oven. When the oven buzzed, she carefully took the steaming bowl out and sat in the chair to eat.

The apartment was Spartan. It was difficult to decorate the walls when any given wall could transform from a flat surface into a bed, a chair, a closet, whatever was needed at a moment's notice. However, the apartment had never struck Dianthe as antiseptic until now. Five minutes before she had come in, anyone viewing the room would have had no idea that anyone lived here, let alone Dianthe.

After getting off the lift, Lolanyo made his way back to the *Pavo*. Dianthe was the most unsociable person he had ever met. It wasn't just that she liked solitude or that she was a misanthrope, it was that she simply didn't have any understanding of how to relate to anyone outside a narrow professional relationship.

No, that was wrong. Lolanyo realized he had very limited experience with Dianthe. A sexy voice at the end of a com link, a person who wanted to be left alone, and a stranger in a broken lift. For all he knew, she was sitting gabbing happily away with her friends, perhaps even her husband. No, he couldn't picture her having a bunch of friends.

His berth on the *Pavo* was small, little more than a bed that folded up into the bulkhead and a closet. Every flat surface bore his mark. Tri-vids he had taken on hikes across nearly a score of worlds adorned the inside of the room, which was no larger than the lift car he had been stuck in with Dianthe.

Lolanyo knew that any thoughts he had of becoming involved with Dianthe were crazy. He had thanked her for doing her job, or at least tried to. She wasn't interested in someone who would be on the station for a day or two every several months. Hell, she probably wasn't interested in someone who lived on the station full time.

It didn't matter. In two days' time, the *Pavo* would leave Oshun and Lolanyo wouldn't be back to the space station for at least six months, by which time his encounter with Dianthe would just be a distant memory. Of course, it had been even longer than that since his last visit to Oshun and he had arrived with images of what the owner of the voice must have been. With the reality of meeting her, though, he would focus on the negatives. Oshun would just be another stop of his tour of duty.

A space station, even one which serves as a transfer point for multiple species, only has a limited amount of room. Even just moving between the ComShed, the Mess Hall, and her apartment, there was a good chance Dianthe would bump into the *Pavo*'s commie again before he shipped out.

Every day, despite her best efforts, she came into contact with scores of other people. Most of them were anonymous passersby, perhaps with the occasional necessary comments. The *Pavo*'s commie should have been no more than one of those passersby. He was actually anonymous since she had no idea what his name was, although she had decided that Lennie wasn't right. It bothered her that she thought she would recognize him if she passed him in the corridors. It bothered her that she was even thinking about him enough to know that it would bother her.

Most of the time they spent in the elevator, he had droned, but there was one point when his emotions and excitement made her look at him differently. He was talking about a purple lake he had seen somewhere in his hiking and his voice just filled up the tiny room with his sheer joy at being in such a vast space.

On her way to work, she stopped on the main concourse with its variety of stores, ranging from the canteen used by the station staff to the shlocky gift shops frequented by the transients. She had been surprised to discover that she didn't have anything for lunch and figured picking something up before work would be easier, faster, and cheaper than hitting the mess hall.

As she was charging her lunch, she saw someone who looked familiar and unfamiliar at the same time. Living on Oshun was strange. There were the people who looked familiar because they were strangers who lived on the space station and who she saw with some frequency, even if she didn't know what they did or who they were. Then there were the complete strangers, clearly passing through on their way from one place to another. Finally, there were the people who looked like people she knew, but weren't. She pegged this person in the last category.

As she exited the canteen, he spoke to her. "Dianthe?"

She realized it was the commie from the *Pavo*. "Look, it's a small space station. Running into you like this is not the universe's way of saying that we were meant to be together. There is no fate involved here. Just somebody picking up lunch and running late for work and somebody else poking around for a souvenir to take on his voyage."

"I wasn't going to say anything about fate. I was just going to say 'hello.' Aside from the *Pavo*'s crew, you're the only person I know on Oshun. I get that you need to be left alone. I just thought I'd say 'hi'."

He turned and walked off.

Dianthe watched him leave and noted that he never turned back to see if she was looking. She felt a vague sense of unease that he didn't look back at her.

She made it to the ComShed moments before her shift was supposed to begin. Erich glanced up at her as she came in, nodded a silent greeting, and turned back to the book he was reading. He had learned long ago that Dianthe preferred to do their shift changes in silence and had given up trying to talk to her. The ComShed allowed a lot of leisure time between ship arrivals. As Erich logged out, Dianthe checked his duty log to see if there was anything she needed to know before starting. It looked like it had been a quiet shift.

She heard the door close as Erich left. She took out her embroidery; she would have a good hour before the first scheduled arrival. Today would be a nice slow day, the sort that could be handled easily by computer.

After she guided the *Jenkins* away from the station, she found herself performing a search for information about Ontal and the fabulous lake the *Pavo's* commie had described. Panoramic pictures of the lake popped up on her screen, the deep purple water set against green and orange plants under a brilliant blue sky seemed more like something from an insane artist's palette than a photograph. Cycling through the pictures, Dianthe noted how few people she saw at the lake. She also noticed that one of the pictures was taken by Lolanyo Oum and the name seemed familiar.

She checked the name against *The Pride of Pavo's* manifest and discovered that it belonged to the communications officer who had been tracking her down. On a whim, she ran a search on his name.

In addition to serving on the *Pavo*, he was a travel writer, describing his hikes on several different sites. His photographs were gorgeous, near professional quality, and demonstrated an excellent eye for composition.

Looking through them she realized that no matter what they depicted ... canyons, lakes, mountains, forests ... they all lacked any humans. Not only humans, any aliens. The only living things caught in any of the pictures were vegetation.

A klaxon called her attention to the imminent arrival of a ship and she saved the information she had found on Lolanyo Oum and turned her attention to bringing the ship through safely.

Lolanyo spent his spare time exploring the maintenance corridors of Oshun. They were warm and cramped, filled with multi-colored pipes. Usually, he had to crawl on all fours to make his way through and he had to be careful to avoid six-way intersections where the floor dropped away. It wasn't a hike, but it was an exploration of new places. And it kept him away from the *Pavo*.

Lolanyo loved the *Pavo* and in fact, as the ship's full name suggested, took great pride in being on board the freighter. However, he found the need to get away from its familiar space whenever he could. When he left Oshun, he knew that he would be on the *Pavo* for at least three weeks, seeing the same people, seeing the same hallways. Lolanyo just felt the need to get away from there whenever he could. See something different. It was why he had signed on in the first place. And the maintenance shafts of Oshun were the closest thing to exploring within 100,000 kilometers. It would have to make do until next planet fall.

As Lolanyo scuttled and crawled his way through the ducts, he sketched out a map and occasionally took pictures, more as a record than to share. A trip like this didn't warrant writing an article, but he still wanted a full record of it for his own use. Who knew when knowing the inner workings of Oshun Station would come in handy.

Despite his vague map, he didn't have any idea where he was in relation to the public parts of the station. He could be behind apartments, the shipping corridor, only feet from where the *Pavo* was docked. He found himself wondering where he was compared to Dianthe.

If he was honest with himself, he would admit that when he had first approached her, a part of him was looking for a fling. Her terse response should have put an end to any pursuit, and in a way, it did. She had made it clear that she wanted nothing to do with him, although she did it in a way he could hardly take personally. She wasn't rejecting Lolanyo Oum, she was rejecting the whole human race. At the same time, he found that he did want to get to know her, learn why she was so, not lonely, because he didn't think she thought of herself as lonely, but solitudinous. It was almost as if she was another place to explore, something new to see.

He let himself out through the nearest access hatch. He was in an unfamiliar part of the station and looked around for a map so he could figure out how to get back to the *Pavo*. Checking his watch, he realized that his leave only had an hour remaining. He found the map and was a little chagrinned to learn he was near the ComShed.

Great, he thought. *Now to get out of here before Dianthe sees me and becomes convinced I'm stalking her.*

He quickly made his way away from the ComShed to the main corridor, successfully avoiding Dianthe. The main concourse was crowded and he blended in with the traffic. When he turned down the corridor to find the *Pavo*'s berth, he was shocked to find Dianthe leaning against the wall.

"Lieutenant Oum, I was hoping to find you." She spoke in a stilted manner, as if the words had been rehearsed instead of the inconsequential small talk that everyone used every day.

Lolanyo stammered something that he knew wasn't coherent.

"I looked at some of your pictures. They are really pretty amazing. I'd . . . I'd like to ask you about them."

Lolanyo glanced at his watch. "Now really isn't a good time. I'm on duty in ten minutes. If you give me your code, I can let you know when I'll have time and we can meet. Here. In the bar. Wherever works for you."

Dianthe didn't think Lolanyo knew how difficult it was for her to come down to the berthing area to find him. It went against everything she knew. He hadn't rejected her, but she wasn't sure she would be able to come back down if he did send her a note. She knew how Erich and the rest of the staff viewed her. She couldn't help knowing. At every one of her performance reviews her boss commented on her anti-social behavior. There was nothing she could do about it and was sure that the only reason she kept her job was because she was good at it. If she ever gave them a reason to fire her, she would be gone in a second.

She knew she was probably wrong, but looking at Lolanyo's pictures made her believe she had found a kindred spirit. Someone else who liked solitude. Someone else who understood what it meant to be alone, but not lonely. She felt like there was a connection and it seemed . . . strange. She couldn't remember the last time she actually *wanted* to talk to someone.

And it was still hard to make the effort. She didn't have the practice. She knew that people could chat casually with each other, but it wasn't a skill she had. Her entire way down from the ComShed she had rehearsed what she wanted to say in the hopes it would come out smoothly and, perhaps, even spontaneously. She had the feeling she failed and now just wanted to hide in her apartment and never come out.

In her apartment, she pushed a button and a chair and table emerged from the wall. She dropped into the chair and pulled out her embroidery. After three stitches, she realized she wasn't concentrating on what she was doing and had to pull the stitches out. She wandered around the apartment aimlessly, turning the vid on before realizing she had watched three shows and couldn't remember anything about any of them.

Instead, she found that she had been having fleeting thoughts about Lolanyo. Nothing particularly concrete, but looking over the couple of hours she'd been in her apartment, they were the only things she could actually remember. She was absurdly proud of herself that she remembered his name. And she had called up one of his pictures on her tablet and had it displayed on the wall. A waterfall cascading through a dense jungle of strange

plants. As with all of Lolanyo's photos, there were no
people, no aliens, no animals in the picture. It was the
solitude of the picture that spoke to her. That made her
feel like she had a connection to Lolanyo. Like he might
understand her.

And it made her feel uncomfortable.

Her compad chirruped at her. She looked down to
find a message from Lolanyo.

Have you ever been on a starship?

Since she was on a space station, it seemed an odd
question, but in fact, she had never been on an actual
starship. All of the ships she had been on had merely
been interplanetary. Dianthe suddenly found herself
with a desire to be on a real starship.

She sent back a short message. Only moments later,
she had a reply.

Come on down to the Pavo.

When she reached the *Pavo*'s berth, she found Lolanyo standing exactly where she had been waiting for
him before his shift had started. Despite herself, all the
awkwardness had returned.

There was something different about Dianthe as she
came around the corner and nearly walked into Lolanyo.
He saw an eagerness about her that he hadn't seen in
any of their previous encounters. It was as if something
had happened to cause her to drop whatever shields she
had put up between herself and the whole human race.
Or at least the part of it that Lolanyo represented.

"I can't give you a very long tour, but you'll be able to
see the main parts of the ship."

She didn't say anything, but followed as he led her on *The Pride of Pavo*.

Lolanyo took her through as much of the ship as he could, showing her the freight hold, mess, sleeping quarters, and bridge. Dianthe took it all in with her customary silence. When he had finished showing off the *Pavo*, they sat in the mess.

"I had expected something like Oshun. I hadn't realized how cramped it is on one of these ships."

"You can see why I need to go for hikes when I make planet fall. After being in such tight quarters, I need to get away from the *Pavo* and her crew. You'll notice how empty the ship is. Everyone is like that. As soon as we hit a planet or a station, we scatter, only coming back to the ship when we have duty. And tomorrow, we'll all come back and spend the next several weeks on top of each other until we get to our next port of call."

"It sounds horrible," Dianthe said.

Lolanyo shook his head. "For you, I think it would be. But not for me. Sure, I would like to have more room. Some privacy. But the *Pavo* gets me from place to place. It lets me see new worlds I'd otherwise never get to see."

Dianthe looked around the small room. The mess was smaller than her apartment and seemed designed to allow up to twenty-five people to eat at the same time. She shuddered at how crowded it must get.

"How many people crew to *Pavo*?"

"Our full complement is about 140. About a third are sleeping at any given time, but that still leaves 95 people active at any point."

"How can you stand it?"

"I'm not you. I enjoy the company of other people. I like the hustle and bustle. I also like being able to be alone. Between our voyages and the time I get to spend on leave, I can handle it just fine. But if I were living a solitary existence ... it would drive me as crazy as if I never had any time alone with just my thoughts."

"But you capture being alone so well in your photos," Dianthe blurted.

Lolanyo considered that for a moment, thought about some of his photos. "Just a side effect of hiking alone. I'm just trying to take pictures of what I see. The undisturbed beauty each planet has to offer."

He looked at her.

"I hope you didn't get the wrong idea about me."

Dianthe shook her head. "I guess I was just projecting my own needs on to you. I think I should go now." She rose from her seat.

"I'm sorry. I didn't mean to mislead you."

"It wasn't anything you did. I saw those pictures and saw what I wanted to be there."

Lolanyo escorted her to the hatch.

"I know I insinuated myself into your life. I'm glad I did. It was good to get to know the person behind the voice I've always heard when I come to Oshun."

"Good-bye."

Lolanyo watched her disappear down the corridor and felt as if she were taking a part of him with her.

She was humiliated and could feel Lolanyo watching her race down the corridor. She wended her way through the crowd, not to her apartment, but to the crew's mess, which was half empty. She grabbed a dy-inant onyx and sat at her favorite table near the back, sipping the golden-black liquid slowly and wondering how she had allowed herself to become so vulnerable to a total stranger in such a short period of time.

He would be leaving the next day and she wouldn't be seeing him again. Her life would be able to return to normal. And yet the thought didn't bring her as much comfort as she would have expected it to. She finished off her drink and thought about ordering a second. Instead, she got up and made her way to her apartment.

Her apartment was quiet and empty, the way it always was, but for the first time, she was aware of the silence. The distant hum of Oshun's environmental machinery seemed like a constant, and annoying, drone. Dianthe turned the vid on and allowed the blather of the talking heads drown out the silence, something she could never remember having done before. It left her feeling disconcerted, almost as if she were someone else.

Eventually she made dinner and went to sleep.

In the morning, she awoke, aware that she had slept fitfully and with vivid dreams of walking in strange, unnatural landscapes with Lolanyo. She got ready for work and walked through the crowds to the ComShed.

She said "Good morning" to Erich, who looked back at her with a stunned silence, and began to scroll through the day's schedule. It was much busier than the day before, with several ships leaving Oshun and several more arriving, either coming to Oshun or making planet fall. Either way, Dianthe, would be responsible for guiding them in from their jump points.

As she prepared to take over the Com, she could hear Erich mumbling instructions into his mike while his fingers tapped their own instructions over the keyboard, sending data to a ship either coming to or leaving Oshun. She glanced at the day's schedule and realized *The Pride of Pavo* would be on it. A sadness filled her.

After a few moments, Erich indicated that the ship had cleared Oshun. He signed out and left the ComShed, leaving Dianthe alone to face the day.

Communication Sub-Officer Lolanyo Oum sat on the bridge, again in his sea of calm as *The Pride of Pavo* prepared to leave Oshun. He passed along instructions from Oshun Navcom, a man's voice, not Dianthe's, to the Commander and relayed questions and status from the Commander back to Oshun.

Lolanyo was disappointed he wasn't being guided out by Dianthe. It would have been nice to have heard her voice, even if his meetings with her were never entirely satisfactory. In six months, he'd be passing through Oshun again, and with any luck, Dianthe's voice would guide him in, even if he knew he wouldn't see her. In fact, he couldn't imagine her recognizing him even if they did cross paths.

"*The Pride of Pavo* preparing for hyperspace departure," he announced to Oshun station.

A slight delay, longer than the radio lag would have accounted for, and he heard Oshun's response.

"The Pride of Pavo *is cleared for hyperspace departure*," Dianthe's voice had replaced the man who had talked them away from the station and Lolanyo felt his heart quicken. "*And when you return, I think I might be ready to sit down with you and look at your latest pictures, Lolanyo.*"

F ISN'T FOR FREEFALL

Donald J. Bingle

"**S**o, how about you, Jake? What was your first time like?"

Tyson froze, then eased back into the shadows, careful not to slip on the soapy wet floor of the shower stall. No way he wanted to be seen by the circle of upperclassmen—jerks, each and every one of them—shooting the breeze by their lockers after Physical Conditioning Class. As a newbie—a plebe—he would be hassled for sure if he was caught overhearing their conversation. He reflexively gripped the damp towel around his waist tighter, as if he could stop them from taking it if they tried—as if he could stop them from doing anything if they tried.

He didn't like the rough-housing and mean-spirited laughter that always accompanied any encounter with "senior pilots-in-training" at the Sky Eagle Pilot Training & iSpace Collegium. Some of the so-called "initiation hazing" went far beyond shared-experience pranks

141

and group-inflicted embarrassment supposedly meant to build macho cohesiveness, and, instead veered into the realms of barbarism and cruelty. Unfortunately, Tyson had to endure the juvenile hazing if he wanted to become an iSpace Pilot. His grades were good and he studied hard; he would make the cut and graduate in four years if the macho ex-military men, work-out yahoos, over-compensating former race car drivers, and adrenaline-jockey tough guys didn't drive him out during his plebe year.

Of course, being smart enough to know that towels snap for the same reason whips crack—the angular momentum of the rapidly uncoiling flexible matrix forces the tip to exceed the speed of sound, generating a mini sonic-boom—was of no practical assistance when you were on the receiving end of a hundred snap salute, naked on the slimy shower room floor, just doing your best to cover your privates and your face to protect yourself and make sure the bullies didn't see you wince in pain . . . or, worse yet, cry.

There was no other exit from the utilitarian shower stall, so Tyson just wedged himself into the dark corner behind the near edge of the open doorway and settled in to wait. He had to be quiet—the ceramic tiles of the stall echoed and amplified every sound. But as he focused on taking shallow, even breaths to evade detection, he realized that the hard surfaces of the floor and stall amplified everything the guys he was evading were saying, too. He could hear every word; he literally couldn't help but eavesdrop.

"So," Jake recounted, obviously winding up his story,

"I gave her just one more quick thrust and, as she settled contentedly, I said 'Yeah, baby! This Eagle has landed . . . *again*.'"

Fortunately, the hoots and hollers and raucous laughter of his would-be tormentors drowned out Tyson's involuntary sharp intake of breath. His momma had warned him, back in South Dakota, when he first told her that he was declining his Ivy League scholarship to go to Flight School at Sky Eagles, that there would be this kind of lewd and scandalous talk. "Locker room talk," she had called it, but he had no idea that it would happen in an actual locker room and that people really talked about such things . . . out loud . . . with a crowd of people shouting encouragement.

But his momma had known, right from the start. When he'd first told her he wanted to become a Sky Eagle, her immediate reply had been: "Remember, son, the Eagle is a bird of prey." He'd been surprised at the time, even upset, at the insult her statement implied about the cadets studying at a respected institution, but now he knew better. Now, it bothered him that he hadn't listened to his momma and now had to listen to such talk. It bothered him even more to realize that his dear, pristine momma even knew about such things.

His disquieting remembrances of his momma's advice were interrupted by Jake's voice once more. "Yessiree. I must have taken that ride a hundred times since, but nothing like that first time." Tyson did his best to suppress both the wave of nausea and the touch of excitement that fluttered through his body as he heard the coarse boast of prowess and ribald cheering that reverberated through the locker room in response. "So, c'mon," Jake continued. "Who's next? How about you, Yoshi?"

"Me?" he heard Yoshi squeak. "There's really not that much to tell." Tyson could hear the embarrassment in Yoshi's voice as he talked, but after numerous shouts of encouragement, talk he did.

"I was young, not yet a man in my father's eyes. And he came to my room one day and said 'You spend too much time studying. You do nothing but read. Your head is filled with science and formulae, but not with life. You must experience things firsthand before you make any life choices, so you know what to expect, what to do.' I flushed. I didn't know what to say. My father had always been very formal. I never spoke to him about such things. I never told him of my desires. It would be too embarrassing! Yet somehow he knew. Then he told me he was going on a 'business trip' the next evening and that I would accompany him, but that I should tell my mother that I was sleeping over at my friend's house overnight and, of course, never say anything at all to her about our excursion . . ."

"Your first time was a 'business trip' with your dad. Yeecchh!" someone hooted. "That doesn't count. That's . . . that's . . ."

"That's disgusting!" interrupted Jake. "I take it back. You're not next. You forfeit your turn . . . in perpetuity."

"We wouldn't want to diminish the father-son bonding experience for you by making you tell us the details," sneered the hooter from before. "I'm sure you have fond memories of your dad's face turning red, his heavy breathing coming in ragged, rhythmic bursts from the couch on the other side of the cabin."

"It wasn't like that," protested Yoshi. "I was just responding to your question. It wasn't my idea to talk about it."

"Here's a hint," continued the hooter. "Next time someone asks about your first time, just lie! Don't bring up your dad. In fact, don't bring up your family at all. Make it thrilling, exciting, exotic. Sex it up for us!"

"I'll tell you what, Yoshi," said a new participant. Tyson was sure it was Evan, a mild-mannered upperclassman who was generally somewhat nicer to all of the plebes than were his companions. "You can borrow my story if you like and just change things around a bit. You know, insert your own dates and places."

"So, it was good for you?" asked Yoshi.

"It was transcendent," replied Evan. "Spiritual, profound, intense, perhaps even . . ."

"Imaginary . . ." interrupted Hoot-Boy, generating a ripple of convulsive laughter from the crowd.

"No," replied Evan in a smooth, even voice. "Life-altering, though, if you—all of you—can imagine that. After my tech proficiency testing was over, I'd gone to Florida for spring break . . ."

"Yeah, that sounds sacred . . ."

". . . and I was on the beach when I saw her in the distance. She was tall, even taller when you got up close, and sleek and beautiful—her curves subtle and enchanting, with the sweetest little tail you ever did see. And

I knew, right then and there, that I just had to get me into that." Everyone else was silent, but Evan chuckled softly, as if to himself. "Let me tell you, that took some doing. I basically just dumped my friends, the guys I'd come to the beach with, and spent all my time chasing her down. It wasn't easy, but I knew a guy who knew a guy who knew a gal ... You get the picture. And finally, there I was on the elevator on my way up to her. It was the last day I was supposed to be in Florida and I was sweating bullets, not because it was hot, though it was, but because if it didn't work out, if there was any kind of problem or delay or I messed up in any way, the ship would sail without me, man. I'm out and I probably never see her again and some other guy, someday later gets what I shoulda had and I miss the sweetest ride of my life."

"But that didn't happen. Everything went smoothly, without a hitch: all the preliminaries; the suiting up for protection, pushing all the right buttons, and getting nothing but green lights. The next thing I know, I'm lying on my back on the couch, looking up at her, soaking up her curves, her exquisite beauty, and I hear 'Just lie back and enjoy' and I do. I simply position my joystick and then relax and she does the rest. First, I just let the pleasant rocking lull me into a sleepy contentment. Slowly, the rhythmic pressure of her revving up begins, my heart rate increases, and the adrenaline kicks in, rousing me into a growing euphoria of happiness and excitement. Then my breathing begins to match her rhythm and comes faster and deeper, and the hydraulics deploy, and my screams of ecstasy mix with her rumbling roar of release, and then I'm panting and my blood-pressure is peaking, and the thrust is maxing out, and I can't seem to even breathe anymore, and then there is a sudden shudder and release and its like I'm floating and she's quiet and life is good."

Tyson found he was holding his breath as the story reached its climax and his towel needed adjusting, but he dared not move. He continued to hold his breath until the crowd of storytellers broke their silence.

Finally, someone gave a low whistle. "Wow," whispered Yoshi. "Thanks for saying I could use your story."

"Oh, yeah," cracked Hoot-Boy, "like anyone would believe you, if you told 'em that."

"Leave him alone," replied Evan. "You're just jealous, 'cause now he's got a better story than you have."

"What makes you say that, lover boy? You haven't even heard my story yet."

Jake interrupted. "So, spill. Put up or shut up. We'll see who's got the better tale."

"Well," drawled Hoot-Boy, "mine's the complete opposite of his and since his is all lovey-dovey plain vanilla, you can bet mine is Rocky Road with Tabasco Sauce."

Tyson grimaced.

"Stop selling and start telling," demanded Jake.

"None of this tall and sleek and subtle curves bullcrap for me. Too delicate for my sensibilities. Naw, my first time was in the back of a 2057 Chevy. Short, fat, with big ol' curves and plenty of room to take care of business, if you know what I mean. Now, of course, I wasn't supposed to be there, which makes it just that much more exciting—you know, the thrill of being caught and all—and there weren't no preliminaries and no protection. I just kinda maneuvered my way in and slam-bam, suddenly things just take off and its real rough and everything is shaking and I'm just grabbing hold of her anywhere I can and she's slapping me about, so I just grab on harder and try to survive the punishment she's dishing out, and it's painful, but it's exciting all the same. Finally, things steady out a bit and then the thrust builds and there's this unbelievable weight pressing down on my chest and I practically black-out, but she just keeps going and going and going until suddenly all the fuel's spent and I just lie back, exhausted."

"Sounds rather tawdry to me," said Evan.

"To each his own," sneered Hoot-Boy. "She was beautiful to me. Short and curvy, that don't bother me. Big ol' fat tail works for me, too. And I gotta say, I still love her fins . . ."

Tyson shook his head to clear it. Did he say "fins?" Was that Hoot-Boy's euphemism for . . . well . . . hooters?

"You like fins?" exclaimed Jake.

"I love 'em," replied Hoot(er)-boy. "They're not just decorative, y'know. Though I love the way they look, protruding out from the main body, all glorious and proud, the rounded edges curving down to narrow points of critical contact. She had three, y'know, which provides structural stability . . ."

"Three?!?" Tyson blurted it out before he could stop himself, dropping his towel in astonishment into the sheen of water still slowly circling the stall drain. Was Hoot-Boy fornicating with mutants or aliens . . . or mutant aliens? Or was three the latest fad in breast "enhancement" surgery? He shuddered at the disgusting possibilities as he reached down for his wet towel.

The entire circle of jerks was standing at the stall door by the time he had recovered his dirty, soaked towel, wrapped it around himself, and turned around.

"Looky here," snarled Hoot-Boy, "it's Plebe Tyson Stafford, spying on us."

Tyson trembled, but did his best to stand up straight and tall. "I wasn't spying. I was taking a shower."

Jake reached over and felt the shower head. "It's not even warm. What, were you taking a cold shower?"

Hoot-Boy chimed in. "Does Tyson take a lot of cold showers?"

"How long have you been listening in?" demanded Jake.

"Long enough," Tyson gulped, "to . . . uh . . . know what you were talking about."

"Plebe spy! Stick his head in the toilet!" yelled Hoot-Boy.

"Yeah," yelled someone in the back. "Make him swirl."

Evan waved his hands to quiet the crowd. "I say we give him a chance."

"A chance to do what?"

"A chance to tell his first-time story," replied Evan. "If it's better than Elroy's," he continued, motioning toward Hoot-Boy, "then we just take his towel and let him sneak back to the dorm naked."

Elroy scowled, but Yoshi voiced quick approval of Evan's idea. Within a few seconds, almost everyone else murmured agreement.

"So spill," said Jake.

"Make it interesting," suggested Evan with a nod of encouragement.

"Give us details," demanded Elroy.

"Lie if you have to," mouthed Yoshi from the back of the crowd, his eyes wide.

Tyson flushed. He couldn't . . . He wouldn't . . . He hadn't . . .

He tried his best to take Yoshi's advice. He'd held hands with a girl once at summer camp in Minnesota. Maybe he could use that as a base, embellish a bit, gloss over the details, and get away with merely a naked streak across campus. But even as he decided to do it, he couldn't make the words come out of his mouth. Not only would he undoubtedly do a lousy job of entertaining his superior officers with his imaginary exploits, it was dishonorable to even try. His "girlfriend" from camp wouldn't ever know he had made things up about her, but it still made him feel dirty to even contemplate doing so. She didn't deserve it. His memory of her didn't deserve it.

He'd admit the truth. Maybe they'd laugh, but just maybe they'd respect him for it . . . or just let him go out of sympathy.

"I won't. I mean, I can't. I can't tell you about my first time, because . . ." He looked at the ground and muttered the rest of the sentence with a sigh. ". . . because I'm a virgin." He looked up to see their reaction so he could be ready to take a defensive position, if need be.

"You're a virgin?" asked Jake, one eyebrow higher than Tyson thought possible.

"I sure wouldn't phrase it that way if I were you," guffawed Elroy.

"But that doesn't make sense," replied Evan. "You came to the moon base on the GMC Spaceways 6000 Rocket Express, just like the rest of us at one time or the other, so how can you be a virgin?"

Tyson didn't understand. Were there amenities in the first-class cabin reserved for recruits that he didn't know about and hadn't taken advantage of? He tilted his head to one side and gave Evan a hard stare. "What's that got to do with anything?"

Evan scrunched up his face a bit before replying. "We were just telling each other stories about our first time aboard a rocket ship. Mine was on one of those two orbit tandem flights they were testing for offering to well-heeled tourists down in Florida." He furrowed his brow even further. "What did you think we were talking about?"

Tyson suddenly felt light-headed. He'd misunderstood; ships were always referred to as feminine. When he'd heard "she" and "her," he'd just filled in the blanks in his mind . . . in graphic detail.

He had assumed; now he was ashamed.

Momma would not be proud of what he had been thinking.

"I . . . I thought you were describing . . ." He stopped. Better to shut up than say what he had been thinking. He looked up at Evan. "Never mind what I thought. It doesn't matter. I'm just a plebe . . . sir." He looked at the faces of the upperclassmen—some blank, some stupid, some hostile—and began to calculate how many toilet flushes he could hold his breath through. Given the lower water pressure and slower swirl rate of a low-grav loo, he'd be lucky if he could make four before gasping for breath. He needed to make sure to time his breaths appropriately during the inevitable hazing to come.

It wasn't like it was his first time.

IF THIS WERE A ROMANCE

Shannon Page and Jay Lake

Haunted, Loren thought. *The man haunts me.*

Not that there was anything sane or rational or even halfway intelligent that she could do about it. Of course not. Furthermore, she wasn't even sure he knew what he was doing.

It was just that he appeared . . . everywhere. She'd be walking down a narrow steel service gallery embedded in the hullframe 280 gardens, wrench in hand, sent to adjust the timing on the mildew pumps—and there he would be. Squeezing past her, his arm brushing hers as his eyes scanned ahead to the great towering falls of greenery that made up the bulk of Ship's biological resources.

Or it would be end of shift and she would have stopped off for a ration of slivovitz in Frame Zero, the generic little bar on Deck 47 near her bunk bay, and he'd be in there, huddled at a small table talking to some officer she didn't recognize. Not that Crew spent much time down here in work gang country.

Or what happened today. She was all the way across Ship's circumference, a full one-eighty from her usual workshift site, at the coreward edge of the habitable area where the passageways began running to anoxic atmospheres and the bulkheads carried exotic gas warnings in a multitude of languages and symbols, running an errand for her gang boss. Even the grav plates were wonky there—Loren had to watch every step, as the bad patches tended to accumulate a lot more dust. And she was lost; the numbers seemed scattered over here, half the hatches not even marked; the passageways didn't follow the normal patterns. They bulged and shifted around to make room for the gardens hullward, but still, why did it have to be *this* complicated?

Loren hefted the carryall of excess He-3 cartridges around to her other hip and sighed. Heavy. Too heavy. She should have brought a waist pack, but she didn't think she'd be carrying them so long. "Blasted things," she muttered. The corner of the carryall dug into her side; the cartridges rattled against one another. Why couldn't Gramma Francesca have sent a runner? She was a biomechanic; skilled far above this sort of makework.

And then he was there. Not a haunting at all, but just about treading on her boots as she turned a blind corner.

"Oh! I am sorry, sir." She reeled back, nearly dropping the carryall, and felt her face flush. Had he heard her?

"Citizen," he said, his voice softer and somehow higher than she'd expected. "My fault. I wasn't attending."

His accent was that of the highest echelons of senior

Crew. This much, at least, she'd expected. His words, though . . . Far more polite than one of her class could ever expect from one of his class.

The Captain would not take as Consort any other than a man of the highest rank, after all.

"No, the fault is mine," she murmured, and struggled to reposition the carryall, ease gracefully past him, not look him in the eye, and show proper respect all at once. As several of these actions were impossible to perform simultaneously, she managed only a hesitant step forward before he spoke again.

"Citizen, your name, if you please?"

"Loren 68. Sir." With an uncharacteristic fit of compulsive honesty, she added, "Work gang Forty-Seven Charlie. Best gang in the decks, sir."

A small smile flickered across the officer's face. "Citizen Loren, do you have a pass for this area?"

She fumbled with the carryall again, then finally set it down at her feet. Holding out her left wristband, she blushed even further as she said, "Gramma Francesca gave me a thirty-minute override. But I'm lost . . ."

He sniffed as he examined the blinking red light on the band. "Very well." Then, taking her hand gently in his and turning it over, he tapped a code onto the tiny keypad at her wrist. The band beeped; the glow changed to green; delicious, startled shivers of craving and delight emanated up her arm from his casual touch. "There you are. Thirty more minutes. Your destination is that way." He dropped her hand—nearly painful, the loss of contact!—and pointed ahead.

"Thank you, sir, thank you!"

"Carry on." With that, he was gone, leaving her a whiff of his scent and a handful of wicked memories.

Two shots of slivovitz down that night, and still sleep would not come. *Haunted.* After an hour of this, Loren sat up in her bunk and turned on the console, then pulled up the entertainment files. Old stories, she liked; the oldest, ones that took place on Earth.

A planet she had never seen.

A planet no one she knew had ever seen.

You'd have to be nearly two centuries old to have any memories of Earth. And, while technically possible, people of that age were vanishingly rare. At least the sort of people she knew.

The Consort probably knew Earthlings among the senior Crew . . .

"Stop it," she whispered, and continued searching through her files.

A Regency romance: a tale of love and unattainability. A man of the highest station, one who is betrothed to a woman of his caste. A simple girl, humble, shy, making her way through edges of someone else's fairy tale. An accidental encounter, and then another; a brush of the arm; a casual exchange . . . Loren laughed at herself, but reread the story anyway, savoring every word.

When she was finished, she wanted to weep.

Of course, everything was backward, just all wrong, here in the real world. Nothing like the stories. For it to be a true romance, the Consort should have offered to carry the carryall today, not sent Loren on her way with a sharp word.

And she should be a stolen child of the aristocracy—a princess in disguise, or hidden, through some astonishing mix-up of fortune. Awaiting discovery of her rightful place . . . and the hand of her prince.

But no. Loren was already in her rightful place, and lucky to have it. Her workshift was not onerous, her teammates were decent and engaging, and Gramma Francesca was a benevolent work gang boss. She'd heard stories, knew how it could be.

So why did she feel as though her life was being wasted, one unendurable sliver at a time?

Gram Keith, the overboss of the Deck 48 work gangs and convenor of all the decks from 45 to 52 in the three hundred series hullframes, had called a general meeting. "Hurry, Citizens, hurry!" Gramma Francesca marched down the bunking passageway, rapping on hatches with her wand, sending tiny jolts of Direction into everyone's right-hand wristbands. "We're starting in five minutes!"

Loren tumbled out of bed and yanked on the suit she'd worn yesterday—no time to turn it in for a clean one—then splashed her face with water from the tiny sink at the foot of her bunk. She dried her hands on her hair, smoothing it down and tucking the excess into the suit's collar. Too much of a rush to find a ponytail holder either . . . a small act of rebellion, or merely independence, keeping her hair long. It was also a colossal pain in the ass, when it came to close work in the deep machinery where the grav plates were variable and the snag hazards multiplied.

No matter. She wasn't going to cut it.

Her head pounding from the slivovitz, or perhaps just the lack of sleep, she grabbed a handful of Pain-Free from the passageway bin on her way out, chewing the chalky tablets as she hurried along with her bunkmates to the ramp leading to the next deck.

"Late night?" Garen had fallen into step alongside Loren. Now he struggled to keep up with her long stride. She wasn't going to make it any easier on him, either.

"Why do you ask, Citizen?"

He nodded at her hand, but it was empty now. So he'd been watching her. As usual.

"You have dust at the corner of your mouth," he said, after a pause that was just a bit too long.

She wiped with the back of her hand, but found nothing. Who did he think he was fooling? "Thanks," she said, giving him a look that said just the opposite.

He sat next to her in the meeting. After she ignored several of his whispered remarks, he fell silent.

Which allowed her to pay attention to Gram Keith, of course. As they were supposed to. Unfortunate that things should be so dull, but such was life.

The bulk of the meeting was to go over the reordered workshift assignments. Loren listened carefully until her own number was mentioned. No changes there. Good.

She was woolgathering again, letting her mind drift to . . . well, to hauntings, truth be told. Tall, slender, pale men appearing at the unexpected ends of passageways, empty service bays, a gentle brush on the inside of a wrist, all accidental . . . when she heard a sharp inbreath next to her.

"What?" she whispered to Garen.

The young man was bright-eyed, his face flushed. "I'm transferred, to your unit. Effective immediately."

Loren stared at him, her heart lurching. Not *him*. "But you don't know anything about biomechanics."

"I'll be support. It's a way up, a way in. You know I've always wanted to do that kind of work."

Then they both jumped as Gramma Francesca sent a small jolt of Control to their wristbands. **Quiet** came through the line, the order emanating through Loren's brain as if it was a thought of her own. Her mouth closed automatically and her attention returned to the announcements.

If this were a romance, Garen would be a prince, fallen from his high station, unrecognizable in humble garb, manure on his shoes, and a painful shyness masking his nobility. Loren would be yearning for the unattainable lord, all the while not seeing the even more fantastic man so close to hand.

No, that would only be true if Garen were the hero of the romance. Not Loren.

No, it could still be true, if Garen were not truly, utterly, miserably horrible. And if the Consort were not so unbelievably, thrillingly desirable.

It could be no kind of romance that had Garen anywhere in it.

Loren turned in her bunk once more, fussing at the covers. The thin blanket seemed too skimpy at times, and all too much at other times.

Not the blanket's fault, of course.

And was Garen really so horrible? Truly?

Yes, he was a pest; yes, he was manipulative and sneaky and weak-chinned and had an odd way of cocking his head when he was thinking . . . but did that make him impossible?

Well, yes, it did. Garen was impossible. Loren knew that much, at least, from the romances. If you have to talk yourself into a man, you don't want him.

Finally giving up, Loren sat up and dialed another entertainment, a period virteo this time with glittering eye candy and wonderful set pieces. But even that failed to distract. Her mind kept returning to its hauntings . . . interspersed with terrifying images of spending every day with Garen, now that he had somehow maneuvered the transfer. The eager boy asking her endless questions, inserting himself into her every conversation, even— shudder—somehow arranging that she should be the one to train him.

Oh, of *course* he would do that. He probably already had! She should apply for a change of workshift immediately. She would talk to Gramma Francesca first thing at lights-up. Anything—she'd transfer to anything. Even to an Outside work gang . . . though "dangerous" barely began to describe Outside work. Ship sailed through hard space, radiation sleeting across Her skin like scalpels waiting to sculpt an unlucky Citizen's cells into monstrous assassins of the body.

The story on the screen before her played on; Loren barely watched. Partway through, a figure caught her eye, and she gasped, did a double take, then ran the transmission back to see it again.

It couldn't be.

An actor in the ancient drama . . . he looked just like the Consort. Tall and slender and pale . . .

No. It wasn't him, of course; the dramas were made in the entertainment division, and actors were chosen from the general Citizenry, men and women and inters just like Loren. And Garen.

General Citizens did not become Consorts to the Captain.

Still, she looked at the scene several times before letting the drama run forward again. The tall actor had a minor role to play; cousin to the penniless heroine. He only appeared in one other scene, and in that one, he was clearly not the Consort.

Of course he wasn't.

Because her life was not a romance. And the Consort was not for her. And if she didn't choose to bond with Garen, or someone else like him, someone actually *available* to her, Loren would spend her life alone. She would not be able to apply for an upgrade to dual quarters; she would not be given celebratory rations of slivovitz every fourth cycle; she would not get to put on the white armband that signified pair-bonding and sometimes provided curfew waivers as well as sundry other benefits.

She would not have anyone to talk to, late at night, when the chattering in her brain refused to die down.

She would not ever understand what love felt like.

Yet if the Consort was not for her, then why did he keep showing up, dangling himself in her line of vision, appearing everywhere she happened to be? Haunting her? Ship was enormous—tens of thousands of Citizens, many hundreds of the upper echelon. Loren had never seen the Captain or any of the senior Crew in the flesh. Only the Consort. Again and again. What were the odds of that?

He was doing it somehow. He was sending her a message. He was powerful. He could do so with very little trouble. But he couldn't do so openly. Not a man in his position. She was supposed to understand.

Even in the entertainments she somehow chose to watch. Why had those particular ones become available to her? Especially the one with the actor who looked just like the Consort?

Of course Loren's life was a romance—it had to be. And of course she was the heroine of it. Except she had understood it all wrong. She was not a classical heroine. Rather, she was the hero. He was the captive, betrothed to the Captain, no doubt against his will. If she would not take charge, if she would not rescue him, then who would?

By the time the entertainment ended, Loren had made her decision.

She rose before lights-up and collected a clean suit from the rack at the end of the passageway, then stole back to her bunkroom and washed her entire body using the tiny sink. Likely nobody would be in the communal 'freshers at this hour; even so, she didn't want to take a chance at being seen. At being asked questions.

Instead of braiding her long hair or tucking it away as usual, Loren left it loose, brushing the strands out with her fingers. In the romances, the heroine had a hairbrush, with a silver handle and boar's hair bristles. Here aboard Ship, in transit for generations, heroines had to make do without. There were no boars, nor silver, to start with. And with standard-issue jumpsuits and heavy black boots, when she really should be wearing gossamer gowns and dainty golden sandals . . .

"Right," she whispered, easing one last tangle from her hair. "And while I'm at it, I might as well wish for a walk in the woods. And a pony."

If they had woods.

Or ponies.

Though of course, if she was the hero, she should have a sword and a suit of armor. Equally impossible. As a biomechanic, at least she could *grow* a pony.

Carrying her boots until she'd left the sleeping area, Loren made it out without waking anyone. Or so she hoped, anyway.

She didn't begin breathing easier until she'd reached the high-speed lifts at hullframe three forty-one, out of her range but not actually a forbidden area. Holding up her left armband to the console, she punched in the override code that Gramma Francesca most usually used to release the workers for temporary assignments. Citizens were not supposed to know these codes, but everyone did. Gang bosses were expected to change them regularly, but the hassle involved was just too much.

So long as everyone kept quiet and didn't steal too much from the stores, everything worked out just fine.

Loren hoped she wasn't knocking over the entire system right now . . . but if she was— so be it. She'd pay the price later, and hope the trouble would be worth it.

The high-speed lift beeped in response to her override code. Doors opened with a whoosh and a clank. The engineering part of Loren's brain noted the clank and was already diagnosing probable cause and likely repair strategies before the part that was in charge at the moment took over.

"No dice, princess," she whispered to herself as the doors closed her into the lift. "This goes well, you'll never repair another lift again."

The hullward decks were unlike anything she'd ever seen before. Loren knew how Ship was laid out; everyone had seen schematics all their lives, and with her biomechanic's engineering training, she understood better than most how the structure was held together.

The beauty of it struck her most. Wide, sweeping open spaces overhead, tied to one another by the thinnest spans of gleaming gossamer-spun titanium while their glittering crystalline panels provided a view of the stars outside. Multideck spans of bulkhead covered in what had to be merely decorative greenery. The very air smelled fresh as if it had not roiled through a million lungs before hers. The long views down to coreward levels unthinkably lower, farther away, demonstrating the grand scale of Ship. Even the color scheme on bulkheads and panels and informational signage was different up here in hullward country: contrasting mauve and a deep green, a combination that somehow conveyed both comfort and majesty. Yes, it was true: Crew really did have it better than the Citizenry.

How pleasant it would be to live up here!

After a minute, Loren realized she had no idea where to go next.

The Captain dwelled at the top hullward level, along the outer hull: everyone knew that. But where? There weren't even hatches up here, much less numbered ones—assuming Loren would know what number to look for.

She had thought it would be obvious. In the virteo romances, the powerful always had red carpets, brazen trumpets, massive doorways. Nothing at all was obvious, though. Loren wandered down a long balcony, stealing glances over the elegant, too-thin rail to the unfathomable depths below, trying to figure out where the center was. The balcony ended in a set of passageways fanning out in a pattern of spokes. She hesitated, then chose the middle way and kept on. Here there were hatches, at least, but they were still not numbered, not labeled.

No signage at all. She could think of several safety code write-ups from that.

Where *was* everyone? It was quiet, too quiet. Did no one live here at all? Was the whole notion of a Captain and a Bridge just a hoax? Ship was vast, and contained multitudes. Right now, anything seemed possible.

Was the Consort a myth, too? No, he was real. A haunting, and so very, very real.

So where were all the people who should be up here?

That question was answered a moment later, when two guards rounded the corner, bored expressions on their faces.

"Citizen," the woman said, her eyes snapping into focus a moment quicker than the male guard's did.

"Ma'am," Loren answered, automatically, her hand going to cover her left wristband.

"Your pass?"

"I . . ." This was it, the moment she had been waiting for. All the sleepless nights, all the dreams, all the desperation of her determined flight up here. "I need to see the Consort. I have urgent business with him."

The woman guard—she had red hair, longer than Loren's, pulled back in a ponytail, and unusually pale eyes—stood a little taller and glanced at her partner. "Your *pass*, Citizen," she repeated.

The male guard nodded and still said nothing.

Loren sighed and held out her wrist. "Gramma Francesca sent me, from Deck 47, in the three hundreds. The errand is urgent, and she programmed my pass quickly— it might not be exactly right." *Of course it's not exactly right— it's not even sort of right. But it's all I've got.*

The woman took Loren's hand, turning it gently, and peered at the left wristband. It was an odd echo of the Consort's action two days ago.

And, oddly, the touch gave Loren the same shivering thrill.

In the privacy of her own mind, Loren laughed at herself. *Now any time someone gives me a new assignment or checks my status, I'm going to giggle like a schoolgirl? Oh wonderful.*

The guard finished her inspection, frowning. She turned to her partner and began to speak quietly in coded language.

The woman was going to deny Loren. They were

going to stop her, to send her back. This was her only chance, and they were going to stop her.

Loren yanked the heavy wrench out of her pocket and held it high, brandishing it over both their heads. "I know it's wrong, and I don't care. I've *got* to see the Consort! I have to!" She reached back; she'd hit the man first, and maybe the woman would run.

The female guard didn't move, didn't speak, for a long moment. Then she drew her weapon in a blur of movement and Loren's world went blank.

Loren awoke in pain—the usual pain, from a stun-blow, magnified by what must have been several applications of Control and Direction to her wristband.

She was lying on a cot in a small holding cell. Had she been sent back to Deck 47? Most likely.

Loren sat up, rubbing her face, trying to ignore the pain. Her head seared with it, and the backs of her eyes, and a stab of agony ran through her left calf muscle. "Oh . . ."

After a minute, the pain ebbed a bit, but still, Loren wished she had a huge handful of Pain-Free. Or a big ration of slivovitz.

Why was her calf hurting so much? Hadn't the guard hit her in the chest, as they usually did?

Loren studied the small room as her vision steadied. No manual controls on the inside of the hatch, just a keypad and a sensor. Yes, a holding cell. Too bad for her if there was a fire or a life support failure. Perhaps a bit more spacious than she'd expected, but since she had never occupied one, merely repaired the isolated airflow systems supporting them, she wasn't entirely sure.

Inside the holding cell was one long table against the bulkhead, with nothing on it; a sink, with no mirror over it; a small sanitary device in the corner, with a ration of wipes beside it. The cot upon which she sat, steel frame with the usual thickness of mattress and the usual blanket. Nothing out of the ordinary, nothing she wouldn't have expected to find.

It took her a while to realize what was different about the cell. The bulkheads were painted mauve, with dark green accents.

After a time, the hatch slid open. Loren crouched on the cot, her knees drawn up, rubbing the sore calf. Her headache surged forward as her eyes snapped to the hatchway.

It was the redheaded guard, alone, and unarmed. She slipped in, then tapped the keypad. The hatch snicked shut behind her.

"What . . ." Loren started, then stopped herself. This whole business had more than a whiff of danger to it. Of things that weren't allowed.

"Quiet," the guard said, unnecessarily. She sat beside Loren on the cot, perhaps just a bit too close, facing her.

From this distance, Loren could see that her pale eyes were sea-gray. It was a striking look, with the lush red hair.

Hair that was now loose and flowing over the woman's shoulders.

"Tell me why you've come here," the guard now whispered, "and I may be able to help you."

"I ..." Loren stared back into the woman's eyes. God, she was beautiful. Loren had been with women before—what girl hadn't?—but it had never done anything much for her. Women together—that wasn't how the romances went, after all. "I told you. I came to see the Consort."

The woman shook her head, but a smile hovered at the corners of her mouth. "Yes, you said that. But you know and I know that your gang boss didn't send you. Look: tell, and I might be able to do something. But quickly."

Loren bit her lip, then told the woman all.

She waited in the cell. After she'd poured out her heart and soul, the woman—Sonia was her name, and it suited her, Loren thought—had nodded, then hugged her tightly. "Be strong," she whispered. "I'll be back."

The next time the hatch opened, though, it was just an orderly with a tray of food. Rations that were neither better nor worse than what she'd get in the gang mess back on Deck 47 or from the dispensers scattered throughout her part of Ship.

She ate the food, though she had little appetite. At least her aches and pains were subsiding.

A few more hours went by. Loren was wishing hard that the cell had been provided with an entertainment console when the hatch snicked open again, and Sonia entered.

The Consort was right behind her.

"Ohhh," Loren sighed, as they both stepped into the cell and closed the hatch behind them. Full of words, she was, thousands of words—and they all failed her, in this moment. The moment she'd been waiting for; the reason she'd taken this risk, risen to this level . . .

"Yes, this is the one," the Consort said to Sonia.

"I thought so." She sat on the cot beside Loren once more, though Loren barely noticed. The Consort stood just inside the hatch, watching her with an unreadable expression. She couldn't keep her eyes off him. He was even more beautiful than she'd remembered.

"Have you told her?" he asked Sonia.

"Not yet. I wanted to be sure."

Now Loren turned to the other woman. "Told me what?"

The redheaded guard took Loren's hands, both of them, and smiled at her. Yes, the woman was lovely indeed. Was everyone so gorgeous here in the upper echelons? Even the workers? Loren shook away the thought. It didn't matter. Of course they were good-looking. That was why they were privileged, right?

"We have an exciting proposal for you."

This is it, she thought, as a thrill filled her chest, saturated her heart with joy. She had been right. The Consort was looking for escape, a way out— he had singled Loren out, chosen her— life was a romance indeed . . .

Even if it wasn't playing out exactly as Loren had hoped, had dreamed, It would be better if it were she and the Consort alone, if it were his hands in hers right now, not Sonia's . . .

But the woman was still talking. Loren had missed the first few words, but snapped to attention at the word "Outside."

". . . never recruit for such missions openly," she was saying. "Too many people think they're strong enough, capable enough, for what we face out there, but they're not."

"Out . . . Outside?" Loren stammered. What?

"Yes." Sonia smiled even more broadly. "It's a new mission, just being formed, to map out our arrival. *In this generation!* The team will be doing planetary surveys. Exploration and mapping. High danger, high chance of injury . . ."

"High reward." The Consort finally spoke again. "And we think you're perfectly suited as the team's bio-mechanic."

Loren stared back at the man of her dreams. Her mind was both blank and racing. Thoughts, half-formed, flitted through her head and then vanished, chased by other, even crazier thoughts. Finally, she managed, "Why me? There must be hundreds of better engineering techs in and out of the bio specialties."

"But none more daring. None with your initiative." Sonia again. "Look at what you've done, all the rules you've broken, the risks you've taken."

"But not . . . that wasn't for going *Outside*." She didn't want to die! Were they insane? Was she going to wake up at any moment, safe in her own bunk?

The Consort laughed. "No, of course not. As Sonia said, we can't advertise for this—we'd get all sorts of fools. You couldn't have known."

"We've had our eye on you for some time," Sonia went on. "When your gang boss first reported that you routinely modified your work logs to cover the fact that you finished jobs faster than anyone else, but didn't ask to take on a new assignment, we knew you had ingenuity, and a strong sense of self-preservation."

"I . . ." Loren stammered. Gramma Francesca had known about the logs? She thought she'd hidden that without a trace.

"And when we reviewed the records of what entertainments you ordered, we knew you were a dreamer, a woman with imagination." The Consort, this time.

"No one without imagination survives Outside." Sonia gazed at Loren, her face serious, pleading.

They meant it, these people. But no, there was no way. Unless . . .

"What is the reward?" she asked.

Sonia beamed back at her, and the Consort smiled and took a step forward. "Name your price."

Loren looked up into his eyes. "You."

His smile fell away and his eyes narrowed. "Don't be a fool, *Citizen*." Her heart sank at the tone of the Consort's voice. "I meant credits, privileges— anything you desire that one of your station can have. Extra rations, larger quarters. Any work assignment you request upon your return."

"I don't want that." Loren felt herself filling with desperate urgency, a sense of recklessness. She had nothing left to lose. "If you've been researching me and watching me all this time, you *know* what I want. That's why you've been following me personally, isn't it? Haunting me. You *know.* And you know I won't settle for some stupid larger bunk and a dozen extra drinks per cycle. You know."

His expression was not changing as she spoke. She might as well be arguing with empty air. Beside her, Sonia looked sad, disappointed. It didn't mar the woman's loveliness any.

"Impossible," the Consort finally said.

Loren stared back at him. Up close, she could see the tiny lines at the corners of his eyes. His hair was thinning, just a bit. His suit, though made of exquisite material, fit him rather too tight around the hips, too loose around the shoulders.

He was not perfect.

He was not the hero.

"Let me go below, then," she said. "Just send me back."

"It's not that simple," the Consort began, but Sonia interrupted: "Yes, it is. We haven't told her anything that isn't general knowledge, or at least general rumor." She looked at Loren. "You can go."

Who was in charge here? Surely the Consort outranked a mere guard? But the man only nodded, and within minutes, Loren was back in the same high-speed lift she'd come up on, carrying nothing but memories and hastily swallowed tears.

Loren slouched in Frame Zero, the small bar on Deck 47, two ration glasses of slivovitz on the table before her. The murmur of conversation surrounded her; she listened idly to it, picking up words here and there, but nothing coherent.

Nothing interesting.

Garen walked in, scanned the room, and saw her. His face broke into a broad grin as he came over to her table and sat down.

"Hi! I haven't seen you in days!"

"Yes. They've got me working over in the gardens at hullframe 280. A big duct rupture. Got to do a bunch of reconditioning."

Garen frowned briefly, then returned to grinning. "I'd love it if you'd show me some day . . ."

"No can do. I can't pull you off of your own important work." Gramma Francesca had him stripping bimetallic windings from old coil drive cores. Yes, her work gang boss didn't miss a trick.

He sighed, then seemed to notice the two drinks. "Oh! For me? Thanks!"

"No." Loren reached a hand out, ready to bat his away if he reached for one. But her tone was enough. Her tone, and her next words: "I've got a date."

"Oh." An awkward pause, as color rose in his sallow, unattractive face. Then he was gone.

"I've got a date," Loren whispered under her breath. "A date with a redhead . . ."

Life wasn't a romance, after all. Not in the usual, traditional sense: with tall handsome knights in shining armor. But that didn't mean it had to be boring.

THE BUSINESS OF LOVE

Kelly Swails

Seth sat on his bed and looked out the porthole window. He and his mother lived in one of the most exclusive sections of the ship *Genesis*, and here all the rooms had views to the emptiness of space.

At least there are some perks to being my mother's son, he thought.

A quiet hum and a whiff of ozone told him the air exchanger had started, and he took a deep breath. He'd read in school that electron storms on terraformed planets smelled like that. He wondered if he'd ever find out first-hand. Sometimes, his girlfriend Chloe would hang out in his room just to watch the stars and talk about life outside the ships.

Chloe. She would hear whether or not she had been accepted to aviation school today. Seth checked the clock on his Messenger. Soon. She would hear soon.

A bell sounded before his door swooshed open. His mother walked into the room, her usual icy demeanor radiating throughout the space. One didn't become CEO of the largest ship manufacturer in the galaxy without being formidable, and his mom fit the description. "We're expected at the Dorsey's suite at six. The president of Billsken will be there, so you need to look respectable. Did Adriana pull a suit for you?"

Adriana was one of his mother's assistants. He pointed to a garment bag hanging from a hook by his closet. "Doesn't it look like it?" Seth looked at his Messenger again. Nothing.

"It's important that you make a good impression on Dr. Fillus," she said. "You're not getting into his university on grades, we all know that, but he needs to see that you aren't a complete dolt."

Seth rolled his eyes. Others might see it as a perk, but special treatment was a downside of being the son of a CEO. Sure, he'd get into one of the most selective schools in the quadrant, but everyone would know he didn't deserve to be there, including him.

"Did it ever occur to you that I am a dolt and so he should know what he's accepting?"

"Don't be ridiculous." His mother ran a finger over his desktop and examined the dust on her finger. "Liza's slacking off. That's the third suite keeper this month."

Seth felt a ping of sympathy for Liza. It must be horrible to work for his mother. *I'll find out soon enough.* "What's ridiculous is the idea of me going there in the first place."

Mom leveled her gaze on him. Most people would sweat under her glare, or at the very least squirm, but he looked her in the eye. Neither of them blinked as she said, "Billsken's business program is the best. You'd need that degree to work in my office, let alone inherit the company."

"Assuming there's a company to inherit," he said.

Mom's gaze hardened and this time Seth stepped back before he realized he'd moved. "If the war with the Sysdian escalates—and all indications are it will—Genesis will be making warships for the next three decades."

Seth looked at her for several moments before looking away. His mother had planned that Seth would take over Genesis Corporation since the day he was born. Probably before then, if he knew his mother. His mind was too preoccupied with Chloe to argue about it now. He checked his Messenger—still nothing—as the bell outside his door rang.

"Expecting company?" his mother said.

"Chloe said she might come over." *Don't make a scene.*

She opened the door to find Chloe standing in the hall. "Will wonders never cease? A young girl who keeps her word." His mother left without saying another word.

Chloe's cheeks flushed as she came inside and the door closed. "Sorry about Mom," he began, then noticed her tear-streaked face. "Oh, no," he said.

"Oh, yes." She handed him her Messenger.

He took it as she sat on his bed and grabbed a tissue from the bedside table. He pressed his thumb to the ID square and an official message from Ithaca School of Flight blipped onto the little screen. *Despite your exemplary academic record, we regret to inform you . . .* He tossed her Messenger onto his desk and joined her on the bed.

"I'm sorry," he said.

She blew her nose. "Not as sorry as me."

He wrapped an arm around her shoulders and brushed a lock of soft hair behind her ear. Seeing her upset made him feel helpless. He tried using his charm to cheer her up. "You look pretty cute when you cry."

She barked a short laugh. "Stop it."

"It's true. You do." Some girls looked like splotchy messes when they bawled, but not Chloe. She looked beautiful.

"Must be something about the way I sniffle," she said.

"Maybe," he said. "Or maybe it's because you're cute at everything you do." He turned her face to his and kissed her.

She returned it before flopping back onto the bed. "Oh, Lords. I've wanted to be a pilot ever since I saw a flight deck with my dad. I saw all those planes and scouters and fighters and I knew then I wanted to fly them, not fix them like he did. And now I won't get to."

Even worse than seeing her upset was hearing her self-pity. "There are other schools," Seth said.

"Ithaca's one of the best," she said. "And it's the closest to Billsken."

"I might not get into Billsken," he hedged. He didn't like to flaunt his mother's connections to Chloe. "Besides, I—"

Chloe snorted. "Please. How much money has your mom donated to them in the past twenty years? You're in."

"—might not want to go there," he finished.

She sniffled and cut him off. "If I didn't get into Ithaca, I probably didn't make Origins or Clarissa, either."

"There are other schools," he said again.

"Only if I want to fly a star-duster," she said derisively.

"Come on, Chloe," he said, a tinge of impatience in his words. "It's not like your life is ruined or anything. If you don't get into any good schools this year you can apply next year. Don't let one rejection kill your dreams."

Anger flashed in her eyes. "Easy for you to say, Mister Heir Apparent. You'll be the head of Genesis Corp before you turn thirty. Most of us aren't lucky enough to have our lives planned out for us, you know."

"Yeah, I know," Seth said, his own anger coming to the surface. "The rest of you get to have this little thing called 'free will.'"

"I'm sorry," Chloe snapped as her brow furrowed. "Sometimes I forget it's not all wine and caviar at the front of the ship." Chloe looked like she wanted to say something else but stopped short. She sighed and said, "I apologize. I shouldn't have said that."

"Don't worry about it," he said before he licked his lips. "Listen, if you want," he said, "I can talk to Mom. She's on the board at Ithaca—"

"Absolutely not," Chloe's face turned hard again. Chloe propped herself on her elbows. "I'm not going to have my boyfriend's mother's get me into school."

"It wouldn't be like that—" he said.

"Then what would it be, exactly?" She gazed at him, her brown eyes full of accusation.

"What's wrong with using the resources at your disposal?" he tried to sound innocent and failed.

"Call it what you want. Having the CEO of Genesis Ships make a nepotistic call is wrong."

"She's right, Seth," a voice came from the door.

Chloe gasped as though she'd been burned and jumped off the bed. "Mrs. Bennet. I didn't hear you come in." Chloe didn't like his mom—Seth couldn't blame her—but she had a healthy respect for her wrath.

"I'm sure you couldn't hear much over your whining," she said.

"Mom," Seth warned. Why did his mom have to be such a bitch?

"I have to go, anyway." Chloe said as she retrieved her Messenger from the desk. "Dad's expecting me for dinner. Good-bye, Mrs. Bennet." She nodded to his mom and slipped from the room.

"Why did you go and do that?" Seth said, not worrying if Chloe was out of earshot or not. "She's having a bad enough day without you picking on her."

Mom shrugged. "It was true. I won't make myself a liar just to placate your . . . girlfriend."

"That doesn't mean you have to say it," Seth said. He took a deep breath and ran a hand through his hair.

She crossed her arms. "What had Chrissy so upset?"

"Chloe," he said through gritted teeth.

"Of course," she said.

"We've been dating for a year. It's time you learned her name."

"Are you going to answer the question?"

Seth stared at his mom. She gazed back, a bland smile

on her face. "She didn't get into Ithaca. I offered to ask you to pull some strings but she wanted no part of that. Not that you would've done it."

"I heard that part." Mom pursed her lips and looked thoughtful. "Interesting."

Seth blinked. Had his mother just admired Chloe? If so, it was gone with her next words.

"It's just as well. She would have been disgraced."

Seth couldn't believe what he had just heard. "Excuse me?"

"The best minds go to Ithaca. Your girl would have washed out. That's not to say she didn't have opportunity here—Genesis has some of the best prep schools in the system—but from what I've learned she's far from the top of her class. The professors there would have chewed her up and spit her out."

Seth didn't know which point to address first. He chose the obvious one. "You won't even learn her name and you've been spying on her?"

"I don't have a choice," she said. "You haven't been forthcoming with information."

"Lords, Mom! I am eighteen. Are you going to check on me my whole life?"

"Are you going to make me?" she cocked a brow.

Anger flared in Seth. His mother always had a way of reflecting everything so that it came back to him. Instead of continuing down that wormhole he said, "I won't listen to you bad-mouth Chloe again."

"Oh?" she said coolly, and Seth wanted to punch a wall. Instead, he took a deep breath through his nose.

"I won't," he repeated. "I love Chloe. Someday I want

to ask her to be my wife. If I'm lucky, she'll say yes." Seth set his jaw. "If you make me choose between the two of you, I'll pick her, and you'll never see me again. You can find someone else to run Genesis."

A flush in her cheeks was the only indication she'd heard him. "Get changed. We need to leave for the Dorsey's in ten minutes." She didn't look back as she stalked from the room.

He flopped onto the bed and clenched his fists to keep his hands from shaking. *What did I just do?* He'd never considered not taking over his mother's company someday, but now that he'd said it out loud, he felt the truth of the words down deep. If he didn't follow his mother's plan . . . well. He smiled. Life would be different. He could still smell Chloe's shampoo on his pillow. Mrs. Chloe Bennet. He liked the sound of that.

The next day, before school, Seth found Chloe studying in the library.

"Hey," he said as he joined her. "You look like you're feeling better."

"My eyes are still puffy," she said.

"I hadn't noticed."

She smiled. "You never notice anything bad about me."

"Maybe that's because there's never anything bad about you to notice."

"Or maybe you're too nice to say anything."

Seth pretended to look around the empty room. "Don't say that so loud. You'll ruin my image." He took her hand and gave it a squeeze. "I talked to Mom last night."

Chloe pulled her hand away. "I told you not to do that," she said.

"Not about talking to Ithaca," he said quickly. "Just about how she treats you."

"Oh." Chloe relaxed and let him hold her hand again. "What did you say?"

Seth recounted the conversation—skipping the marriage business, of course. No reason to spring that conversation on Chloe yet.

Chloe's face fell. "That sounds like a horrible fight."

"It wasn't our worst," he said. "And I meant every word." Seth shifted in his seat. "I kind of expected you to be happy. Or something. I mean, I just told my mom off and picked you over her and all that."

"I know," she said, her brow knotted. "And I think it's awesome you stood up to her. Especially on my behalf. It means a lot. It's just . . . well." She bit her lip. "She could make life really hard for me. Or my dad."

Seth blinked. He hadn't thought about that. "She wouldn't."

"Are you sure? She's basically my dad's boss—"

"There are about fifty layers of management between them," he said.

"Thanks for the reminder," she said.

Eric squeezed her hand. "You know I didn't mean it like that. I meant . . . well . . . why would she care enough about your dad to fire him?" He knew it sounded elitist as soon as he said it, and he cringed against Chloe's response. To his surprise, though, she didn't call him on his snobbery.

"It'd be a roundabout way to hurt you," she said. "If she fired my dad we'd have to leave *Genesis* so he could find another job."

Eric hesitated a moment—*would she?*—before shaking his head. "No way. That's not Mom's style. She's more 'in-your-face' than that."

She scrunched her face. "Your mom's a hard person who's used to getting what she wants," she said. "If she doesn't like that we're together, she'll find a way to keep us apart."

He didn't want to think too hard about his mother's machinations, especially where Chloe was concerned. Chloe's rejection letter from Ithaca blipped through his mind. *She wouldn't. Would she?* Seth shook his head against that thought and changed the subject. "Have you thought about what to do about next year?" Seth said.

Chloe rolled her eyes. "You really know how to push a girl's buttons."

Seth released her hand and smiled. "What can I say? I'm a romantic kind of guy." When she laughed, he said, "Seriously, though. Have you thought about Billsken?"

"Not really. They don't have an aviation program," she said.

"I know. But maybe there'd be something else you could major in. Or you could go there for a year and transfer to flight school. Something."

"I'll think about it," she said.

"That sounds convincing," Seth said. He tried not to sound as hurt as he felt.

"I know," Chloe said as she rubbed her eyes. "I have a lot to think about right now." She smiled at him. "You could always apply to flight schools and come with me."

Seth snorted. "With my grades? Not likely." A few students trickled into the library and he checked the time. "School's about to start. Promise me you'll think about what I said, okay?"

"I promise."

"It's all gonna work out."

"It's all gonna work out," she repeated. To her credit she sounded like she meant it.

After school, Seth walked to Chloe's section of *Genesis*. He didn't come to the back of the ship often, and as always, the differences between this area and his surprised him. It wasn't dirty, exactly, but the walls and floors were dull and shabby and looked older than they should. The narrow corridors made him feel claustrophobic; the lack of portholes made the sensation worse. He rang the bell to Chloe's quarters. She opened the door and smiled.

"Hey, I was just about to Message you," she said as she yanked him into the cramped living room.

He smiled and hugged her. "I'm glad to see you're in a better mood."

Chloe's smile widened. "I am. During Physics class today I had a brilliant idea," she said. "I can learn to fly in the military."

Seth's smile faltered as his stomach dropped. "What?"

"They use fighter pilots! I don't know why I didn't think of it before," she said.

Seth couldn't believe what he was hearing. "Probably

because we're at war with the Sysdians and you don't want to, you know, *die,"* he said.

Chloe waved away his words. "At Ithaca I wouldn't get into a cockpit for two years. With the military I'll be in space in six months." She jumped up and kissed him. "Isn't that great?"

Seth's fingers shook as he put his hands on her shoulders. She couldn't join the *military!* This wasn't how he saw their future. He had to get her to see reason. "Don't you think you should talk to your dad about this? He'll never go for it."

"I already did. He loves the idea," she said. "Especially since they'll pay for college once I'm out."

Seth felt short of breath. "This is a huge decision. Take a few days to think about it."

"What's there to think about? I'll learn to be a pilot and they'll pay for school," she said. "I stopped by the recruiting office today."

Seth blinked as his stomach clenched. "What?"

"The recruiting office. I signed up today. I leave for training right after graduation."

"What about Billsken?" Seth blurted. He knew he sounded selfish but he didn't care. Since talking with her that morning, he'd convinced himself that Chloe would join him at college and they'd live happily ever after. Seeing her overwhelming happiness now dissolved his fantasy.

"What *about* Billsken?" She said, confusion replacing the happiness on her face.

"It's just . . . well." His mouth felt dry and he swallowed. "Do you have anything to drink?"

"Sure," she said. She went to the kitchen and came back with a metal cup of water.

He gulped it down in two swallows and licked his lips. "I sort of thought we'd be together at Billsken," he said.

"Just because I'm in the military doesn't mean we can't be together," she said.

"And just when are we going to see each other?" Seth said. "Your drill sergeant's not going to let you leave campus every night to hang out with me."

"What's your problem?" Chloe said as she blinked. "I can't believe you're not happy for me." She crossed her arms and scowled. The look of determination in her eyes chilled him. She really meant to do this. "I guess all that talk yesterday about me getting into another school was bullshit?"

"That's not fair and you know it," he said.

"Whatever," she said. He had never seen such cold fury in her eyes before. "You didn't want me to get into another flight school because you knew it'd take me away from you. You wanted me to follow you to Billsken the whole time."

"Last I heard, the casualty rate of flight schools were less than one percent. What's it in the military? Thirty? You do the math." His voice shook and he looked away. He didn't want her to see the tears in his eyes. "What's wrong with worrying about your girlfriend? What's so bad about wanting to be together forever?" Seth said.

Chloe's features softened. "Nothing." She grabbed his hand and intertwined her fingers with his. "But I have to do this. I would really like your support."

"You could have waited until you heard from the other schools," he said.

"I don't think it would have changed my decision." She squeezed his hand. "Signing the paperwork felt right."

Seth shook his head. "I don't want to lose you."

"Don't think about that," she touched his face. "Promise me you'll focus on the bright side. Okay?"

"Okay," he said even though he couldn't see one.

Chloe checked the time. "Dad's going to be home soon. I need to start fixing dinner."

Seth nodded. "I'll call you later."

"I'd like that," she said as she kissed him good-bye. He watched her dance around the living room as the door *swooshed* closed between them.

Seth managed to make it to the middle of the ship before his thoughts caught up to him. *Chloe's joining the military. She could get maimed or killed. I could never see her again.* Helpless anger welled up inside him and he punched the wall. The impact reverberated all the way up to his shoulder as pain exploded in his hand. He welcomed it; he could deal with physical pain way better than watching Chloe throw her life away. He rubbed a bloody knuckle as more thoughts tumbled inside him. *This can't be happening. This shouldn't be happening. She should have gotten into Ithaca. She had the grades, I know she did, I don't care what Mom says.*

Seth's breath caught in his chest. He'd said it himself: his mother was on the board of trustees at Ithaca. What if she'd kept Chloe out of the school? If she had done that, it wasn't too far to think she could pull strings and keep Chloe out of all the flight schools. His body tingled and he forgot about the pain in his hand. He needed to know the truth.

By the time Seth barged into the executive offices of *Genesis* and walked toward his mom's office, his anger had gone from supernova to black hole. He intended to find out exactly what his mom had done to Chloe.

"She's in a meeting," his mother's assistant, Linda, called from her desk.

"I don't care," he said.

"She can't be disturbed," she said. She sounded—not scared, exactly, but tense—and Seth stopped.

"I don't care," Seth said again.

Linda blanched. Apparently, she'd been on the receiving end of his mother's tirades enough to know that this interruption wouldn't go unpunished. Seth felt sorry for her, but not sorry enough to schedule an appointment. Lords, it was only his whole life. His mom could stop working long enough to answer his questions. He scanned his thumb on the pad by the door. It opened to reveal her flipping screens on her desktop.

"Thought you were in a meeting," he said as the door *whooshed* shut behind him. The air felt cool against his skin, and he could smell his mom's cup of hot tea from across the room.

"I didn't want to be disturbed," she said. She didn't look up.

Her distraction flared his anger even more. "What did you do to Chloe?"

She looked up, her face unreadable. "What do you mean?"

"Chloe's joining the military to become a pilot."

She gave him a cool look. "What are you suggesting?"

A muscle in Seth's jaw twitched. "I think you know."

She turned her attention back to the desktop. "If you have something to say, say it. I can't listen to your yammering all afternoon."

Seth clenched his fists and opened the scab that had begun to form on his right hand. "Did you keep Chloe out of Ithaca?" He said as his knuckle throbbed.

"It sounds like you're trying to blame me for a smart decision on Chloe's part."

Seth threw up his hands. "What part of Chloe getting killed is a smart decision?"

She flipped a screen on the desktop. "Are you saying she's not smart enough to stay alive in the military? I expected you to think more of her."

Seth took a deep breath to collect himself. *Don't let her goad you.* "Answer the question."

"Does it matter?" She flipped another screen and shuffled a few others around.

He seethed. He should have known better than to try and direct this conversation. The only game his mom played was her own. "You know it does. You never liked Chloe and you don't want us to have a future together."

"It doesn't," she said again, a faint look of smug superiority on her face. "Let's say for the sake of argument I did. You should thank me for showing you who Chloe really is."

Seth's heart beat hard. So she *had* made a call. This is as close as an admission his mother ever gave. "*Thank you?* For what?"

Mom leaned back in her chair and ran a hand over her severe bun. "Girls like that don't have as many choices in life as you do," she said. "She held you back."

Seth gaped at her a moment before saying, "Girls like her."

Mom's eyes flashed. "Girls from the back of the ship. The ones that attach themselves to rich boys and expect that life will be full of beef and champagne."

"Chloe's not like that," Seth said through gritted teeth.

"She's not?" Mom said as she smirked. "Then I suppose it's a coincidence that this mechanic's daughter who wants to be a pilot just happened to fall in love with a boy whose mother owns the biggest fleet of spaceships in the quadrant? A boy who will, also coincidently, one day own that business?"

"Chloe's not like that," he said again, this time with even more venom. *She's not. She loves me. She wouldn't have used me like that. Mom's playing her usual mind games.* "I told you I wouldn't listen to you disparage Chloe. Don't ever talk about her like that again."

"Besides," mom continued, "if she really loved you as much as you loved her, she'd have stayed here for you."

"Don't make her the bad guy in this—"

"She'd have followed you to Billsken. Do you really want a woman who puts her career before you?"

Seth anger turned cold. "Sounds like you, Mom," he spat before turning and walking from the office.

He seethed as he left her office. The events of the past few days tumbled in his mind. Billsken, Ithaca, Chloe, his mother, his choreographed future. Seth knew two facts for certain: he loved Chloe, and he wouldn't allow his mother to run his life any longer. He looked at his Messenger. If he hurried he'd make it. He jogged to the business district of *Genesis* and arrived at the recruitment office just as an officer turned off the lights.

"Excuse me, sir," Seth said, his heart pounding. "I'd like to talk to you about joining."

The man weighed Seth with his eyes. He must have seen Seth's resolve, because he spoke a code word and the lights came back on. "Come on in, son, and let's talk about it."

Resolute tranquility enveloped him. "Nothing to talk about," Seth said. "I want to join." As he spoke the words, he knew what Chloe had been talking about. This felt right. *If Chloe loved you she'd have followed you,* his mom had said. Maybe. Maybe not. His mother hadn't bargained on Seth loving Chloe enough to follow her.

MUSIC IN TIME

Dean Wesley Smith

The bright light from the Benson Space Station sundeck made the inside of Scott's Tavern as black as the insides of an ore carrier. The thick musty smell of the bar, comfortable herbal smoke, and, rich odor of beer wrapped around me like a whore's arms, dragging me into the dark. It was cool inside, making sweat break out on my forehead.

A whole lot cooler than that stupid sundeck. Whoever thought of putting a station tube made of mostly windows open to the closest sun on a space station should be shot. Idiots in bathing suits actually laid on lounges, more than likely frying what little brains they had left.

I let the door slam behind me, closing off the sundeck heat, and stood there for a moment, fighting for my eyes to adjust, letting the cool air relax me. I knew Scott's Tavern wasn't really dark, but until my eyes adjusted, it sure seemed that way.

"Yo, Danny," a voice said from the shadows in the direction I knew the bar was. "Bright out there, huh?"

The voice was Carl's, the owner of Scott's Tavern. Carl had bought the place after Scott died in a shuttle accident a few years back.

"Like walkin' on the damn sun," I said.

My eyes had adjusted enough for me to see the tables and chairs, so I started toward my normal bar stool. Carl was already sliding a beer onto a coaster just like he had done for me hundreds of times over the last few years.

I could see the shadows of a couple at a table, and one woman bent over her drink at the bar, two stools down from mine. Steve usually sat on that stool later in the night. Steve actually had a real job on the unloading pylons. Middle of the afternoon was too early for him.

I had no job, hadn't found one in a year of searching, and had basically given up at this point. I was going to die on this stupid space station orbiting a star with a name I can't even pronounce. This morning I hocked my old guitar. I used to think I was going to take the Old Earth Country Music world by storm. I dreamed of selling millions, having fans want my autograph, be in demand by women, the whole deal.

Fat chance that was going to happen. I couldn't even find a damn job flipping burgers or cleaning up shuttles or mopping the stupid hallway floors.

I had used the money from the guitar to buy enough food to last for a week, and I had enough money left over to drink myself into a blind drunk tonight. What I would do for tomorrow's drinking money I would worry about tomorrow.

Damn, I was going to miss that guitar. It had been like a best friend to me for twenty years. My first and only wife told me I loved the damn guitar more than her, and the bitch had been right about that toward the end of our marriage.

Man, how had I gotten so low as to hawk my guitar for food and drink money?

I shook the thought away, ignored the twisting in my stomach that I had made a fatal mistake, and climbed onto the stool. Coming to this stupid space station had been my fatal mistake. The promise of a gig here fell through twenty minutes after my ship arrived and I've been stuck ever since.

I grabbed the beer and held on for dear life. The glass was cool and wet and felt damned good after the heat on that sundeck. Actually, it felt good for a bunch more reasons than just the heat. I downed half, letting the wonderful taste wash away some of the regrets like I had taken a big-ass pill.

I then took out the fifty station credits I had on a chip and slid it across the bar toward Carl. "When that's gone, kick me out of here."

"You got it," Carl said.

He started to pick up the credits when the woman two stools over said, "Hold on a minute."

Both Carl and I glanced at her. Even with my eyes still not completely adjusted to the dim light yet, I could see her well enough.

She had on the traditional space wear business jacket, dark shirt, no tie. Her pants matched her jacket, and I could tell she spent far too much time on her short, blonde hair.

I couldn't get the color of her eyes, but I was betting blue.

She was shorter than I was by a distance and looked to be athletic, not extra hyped up like some women were today. She seemed natural and aging normal, just like I was. I liked that.

She didn't look the type to be in Scott's place at this time of the afternoon, let alone picking up some loser like me. I hadn't had a real woman look twice at me in longer than I wanted to think about.

More than likely that was because I had nothing to offer any woman, hadn't cut my brown hair in half a year, and didn't have a non-wrinkled shirt to my name.

"That one's on me," she said, indicating my half-finished beer. "And you may not want another after what I've got to say to you."

Carl and I both just stared at her, then finally Carl just shrugged, as any good bartender would, took the price of my beer from the chip in front her, and turned away.

"And why would something you've got to say stop me from having a few drinks?"

The woman shrugged. "I got a job for you if you're up for it."

My stomach clamped tight at the idea of getting a job, earning enough to get my guitar back. Could something like that actually happen? Could I actually get so damned lucky?

I stared at the woman, her thin face, and faint smile. I had never met her before, that I could remember, and I couldn't imagine what kind of job she might have. Or what type of job that would need a drunk from a bar to do.

But damned if she wasn't good looking. Even a loser like me could notice that I suppose.

I turned back to my beer and took another long drink, almost finishing it. My fifty credits still sat on the bar in front of the beer, waiting for me to drink it away. And I had no doubt I was going to do just that, even with a nut case sitting two stools down from me. But it was nice of her to buy me the first one.

She scooted her stool back with a scraping sound, then reached down into the darkness below her and pulled up a guitar case. She put the case up on the bar between us. "I think you lost this."

I stared at the old case, the once-broken upper latch, the faded sticker from a trip I had taken to the New Mexico Star Cluster for a gig ten years ago. I had figured when I walked out of that pawnshop this morning I would never see it again.

My stomach felt like someone had kicked me.

"My guitar," I said, my voice soft. I wanted to reach out and clutch it like a long lost child, but instead I just turned to stare at the woman. "How did you get it?"

"I bought it out of hock for you this morning, on the assurance to the man in the shop I would take it to you." The woman laughed to herself. "I had to pay him a little extra to let me take it though."

She slid the guitar another few inches toward me.

"It's yours. All I ask is you consider doing one job for me in return."

I looked at the case, then back at her. "A few answers first. How did you know I had hocked the thing? And how do you even know I want it back?"

She sort of shrugged and smiled, the smile of an insurance agent.

I was right. Her eyes were blue. I wondered if any of her appearance was actually real. It looked real, unaltered. But with enough money, looking natural could be bought these days and she looked like she had enough money to do just that.

"I happened to see you coming out of the pawnshop, so I went in and asked what you had sold. When I heard it was your guitar, I knew you could help me."

"And how would you know that?" I asked, doing my best to not get angry at some woman who was trying to give me back my guitar.

She stared at me, then said flatly, "I'll be honest with you. Coldly honest if you can take it."

I nodded and looked her right in the eyes.

"No one with your talent, your former career, would ever give up their instrument," she said, not looking away from my gaze, "without being flat on the bottom, with no hope. And right now I need someone with talent who thinks there is no hope."

I figured right at that moment I had two options. I could let my normal pride make me turn away from this woman, ignore her, or I could laugh. And since my guitar, the special Earth-made guitar I had hocked just a few hours ago, was sitting on the bar in front of me, I figured laughing was the better option.

"Am I right?" she asked.

I finished off my beer and turned on the stool to face her. "Oh, lady are you right. With the money from the guitar I bought food for a week and that money right there to drink tonight."

I pointed at my last fifty station credits.

"After the food and money are gone, I'm done. I'm about to be kicked out of my room in the workers section of the station since I haven't paid in three of months. I've borrowed from every friend and some strangers, and more than likely I'll be sleeping in some station shelter in the outer ring in a week and eating handouts or from garbage before it gets recycled."

I held up my empty beer glass, caught Carl's attention, and motioned for him to bring me another. "Friend, I don't know about the talent part, but you found someone with no hope."

The woman nodded, then stuck out her hand. "Mr. Danny Kenyon, my name is Alexis Pierce. Just call me Lex."

I reached out and shook her hand. Her grip was firm, like she had done a few years of good solid work. But at the same time there was a softness to her hand and I held the grasp a little too long as I looked into her eyes.

She didn't look away.

I felt disappointed when I let her hand go finally. I was sure attracted to this woman for some reason.

I stared down into my beer, now feeling embarrassed. "Lex, I don't know what to say."

Carl brought me another beer at that moment, and Lex, bless her heart, paid for it, indicating that Carl should take the price from the money in front of her on the bar. Lex was going to make my fifty credits last a little longer than I had hoped at this rate.

"Just listen to my offer," Lex said. "You don't have to say anything yet. And no strings attached." She shoved the guitar a few more inches my way. "Better put that under your chair before we spill something on it."

I picked up my guitar and slid it to the floor between my legs. I had sat in many a bar over the years in many a different solar system and space station with the guitar in its case in that same position.

Me and my guitar had seen a lot of bars and a lot of light years. It felt good to have it back.

No, better than good. It felt great. I was whole again. I decided right at that moment I'd head for garbage cans to eat and sleep in the hallways before I pawned the thing again.

"Thanks," I said. "I'd offer to pay you back, but I doubt I'm going to be able to do that any time soon."

"Just considering my job offer is all I ask in return," Lex said. "I'll call it even if you do that."

"Lex, I've been looking for any job for the past year. So I'm more than willing to listen. Fire away."

As I looked into her eyes I felt even more an attraction. Was she drawing me in with some chemical or some special way she looked? I could see no reason why she would, but I had better be damn careful. Men have disappeared around the systems over far less than a good-looking woman with a fast pitch.

"I need you to play a series of concerts for me."

I laughed again. "For who? I haven't had a gig in three years."

"After I got your guitar this morning I made some calls about you," Lex said. "The information I got is that you're talented and could have made it all the way to the top, but drank it all away."

"That and a few other bad breaks," I said, stung by her words. What did this blonde bitch know about how hard it was to push ahead in the music business day after damned day, sleeping in tiny shuttles, playing in station bars for drunks? It wasn't until everything fell apart that I really started drinking.

Lex shrugged. "What happened in the past doesn't matter to me. I just needed to know you were good, that you could play, and I discovered you can. And that you can write your own songs as well."

I stared at her, then smiled. "You didn't just happen to see me come out of that pawnshop, did you? You've been following me or something."

Lex laughed. "No, not really. I just had some good contacts in pawnshops around the stations in this system. The pawn dealer contacted me."

"Why?" I asked.

"I'm sort of a talent agent," Lex said. "My job is to find talented people who have hit bottom, give them one special job, and a new chance for the future."

I kept staring at her, fighting the attraction, trying to not really ignore everything she was saying. Even with my eyes now used to the dim lights of the bar, I just couldn't get a read on her. She looked like an agent, she was sneaky like an agent, and she dressed like an agent. And she tossed money around like an agent. And over the years I had been around enough booking agents to know not to trust them with a mouthful of spit.

"Look," Lex said, scooting over to sit in the chair next to me.

Her wonderful soft smell shocked me. I wanted to lean away and get closer at the same time, so I just stayed centered, holding onto my cold beer like an anchor in a rough sea.

"I'm willing to give you a half million Intersystem Credits for ten concerts over a fourteen-day concert period. I need you to play about twenty or so songs per concert. I don't even much care which songs they are. Covers or your own originals."

"Lady, you are totally nuts," I said, turning back to face my almost empty glass of beer, doing my best to ignore her wonderful smell.

"You promised you'd listen to me," Lex said. "That's all I asked for the guitar."

I moved my right leg and bumped it into my guitar just to make sure it was still there. It was.

"All right," I said, "you're willing to give a washed-out guitar player a half million Intersystems to sing a few songs. What's the catch?"

"The catch is the location of the concert tour," Lex said, glancing at Carl to see if he could hear. He couldn't since he was down the bar cutting up limes for his fruit tray.

"So, I got to go out to the frontier or into the Farms or something like that?"

No way I was going into the Farms. They were the systems occupied by the only aliens humans had run into. The aliens looked like a cross between a black beetle and mass of mud shaped like a deformed cow, which is why humans called their systems the Farms. And from what I hear, they smelled like a sewer. I was fairly certain they had no desire for human country music.

"No, actually, your part of the tour will take just over two weeks each way, all done in a first class luxury cabin. But here in the human systems about ninety years will pass before you come back."

This woman was keeping me entertained, I had to hand her that. I hadn't wanted to laugh this much since I found a hundred credits on the sun deck on the way to the bar three weeks ago.

"I'm a talent agent here in this time period for this section of the Consolidated Planets," Lex said, talking fast and low. "In this time period the Consolidated Planets have not yet been formed, and except for a few high-ranking officials, no one here knows it will even exist in the future. There's a great demand for original old-style Earth music and musicians in the future and this is as far back in time as we talent agents are allowed to go."

I decided to play along with the nut case for a minute. "So how come you just can't beam me into the future and have me back for my next beer?"

"Space and time travel don't work that way I'm afraid," Lex said. "You'll be gone your time about six weeks total, but because of the speeds involved, and a whole bunch of stuff I don't really understand about time travel, about ninety years will pass here. That's why we look for musicians who have nothing to lose and very little family. Of course, it's a help that you are also very talented. Your talent, to be honest with you, is one of the reasons I can offer you as much as I can."

"Thanks, I guess."

"Look," Lex said, leaning forward. "I don't expect you to believe me. I wouldn't believe me if I lived in this time period. But I do want you to think about it. You'll play ten concerts, to audiences as human as I am a very long time into the future. You can stay in the future as long as you would like beyond the tour, maybe never come back."

"Stay?" I asked.

"Sure," Lex said, nodding. "You can stay for a week, or a year. If you stay a year it will be ninety-one years passing here. If you decide to stay in the future and make a career there, your money for this can be transferred forward. But if you do decide to return to here, you won't make it back until at least ninety years into this future."

"And a half million will be worth nothing then, right?"

"Actually, no, with some minor bubbles, money in the systems stays amazingly stable all the way up and into my time period in the Consolidated Planets."

"And I'll be too old to spend it when I get back."

"No," Lex said, shaking her head, "You'll only be six weeks older than the day you leave. Just ninety years will pass here. Again, I don't expect you to believe me, but at least think about it and meet me back here tomorrow."

Before I could say anything, Lex handed me five hundred station credits. "This should help get your rent caught up. Thanks for considering this."

I stared at the money in my hand like it was a snake that might bite me as Lex slid off her stool and headed for the door.

Five hundred station credits was about 50 Interstellar Credits. She was offering me a half million Interstellars. That was a lot of beers.

I watched her walk, wanting more than anything to jump up and follow her and never let her from my sight. But the money in my hand froze me to my stool.

When she opened the door to the sun deck, she was gone into the bright white light.

"Wow, she was a looker. Was she as weird as she seemed?" Carl asked, glancing down the bar at me.

I took another look at the five hundred station credits in my hand, then stuffed them in my pocket. "You have no idea," I said, finishing my beer and motioning Carl for another. "You have no idea at all."

As it turned out, Lex's offer, my guitar, and the money in my pocket put me right off the idea of drinking the night away. I had one more beer, grabbed a take-home Old Earth style pizza on the way to my room, and then surprised the dump's manager with payment in full for all the back rent.

I was living in such a slum that even after the pizza and rent, I still had enough money left over to last for almost a month if I watched the drinking. Maybe by then I could find a job. A real job, not the crazed thing some good-looking woman had talked to me about. But at least she had bought me some time.

I dropped the pizza on the old scarred coffee table, then brushed some food wrappers aside and dropped onto the couch. I opened up my guitar case like I was standing at the door of a blind date. Inside was my guitar, just as I had left it this morning at the pawnshop.

I held it to my chest for a moment, just letting myself believe that it was actually back in my hands. Then after a few quick adjustments for tuning, I strummed a few chords before putting it back in the case.

How had I let myself get so low?

And why did some woman I didn't know go through the trouble of getting my guitar back for me, not counting the five big ones she had tossed my way? She couldn't be serious about the job.

There had to be something else going on.

I took a piece of pizza and worked at it, thinking over any possibility of a scam, which was unlikely since I had nothing to take in a scam. After a second piece of pizza, I still hadn't come up with anything that made any sense at all.

I was exactly what I seemed on the surface, a washed-out musician who liked to play in the style of old Earth country. I had nothing to scam. I was worth exactly the amount she had given me and not one credit more.

So, with a quick bite out of a third slice, I went out the door and down to the manager's office to use his com device. I used to know a guy who was one of the brainy types, read a lot; actually had a major education from somewhere. He had done soundboards on a tour I worked once, and we drank a few nights together. He'd understand this time travel stuff and if it was real or not.

I had to give the manager the fifty station credits I had planned to drink earlier to cover any intersystem charges. I hoped like hell the call was going to be worth that.

"Steve," I said as he came up the com link. He looked about the same, maybe a little shorter hair, and he still hadn't had his lack of chin fixed. "This is Danny Kenyon, from the Country Old-Style Planetary Tour back a few years. Remember me?"

"Uh, yah, sure Danny, how are you?"

I knew he didn't remember me, I could see it in his eyes, but at this point, that didn't matter. At least I didn't owe him money, so he wasn't either cutting the link or asking for his money back just at the mention of my name.

"Sorry to bother you, Steve," I said, "but I got this dumb science question that a few friends and I have been arguing about, and I figured if anyone would know the answer, you might."

"Fire away," Steve said. "I took some science classes back in college." Clearly not talking music or money made him relax a little, even though he didn't remember me.

"Okay, promise not to laugh too hard," I said.

He laughed and said, "Promise."

"Okay, my friend was telling me that time travel is possible and in the future we might actually invent it. Does that sound stupid to you or what?"

"Not at all," Steve said. "Lots of scientists over the years, starting with Einstein back on Old Earth, thought that time travel might be possible. But a lot of factors would have to be solved and we're no where near that kind of major breakthrough."

"You're kidding?" I said, shocked. "It might actually be possible in the future?"

"Possible yes," Steve said. "Likely, probably not. Not in our lifetimes anyway."

"Well, damn," I said. "I lost that bet. Thanks, Steve."

"No problem," Steve said, "take care of yourself, Danny."

I shut down the com link and headed back to my room, thinking over what Lex had said. It was possible. How completely crazy was that?

By the time I had finished the pizza and played a few songs, I had decided to go back to Scott's tavern and meet Lex tomorrow. What could it hurt, as long as she didn't ask for her money back?

Just as the day before, it took my eyes a moment to adjust inside the dark bar from all the light in that stupid sun section of the station. I had managed to finally get some sleep and by the time I reached the bar I was slowly getting angry. I might be broke, but I'm not completely stupid, and Lex, for some reason, was trying to get me to buy a huge pile-of-shit story.

I just didn't know why.

As I headed across the dark bar I felt like I needed a beer more than just about anything, especially after the hot sun beating down on me in my walk through that sundeck ring.

I could see through the darkness that Lex was sitting

on the stool beside my favorite, sipping on something. Just the fact that she was there again surprised me.

And actually made me happy.

I hated that I was attracted to a nut case. Just hated it.

My former wife had turned into a nut case, swearing there were aliens in every station, on every planet we visited, and that they were watching us every minute. *Invisible aliens.*

She blamed the aliens for our divorce. She was partially right.

Carl was behind the bar as always. Otherwise, the tavern was empty.

"Danny," Carl said, slipping a beer onto a napkin in front of my stool. "Good to see you."

"Give my eyes a minute," I said, "and I might be able to see you back."

Carl and Lex both chuckled at my stupid joke, then Carl moved back down the bar to keep working on the evening preparations.

"Thanks for the loan," I said to Lex after taking a sip of the wonderful, cool beer. "Again, I'm not sure when I'll be able to pay you back."

Lex held up a beautiful hand. "No need to even think of paying me back. The money was like an option on your time. I wanted you to consider my offer."

"Well," I said, taking another sip of the beer. "I considered it. I even called a friend who confirmed that time travel at some point in the distant future would be possible."

Lex nodded. "It is."

"So how far forward would I be going?"

"A very long ways," Lex said.

"How far?" I asked.

Lex glanced at me, then at Carl to make sure he was far enough away to not hear.

"Fourteen thousand years."

"Not possible," I said, turning back to my beer. "Humans won't be around for that long."

"Oh, they very much are and have a real desire for Old Earth music like you play."

"So why not go back another six hundred years and get real Old Earth musicians?"

"Not allowed to," she said.

"So explain to me how it works," I said. "Since you're asking me to give up my life and climb into something that flies through time, I better know at least some basics about how it works."

Again, Lex stared at me for a moment like I was some alien thing. Clearly, other dead-end musicians she had offered this to hadn't bothered with any homework.

"I really don't know how it works," she said. "At least not the science of it. Something about folding space." She glanced down the bar to make sure Carl couldn't hear what she was saying.

Damn, I just couldn't get the attraction I was feeling toward her out of my head. She had to be doing something to me. I hated agents and she was an agent. I couldn't want to sleep with an agent. That would be like sleeping with some mud-cow alien on the Farms. But I still just wanted to lean forward and kiss her.

Had to be the reaction to the money.

"The Consolidated Planets are a group of about forty

thousand systems banded together for safety and trade. The Planets as an organization has been in existence about ten thousand years now."

I was too stunned at the number to say anything since there were only about fifty colonized systems now.

She went on. "Travel between my time and this time is done only by people who have no ties or family because of the time loss issues."

"Okay, that makes my brain hurt," I said. "So you have no family, no husband waiting for you back home?"

"None," she said. "If I did, they would be long dead by the time I returned from one trip. The time lag works both ways I'm afraid."

"Okay," I said, not liking the sound of that either, but deep down happy she didn't have anyone.

Lex went on. "Only two weeks will pass on board the ship, but decades will pass on the planets at either end of the trip, forty-five years on the trip there, forty-five years on the trip back here."

I finished my beer and held up my glass until Carl saw it and nodded.

"I see why you need someone with no ties to here."

Lex nodded and again I resisted the urge to just kiss her. She put her hand on my hand and the soft feel of her skin sent a shock through my system.

"Are you drugging me?" I asked, looking into her blue eyes.

"No," she said, smiling. "Not my style. Just trying to do a job."

"And this attraction I'm feeling to you is part of the job?"

She pulled her hand back and shook her head, looking away. "Never happened before."

I wanted to believe her but I wasn't sure that I did.

Carl slid another beer in front of me. Again, Lex bought.

I stared at her, then decided I still needed a few more questions answered. "So, what planet were you born on?"

She smiled. "One named Small Five about two hundred light years from here. It hasn't been discovered or explored yet in this time period."

"So, how many trips have you made to this time period?"

"This is my second."

"Ninety years each?" I asked, staring at her. "How old *are* you?"

Lex laughed. "Actually, in real time just three years younger than you are. I'm thirty. Time passes normally on either end. I'm still aging just like normal. But if you took my birth date on my home world, I guess you would say I'm a lot older than you."

"We'll just leave it at thirty." I took a big drink out of the beer to try to give myself time to think and also not look at her. The attraction between us seemed to be growing by the minute, at least on my side.

"It's a job," Lex said, clearly feeling she needed to explain even more. "I meet interesting people like you and I do a service. In a few years I'll retire back to my time. There are some beautiful places in the future among the Planets."

"There are beautiful places here in this time, too," I

said. "Granted, I haven't seen many of them lately, but I know they're here."

"Take this job," Lex said, "live a couple of months like you've never lived before, see planets you can't even imagine exist, play ten concerts and then come back rich, with enough money to see the places you want to see and start your music career over under a new name."

"Ninety years from now."

Lex nodded.

"So why? Why me?"

Lex actually laughed at that. "Honest question. We want to hear you play concerts. That's all. The Consolidated Planets love any type of Old Earth music, and have gotten very little of the style of music you play before. That's why we're willing to offer someone of your talent so much money. Trust me, we'll make a profit on you."

"You've gotten people to go with you for less?"

"Oh, sure. One burnt-out rocker went out about two years ago with only the promise of a lifetime supply of food and drugs."

"And how did it go for him?" I asked, before it dawned on me Lex would have no way of knowing.

Lex shrugged. "He's still in transit."

"Still in his first day on the ship?"

"More than likely," Lex said. "He won't arrive for another forty-three years this time."

"Oh," I said. I was starting to catch on how it worked.

"What I told you is the limit of my knowledge about this stuff," Lex said, her voice soft and sincere sounding. "I've been totally honest with you. I just fly in the ships and hope someone somewhere knows what they are doing."

"I know that feeling," I said, smiling at her. "I'm the same damn way with these spaceships that flit from system to system now."

"So you understand?" Lex asked.

"Not a bit of it," I said. "But what the hell difference does that make, right?"

"Right," Lex said. "So what do you say?"

"Give me an hour sitting here alone," I said, "and I'll give you an answer."

Lex nodded and slid off her stool. I really didn't want her to leave, but I had to be outside of her wonderful smell, those driving blue eyes, to think clearly.

A moment later, the tavern was lit with bright light as Lex went out onto the sundeck.

"The way you two were talking," Carl said, "it seemed important."

I shrugged and finished off my beer so Carl could bring me another. "She's just offering me a gig is all."

"Fantastic," Carl said, his face lighting up like someone had just given him a hundred buck tip. "It's about damn time you got back on the horse."

"Not even sure what a horse looks like anymore," I said.

Carl laughed as he slid another beer in front of me. "Man, I heard you when you opened for Baked Pie in the Princeton System in the Baseline Theater. Trust me, you know the horse."

I stared at Carl, actually looking at him for the first

time in the two years I had been coming into this place. "You were at that concert?"

"Sure was," he said. "And I saw you over on Mercer as well, when you opened for Craig S. and the Princes. I even bought a hard disk copy of your first song collection."

"Only collection," I corrected.

"First," he said, smiling at me.

"Man, I didn't even think you knew who I was."

Carl laughed. "I let people in my bar do as they want. But I can tell you I was a huge fan of yours. You were just ahead of your time is all."

"Yeah, ahead of my time playing Old Earth Country," I said, sipping my beer. It sure seemed that time was an issue a lot lately.

"No man, honest," Carl said. "Things have changed, your original songs would take off now."

"I sure hope you are right, my friend."

"Oh, I am," Carl said, smiling. "Take the gig, get back on tour. I'll miss your business, but I can buy the next collection and play it in here on busy nights."

It had always seemed that my songs, the only songs I really wanted to play, were just a little too "edgy" for most Old Earth Country fans a few years back.

"Man, this is exciting that you're getting back to playing," Carl said. "Just tell me when and where your first concert is, and I'll be there, right in the damn front row. I know a bunch of fans who will do the same."

"Well, right now everything's a little up in the air," I said.

Carl smiled real big. "Just let me know."

With that he turned and walked down the bar, going back to his prep work for the nightly crowd, leaving me to my thoughts.

I couldn't believe how much things had changed for me in simply a day. I had an offer for a short tour that I didn't really believe, yet part of me accepted.

And I had been reminded I still had fans, few as they may be, but they were still out there, and they remembered my work.

I glanced down the bar at Carl. I doubted he had any idea how important his comments were to me. Hell, any fan's comments to any artist, in any field were important. When the money runs out, the recording contracts are cancelled; all musicians have left are fans to keep them going. Fans. They are everything.

I sipped my beer and sat there, remembering the concerts, the feel of making people happy with my music, the disappointments and setbacks on the business side, and finally, all the loneliness, hitting rock bottom yesterday when I hocked my guitar for money.

Lex had been right. I had nothing to lose by taking her offer.

I glanced down the bar. Nothing to lose except fans like Carl, who still remembered.

Carl's dream had been to own a bar. He'd told me that right after he bought the place. He was scared to death, and at the same time as happy as a little kid at Christmas. It couldn't be easy running a bar off a sundeck on an old space station orbiting a star with a name no one could pronounce, but he was doing it, making it one day at a time.

I shook my head. Man, that was admirable. Maybe

Lex was right, maybe I had given up and dove into the bottle a little too soon.

And now I was getting a second chance. Granted, no one like Carl would be around to remember me in ninety years, but it was still a second chance.

Maybe my songs would be dated by then, I would be dated. Wouldn't that be ironic, a musician who was ahead of his time coming back dated?

Again, that time thing.

I glanced down the bar at Carl. I hated to lose my fans, even the few who still remained. I hated the idea of coming back and starting over and being dated then. For me, it would only be a few months, but I wouldn't recognize most of anything.

There had to be a way to get everything. I was always accused of wanting everything, and I guess this time was no different.

I started to take another drink from my beer, then looked at it and sat it back down on the bar napkin. I pushed it to the inside edge of the bar away from me and said, "Hey, Carl, could you bring me a diet soda of some kind?"

Carl looked up, the smile on his face huge. "Coming right up."

Thirty minutes later, when Lex came back through the door and stood for a moment letting her wonderful blue eyes adjust, I had my plan pretty much worked out. It was going to cost me a pretty penny to pull off, but if it worked, I just might get the best of both worlds, Lex's and mine.

And if I got lucky, maybe I'd get Lex as well. As I said, I wanted everything.

Lex slid onto the stool beside me and Carl brought her a diet drink as well. I sipped mine, some sort of drink that tasted like lime only sweet.

After Carl moved down the bar, Lex pointed to my drink and smiled, looking into my eyes. "I see you've made a decision."

"I have," I said. "But hear me all the way out like you asked me to do for you. Okay?"

"Okay," Lex said, a puzzled look on her face.

"Your entire problem with finding people here on Earth to play out in the Consolidated Planets is time. Right?"

Lex nodded.

"And Carl said that my songs had been ahead of their time," I said.

"I think he was more than likely right," Lex said. "I listened to your first collection. It's amazingly good."

"So here's what I want to do," I said, plowing on and ignoring her wonderful compliment. "I want to take you up on your offer, but I want to postpone when I leave."

Lex really looked puzzled, but she didn't say anything, letting me go on.

"I want to try to make a comeback right here, right now, first, before I leave. And I want you to be my manager and backer with the money you'll pay me to leave to the future."

With that, Lex sort of rocked back and got a distant look for a moment.

So I just went right on talking. "In exchange for you helping me get going again, right now, doing a little bankrolling, I'll help you recruit some top talent for your Planets tours. And if I don't make a comeback here, I'll take less than what you offered me now in a couple of years."

"And if you do make it big?" Lex asked.

"We both get rich and we'll just fake my death when I get as far as I can here, and then head out to the Planets together to make some real money. But the key is time."

"A win-win situation for you," Lex said, staring at me, a slight smile creeping into the edge of her perfect lips.

"For both of us," I said. "Think about it. You get me cheaper if I don't make it, we both make money if I do, and I get not one, but two chances to make a comeback. Now and in ninety years. All that is lost is a little time on this end."

Lex laughed and nodded. "You know, that sort of makes sense."

I looked her directly in the eyes and reached out and took her soft hand. "Eventually, my songs won't be ahead of their time."

"Timing is everything," Lex said, nodding, squeezing my hand softly in hers. "You've got yourself a manager and a bankroll."

While keeping one hand in hers, I held up my glass with my other hand and offered a toast.

Lex picked her glass up, smiling at me.

"To time," I said, "the real solution to everything."

"To time," she agreed, tapping her glass against mine.

Then she put her glass down and with her free hand pulled me close and kissed me.

And for me, right at that moment, time just stopped. And I had no desire to restart it.

DANCE OF LIFE

Jody Lynn Nye

A clash of wrist cymbals made us all turn toward the door of the grand ballroom. I, Prince Ergal, waited within the sacred globe of light for the arrival of my brother, Prince Aiechell, and his bride to be, beautiful Ndera, whom we had all known for two years, and loved since we first met.

I, especially. Alas.

Negotiation between our two ancient houses to agree on terms was cursory; no one would stand in the way of a genuine love match. Ah, would that I had been so fortunate, but once she had met Aiechell, she never looked again at me. There had been so many other advantages to the marriage. I could not object, though my soul cried out to her every time we met. I did my best to keep my jealousy subdued. It would show in the color of my skin. I was truly happy for Aiechell. If I could not have Ndera, then he was the only other choice in the galaxy I would make for her. I kept myself as green as possible to show happiness as the ceremony commenced.

A Terran dancer led the wedding procession into the room. Around and behind her floated an envelope of dark carmine red, a color of celebration on our world, the fabric cut to simulate the wide, soft wings of flesh of our bodies. The pale golden skin of her face, hands, and feet, and long, deep brown hair flowing from her scalp seemed to contrast oddly. All things about humans were odd. Their manipulative digits lay at the end of bony arms that looked too exposed without the spans of our wings, whereas we had sensors and digits at wingtip and on the front of our bodies concealed in a nest of silky blue hair ten or twelve centimeters long. Unlike us, their faces were on round, bony heads at the top of their frames instead of a third of the way down where it could be enfolded protectively in our sails in case of threat. That was the primitive reaction, naturally. We've had better protective devices for centuries. And Terrans' feet faced the wrong way, their ankles at the back instead of at the front. I wondered how she kept from falling over.

The dancer circled the chamber again and again, clinking her wrist instruments in a hypnotic rhythm. Ndera's honor attendants, both male and female, swept in behind and took their places around the globe. In spite of the gravity, which was heavier than on Soteial, they moved with grace. They were happy. Their skins glowed brilliant emerald, turquoise, and teal. Aiechell's contingent, who greatly outnumbered them, followed, emitting slightly more somber hues. In their wake came

Aiechell. His face was solemn but his brown eyes were wide with astonished pleasure. I had never seen him so happy.

He took his place beside me and bumped me with his left wing. I bumped back. In spite of the envy I felt, I loved him and wished him well. Our eyes fixed upon the door.

As if weightless, Ndera floated into the room. The soft barbels on the top of her wings flowed backward like streamers. She had dusted her skin with powdered crystal and gold. When she passed through the walls of the sphere of light, the whorls and curlicues glittered. She was dazzling. Aiechell let out a breath that deflated his body and moved to stand at her side. Our mother, Queen Denoa, spread out her wings in greeting, and began the traditional ceremony of marriage.

Outside two quarter-arcs of the translucent walls of the enormous chamber, beings of several species stood gazing in. They were not invited, but as they were passengers on board this intersystem liner, they were curious about our joining ceremony, which had taken up most of the time and attention of the event planner and his staff for over a month, Terran-reckoning. Vondyk had asked permission to allow them to watch, in the name of interstellar cooperation. We were as curious about many of these races as they were about us, so Aiechell had given his word. It was the first royal Soteian ceremony to take place off-planet. In a cultural exchange that would benefit our system as well, visuals of the event would be beamed to many worlds.

We were here because Ndera had expressed a wish

for what the Terrans called a "destination wedding."
Aiechell denied her nothing; besides, it sounded like
fun. The gravity was higher aboard the Terran-flagged
luxury liner, but beyond that, we lacked no comfort.
Even though the trip would be three months long, a sig-
nificant part of our lifespans, it was worth it to secure the
marriage. Ndera's family tended to live almost five years
longer than my family's span of thirty or so years. It was
not only her beauty and charm that made her attractive to our very choosy parents. The interchange of cells
between her and Aiechell would add vigor to their de-
scendants, increasing the length of the lives of the royal
line, including Aiechell himself, while correspondingly
shortening hers.

We Soteians breed easily and freely among ourselves.
I already had three offspring, two extant and one in the
womb, with females from approved families. Both my
sons and my incipient daughter would have attractive
traits, though unless something terrible happened to
Aiechell, my line would not be needed to carry on the
dynasty. I loved my brother, and I truly did not want
to occupy the Pearl Globe and rule our continent. That
throne was his, and that of his eldest child he would one
day have with Ndera. I only hoped to find a lady to be
my permanent mate, for what time I had in this sphere
of life. Our species is not long-lived, which was never
a concern until we discovered space travel, only thirty-
two years ago. All of our long-range ships are generation ships. The thirty years, forty years if we are lucky,
that we live seems sadly inadequate when the vastness
of space is surveyed. We were never dissatisfied before.

Now came the moment of life-sharing. Aiechell and Ndera opened their wings forward and pressed together, face to face, along every centimeter of their bodies. I heard Aiechell's deep baritone voice murmur within the folds of flesh. What a bride and groom said to one another within that intimate embrace I did not yet know. We life-share only once. During that moment a chemical exchange occurs that averages out our immune and endocrine systems. Barring accident or illness, it means that each of them would now live exactly the same length of time as the other, so neither would be left alone in this world after the departure of the first. I had read harrowing stories of long widowhood, and they always left me woeful with sympathy.

Soon, Ndera's turquoise skin and Aiechell's dignified green shifted until they were precisely the same shade of aqua. They had become one life. Ndera's lifespan was shortened, but Aiechell's was lengthened to precisely the same extent. They would be together now for all their days. I began the traditional chant, wishing them well and healthy and fruitful through the days of their marriage. The rest of the wedding party added their voices until the glad sound rang off the ceiling of the chamber. The human dancer chinked her cymbals and twirled at the perimeter of the circle like a joyful satellite.

When they parted at last, Ndera's huge brown eyes were bright. She looked more beautiful than ever. Within moments the matching hues faded back to their normal colors. The wedding party joined them in a circle, the flesh of our wings pressed up against loved ones on either side. The bride and groom glowed with happiness, their eyes fixed upon one another. My mother sang her joy. I was bereft. I slid out of the group embrace as swiftly as I could.

"Thank you all for witnessing our marriage," Aiechell boomed out. "Enjoy refreshments and entertainment!" He gathered Ndera in his large wings. She nestled to him as though they were truly one flesh. They whispered softly to one another. I could not distinguish their words, but they were not meant for me anyhow. I turned away and floated toward the blackened far wall, away from the strange onlookers to either side. I craved privacy.

At the perimeter, I gazed at nothingness, or so I believed, until a dot of light flared and died. I flinched with surprise, and let my eyes focus on what lay beyond the ship. Arches and veils of light stretched across a full sixth of the sky. The spans were twisted into fanciful shapes. If I let my fancy reign, I could distinguish animals or plants, as if I was looking at clouds. Bright dots of white, some mere pinpoints, spangled the clouds of light like jewels. I saw colors I never dreamed existed, reds, blues, golds, in eternal dances of light and darkness woven together. The view filled my soul with wonder. Suddenly, the three months of my thirty-year lifespan that the journey required was worthwhile. I drank it in, feeling it nourish my soul. A soft voice at my side startled me again.

"That's the Centaur Nebula, my lord. It's about twelve light years away."

I turned to behold a pair of large brown eyes, but these belonged to no Soteian. It was the Terran dancer.

"It's wonderful, isn't it?" she asked. Her voice was slow and deliberate. Her command of our language was stilted, but the movements of her hands echoed the sway of our wings perfectly. "Any closer and it would consume us in a firestorm of radiation, but in a way I wouldn't mind, to be part of the stars' birthplace. Don't you love it?"

I fluttered my wingtips in agreement. "It is magical."

We stood together as she pointed out features of the shifting curtain of light. I absorbed it all, the brilliance and the soft voice speaking into my ears. She showed me clouds of glowing dust out of which nascent star systems were bursting. I could almost see them grow as they consumed the raw matter around them.

"I've seen it three times, and it never gets old," she said.

We had been in transit over six weeks to reach the cruiser, and another two weeks to reach this point. I had celebrated a birthday along the way. I was shocked. "Three times! How old are you?"

"Twenty-nine," she said. "How old are you?"

"Twelve."

She tilted her head. I read it as an expression of curiosity. "Really? Is that young or old for your people?"

"Neither," I said. I blew through my lips. "It is . . . old to be unmarried."

"I thought so," she said.

"Why?"

I must have delivered my question too forcefully, because she backed up half a meter. Her mouth drooped into a downward crescent.

"I hope I didn't offend you. I was watching you during the ceremony."

"What were you thinking?"

"I felt sorry for you," she said softly. "You wanted her for yourself."

Very true. I did not want her sympathy. I turned half away. "Alas, I did. Could you tell?"

"Everyone could tell," she said, softly. "She is very beautiful."

I met her gaze sternly. "Why do you think so? She is not of your species."

She tilted her head. I realized her eyes and mouth were on the same level with my own. For a Terran, her mouth was pretty, too, with curved pink lips and funny little square teeth. "I can tell beauty. That nebula is beautiful, even though it's not my species, either. Come with me." She led me across the room to the other wall that was opaque to the curious public. I focused to see through the strong spotlights that beamed at all angles around it. To my eyes it seemed to be filled with star clusters, but more vividly colored. As I came closer, I realized it was a tank of water, filled with small images of we Soteians, floating and dancing and interacting, head barbs and backward-turned feet wiggling gently as they went. "They are beautiful, too."

I halted and glared at the dancer.

"Is that meant to be an insult?"

Her warm eyes assumed an expression of worry. "No, it's a compliment. They are Terran animals. The event manager thought you would like them because they resemble Soteians. They are called 'angelfish'. They are lovely, aren't they? Don't be judgmental; leave yourself open to the experience."

She was so kind I found it impossible to be angry. In

her warm eyes I saw sympathy, but also a fellow seeker of new experiences. I leaned close to the tank until my eyes nearly touched the glass. The outline of each fish was roughly triangular, with translucent feathery fins. They did resemble Soteians in profile, since we walk with our faces thrust forward and wings trailing behind us, though somewhat exaggerated, their eyes and mouths taking up a disproportionate area of their bodies.

"See?" she said. "Even your little feet look like their ventral fins. At first when I saw you, I thought you must be able to fly like these fish."

"In truth, I wish we could," I told her. "Gravity on our world is lighter than yours, but not light enough to carry us as effortlessly." From macrocosm to microcosm, I let my attention be drawn into the wall-sized tank. The morsels of color danced through the water, almost hypnotizing me. I realized that the Terran girl was watching me. I smiled at her, appreciating her kindness in taking my mind off my sorrow.

"What is your name?" I asked.

"Estela. What may I call you, lord?"

"Ergal. How is it that you speak our language so well?"

She pointed to the base of her throat. A crystal pinpoint glittered there. "I have an implanted translator. When you act/speak language, it tells me what you said. I formulate my reply, and it gives me the sounds to say and the movements to make. I tried to learn some of your language before you came, but I'm glad I have a cheat-sheet." She laughed, a husky gurgle that I found oddly appealing.

"Well, you are very graceful," I said.

She smiled. "I am a dancer, not a linguist. I am glad that you can understand me. Do you want me to dance for you?"

"Yes." I wanted to see her body sway as it had when she danced around the sphere of light, then I thought of Ndera again. "I mean, no. Come and watch the stars with me again. I enjoy your company. Do you mind?"

"Not at all," she said, automatically. "If it is your pleasure, I will. I love to look at the stars."

"Do you have other duties that I am keeping you from doing?" I asked.

"Well, no. I . . . my contract requires me to do anything that I am asked by your party. I mean, apart from self-destruction or mutilation. Any of you. At the moment, you are the one asking."

I was horrified, but I kept my color neutral. "Quite a contract."

Estela twisted her pretty mouth. "I wish I had read it more carefully before I signed it," she said, with a deep exhalation of breath. "Ten years of my life. But it has not been all bad."

Something in her expression said that some of it had. I was about to ask more when a soft, ringing chime sounded through the room.

Estela beamed, showing her flat teeth. "Come on! They are turning off the gravity at this end of the ship. You'll have your chance!"

"To do what?"

"To fly!"

She touched my wing. I felt a warm force emit from

her hand and rush through my entire body like a wind-storm. With a gasp she jerked her fingers away, her face suffusing almost to the color of her carmine drape. "I am *so* sorry."

I wanted to ask her what she had felt. But I did not want to add to her humiliation. She was required to do whatever we asked, to the point of self-degradation. One with her dignity and charm should not have to exist under such intrusive strictures. Her pretty mouth formed into a crescent open at the top.

"Come on, angelfish!" she said. "Fly with me!"

I felt the shining floor drop out from under me.

There were legends among my people that we were once free of the fetters of gravity. I had experienced weightlessness briefly as our ship lifted off from Soteial, but we had been strapped in tightly. By the time the crew let us move around again, artificial gravity had been es-tablished and was never turned off. But here, Terrans in black, close-fitting garments came from the service tun-nel and kicked off from the floor. They zipped into the air like flying lizards. With outstretched hands they en-couraged my family to join them.

Ndera let out a squeal of delight as Aiechell pulled her upward. They sailed together like a pair of leaves, twirl-ing and tumbling end over end. They looked so happy.

Estela coaxed Raciel, an aged aunt of my mother, up-ward, and twirled her through the room, skillfully avoid-ing other people and the furniture, which was held in place by magnetic bolts. Estela whispered to her as they rose.

"That's it," she told my aunt. "This is fun! Let yourself relax. It is perfectly safe. Small children do it all the time."

The fear on the old female's face gave way to pleasure, and she let out a bubbling laugh. I was delighted. Aunt Raciel could be dour and obstinate, but Estela had the skills to coax her into a good mood. And me. When the two of them passed me, Estela took hold of my wingtip fingers and pulled me along. The tingle raced through my body again. In wonderment, I almost forgot the sensation of weightlessness. Aunt Raciel let go to flutter on her own wrinkled wings. I stayed with Estela.

Estela flew around the enormous chamber, coaxing my brother's guests to let go of the walls or floor and soar freely. Soon, the room was full of Soteians boosting off, tumbling, wings spread, their eyes glistening and mouths open with joy. She led us all like a mother teaching winged lizards to fly. I stayed close to her, not wanting to miss a moment. She was right; I could see beauty in strangeness, especially her strangeness. I even liked the deep red flush blooming on her cheeks.

"Dance with me, angelfish!"

Again, she took my wingtip fingers in hers. We twirled together. I felt a heat from her that excited me. Music played from concealed speakers all over the room. Spotlights tracked us, created intersecting beams of color and shadow, but the best part were the twin sensations of floating and of Estela holding onto my hands. I never wanted the moment to end.

"This is what I live for," she said. "These are the times when I feel the most free."

"I understand," I said.

She smiled into my eyes. "I think you do."

"A good creature, for all she is Terran," Aunt Raciel murmured in our language as she wobbled by.

Estela let go of me and disappeared into a mass of Soteians clustered upside down around the central chandelier. They burbled with laughter as she organized them into a game. I caught my aunt near the wall of stars.

"Did you feel a shock when you touched the Terran girl?"

Aunt Raciel peered at me and her thin cheeks puckered. "No, dear. I am too old to be interested in dalliances." Her large brown eyes were curious. "Is she meant for you?"

"Of course not!" I exclaimed. "She is Terran. I am Soteian."

"Ah, but look at your color. You are emerald green. That is a healthy sign. Now that Aiechell is wed, you can take your pleasure where you choose. If she makes you happy, why not?"

I looked at my skin. It was as green as the old female had said. I hadn't been this shade since the last time I had fallen in love.

"It is just the party," I protested. "I am enjoying myself." And in truth, I was. I would never have thought that I would, having lost Ndera.

With mock irritation, Aunt Raciel pushed me, and I tumbled away from her. "Don't be a fool, Ergal. Twenty parties would not have cheered you up. If there is something about that Terran, you ought to allow yourself to find it out."

I felt shy about pursuing Estela. The Terran had a job

to do, encouraging everyone to have a good time. I was only one of the crowd, I reminded myself. Still, every time her eyes met mine, I saw a curiosity there and–did I imagine it?–a warmth that was reserved just for me.

I was deeply happy. I had seen more beauty today and felt more strong emotions one after another than in several years combined. My relatives shooting around the room did look like the angelfish in the tank wall, and as brilliantly colored. Our wings, for once, *were* wings, giving us thrust, helping us angle sharply to veer away from the walls, and making great, cupping sails to hover lazily in one place. When parts floated that didn't usually float, I observed things I had not noticed before, such as the three ladies who were carrying children. The bulges of their pregnancies seemed exaggerated in size and mass when they angled into a turn. I had never seen them as beautiful as they were in that moment. Flying transformed my perspective. I reveled in my new knowledge, and all thanks to Estela.

That shock of energy had intrigued me. In fact, it was like a caress. I had never felt anything like it before, not during any affair with one of my many ladies, or when I thought I was in love with Ndera.

I found myself in a circle with Ndera and Aiechell. They held to each other by feet hooked backward, swinging one another's mass through the air with a thrust of their wings and laughing. I thought I would feel pangs of agonized loss, but I was surprised to note how much my feelings had blunted. I was in love with a nebula, a sensation, and a new way of looking at things. I had found a joy of my own in the freedom.

"Thank you, brother," Ndera said, caressing my face with her wing. She and Aiechell sailed away. I watched after them, wondering why I did not feel sorrow.

"Don't worry," Estela whispered, as she came to swoop around me like a lizard of prey. "You will make someone a wonderful husband one day."

She fluttered away. This time I pursued her, hoping to catch her alone by the glass wall overlooking the nebula. I must speak to her. I must know what she felt.

Instead, I heard the soft chime come again. Estela and other employees hastened to each of us in turn, making certain we were upright when the gravity slowly returned. I felt the pressure grind against me, forcing me to the floor. My weight almost caused my slender feet to buckle underneath until I made them remember they did this every day. I am not ashamed to say I felt deep sorrow at the loss.

Estela touched down like a bubble and glided to me. "Are you all right?"

"I am wonderfully well," I assured her. "I would live for that, too." I flapped my shoulders to cool my face. "How well you guided us! Those who would fear were led to forget it. You made us all feel as if it was easy to fly."

She held up the folds of her garment. "You are made for it," she said. "I wish that I was. This is just a costume."

"I had forgotten. Your limbs move like ours, but they aren't shaped the same." I was consumed with curiosity. "I have never met Terrans before. May I see you?"

She let out a small sigh, and her eyes dropped from mine. "May I have privacy, lord?"

I felt terribly abashed. But I couldn't help myself. "Of course," I said. "Is there somewhere else you wish to go?"

She glanced around. Nothing of an opaque nature presented itself. "I think we'd have to go into the servers' tunnel."

But that was busy with Terrans and other species coming and going with food and other supplies.

"Come here," I said. I stretched out my wings to their farthest extent and made a cylindrical tent around her. Reluctantly, she complied.

The garment unfastened at shoulders, wrists, and ankles and slid to the floor. Without the enveloping cloth, her frame was pale, skinny, and bony. Where we have manipulative digits concealed in the mass of hair on our chests, she had soft, round protruberances whose slight movements mesmerized me. In truth, a Terran's body was shaped like a Soteian's without wings. If she held her arms up and behind her, her skeleton would be very much like mine but for the backward feet. I had heard of the 'seeding theory' of the universe. Was there truth in it? Were we actually long-distant kin? I wanted to touch her, draw her to me, and feel the lines of her body against mine. I leaned closer.

Her face turned scarlet, which I knew was not a look of pleasure. Humiliation was writ large on her face. I was abashed and sorry, but also fascinated. I had observed something about her midsection, the same as some of the Soteian guests. "I apologize. You may dress again. You are beautiful, too. You . . . you are with child?"

She kept her chin thrust out as she stooped to retrieve the mass of red cloth. "Yes. That's not covered by my contract. I am going to have to work extra to pay for him when he is born."

I burbled sympathetically. "How long is your contract to run?"

"Four years," she said. "He will be born here. That's not so bad. There are good doctors on board, and tutors for passengers' children. He'll get a good education."

"Then, what?"

I realized my inquiry was getting personal, but I did not know how to change the subject. She did it for me.

"What now for you?" she asked, covering her embarrassment as she refastened the drape at her shoulders.

"Nothing," I said. Once again, I felt the emptiness of the years to come stretch out ahead of me. "I belong to the advisory council of several companies, which all run perfectly well without me. I have provided for the ladies who have and are going to have my children. I have two sons, and a daughter on the way."

"How nice for you," she said, as I unfolded my wings and set her free. "What would you do if you could?"

I respected her strength. I had just embarrassed her, and she was still trying to draw me out. I glanced over her shoulder, and was rendered breathless by the view. I touched her gently on the shoulder, careful not to touch her skin.

"More of those," I said, sweeping my wings widely toward the window. "Between the soaring and the stars, I have never felt so alive." I looked at her warmly. "And you. You have been my guide to things strange and exciting and wonderful. I will forever be your 'angelfish.'"

Estela laughed. She leaned forward to press her lips upon mine. I felt that shock again.

Impulsively, I wrapped my wing around her. "Come and see the stars with me, Estela. It would not mean the same if you were not with me to help me understand the wonders before my eyes. I want you to be with me forever. Can you not feel it when we touch? That electricity? It was happy chance that put us here together."

Estela looked at me sadly. "It isn't real. You only felt the excitement of the moment." With a graceful turn, she whirled free of my wing. "I have to go."

I reached for her, but she eluded me. "What would it take to buy you free?" I blurted.

"Absolutely not," Estela said. Her cheeks went red again. "Then you would own me." She strode away from me. I followed, desperation weighing as heavily on me as gravity.

"I would give your freedom to you," I begged. "As wages. To be my guide in this universe. You have seen so much more than I have. I have only a few years ahead of me. By the time I am gone, your son will be grown and we will all have enjoyed the beauties of this galaxy, both large and," I gestured toward the fish tank, "small. Show me. Please." I caught her fingers again with my wingtip and held it firm. The wave of sensation flowed through me. "You can't tell me you don't feel that, as I do. You gave me joy, and I have fallen in love with you."

She turned and searched my eyes. "I do feel it. If we met at another time and place, I would say the same to you, but you are just reacting to the excitement of the moment. You are a wonderful person. There is no one

else I would have enjoyed sailing the stars with more
than you, but I can't go with you."

"Do you really want to stay?" I asked. Others were
staring. I dropped my voice. "I plan to explore the universe in the years I have left. Come with me. What
would it take? How much have you saved? Could you
buy yourself free without me?"

"No," she said. The corners of her mouth pointed
downward. "It wouldn't be possible. I don't have enough.
I would be tempted. But I advise you not to do it." She
laid her hand on my chest, and I grasped it with those
fingers. Her eyes appealed to me. "Really. I'm not un-
happy here. People get emotional at weddings. I've seen
plenty of spur-of-the-moment proposals at these events.
In the morning you'll be sorry for the impulse." The bitter expression on her face hurt me. I must be doing exactly what other males had in the past, but I knew it was
different for me. She was meant to be mine. I looked
deep into her eyes.

"I can save you from this. Can you bear four more
years of humiliation?"

"Which you added to, if you recall, lord," Estela said,
holding her chin high.

I was ashamed. I had. I had allowed my curiosity to
overwhelm good sense and regard for her decency. "I
am sorry. I am no better than anyone else. But I meant
what I said. I love you, and I want you to come away
with me."

Estela put on a hard face. "Go on. Enjoy your party. I
have to dance for the bride and groom." She didn't look
at me again.

I knew I was right. Having her by my side was the missing part of my life. Ndera was beautiful and loving. She could have given me splendid children, and we might have had years of passionate coupling, but when this cruise ended she and Aiechell were going back to Soteial forever. The heavens above our world were dull compared with what I beheld from the glass portal. I knew more was out there to see. And I wanted to fly again, but only if I could fly with Estela.

I knew why she refused my offer. She had no doubt been promised such things again and again by other guests who were beguiled by her charm and grace in such an emotionally-charged atmosphere. She was a functionary of this cruise line, another means of eliciting enjoyment from the passengers in exchange for the exorbitant fares charged by the travel company, as much as the food service, the accommodations, and the music. She had come to understand how fleeting was the attachment of passengers to the staff that served them. I didn't want her to serve me. I wanted her by my side, as an equal. I had made a mistake, but I would not make another one.

"You could get her fired," my aunt said, appearing at my side. "Then she would be free."

"No! That would just insult her more than I already have."

"You'll have to give her the means to float away from you if she chooses."

"I will give her her own ship if she wants." In fact, I liked the idea, now that it had occurred to me. I had plenty of money. "I will travel as a passenger. Then she can drop me where she wants if she tires of me."

My aunt opened her mouth to an amused O. "This is the most intensity I have seen in you since your first son was born. It is a shame that you can have no children with this one."

"I will be the father of her son," I said. I threw my sails back and marched firmly into the circle of onlookers watching Estela dance.

With the false wings of red cloth she was as graceful and powerful as the nebula. She threw herself into the dance as if pouring out her life. Aiechell and Ndera, wings pressed together, were rapt. I glanced at them briefly, but my gaze was drawn by Estela. I loved every line of her. What did it matter that we had been born under different stars? Our souls both longed to range. I wanted to see the universe through her eyes.

When the music came to a halt, Estela dropped into a graceful curtsy before the happy couple.

"That was wonderful," Ndera said. "Thank you for giving us this gift. Your presence has made our wedding day even more joyful than I dreamed."

Estela listened for a moment to the translator in her throat, then rose to bow in the Soteian style, her arms waving at her side. "I am honored," she said.

I strode forward. I hesitated a moment, but with one more look at Estela's sweet face, I pressed on. "I have an announcement to make, my brother and sister."

Aiechell turned to me. "What is it, Ergal?"

"I want this Terran female to marry me."

Estela rounded on me as fiercely as a Soteian woman might. She curled her hands on her hips. "What if I don't want to marry you?"

"Then you will lose your job," I said calmly. "Did you not say that your contract requires you to follow any order given you by our guests?"

Her mouth dropped open. "Yes, but . . ."

"If you obey my instructions, you will be my wife, and we can fly away together. If you do not, you will be breaking your contract, and will have to leave this ship anyhow. So you may as well come with me. What do you say?"

She gawked at me. Murmurs rushed through the crowd. Suddenly, a fleshy, pinkish-skinned Terran male, clad in black except for the white front of his tunic, appeared in the circle of Soteians. He pressed his hands together and dipped his head. His eyes were a watery blue with black dots at the center. I had met him before. He was Vondyk, the event planner for the cruiser.

"Is there some trouble here, my lords and ladies?" he asked in an unctuous voice.

"Yes," Aiechell said, waving an imperious wing. "My brother requests to marry this Terran female. By the terms of our agreement with your shipping line, she must comply, but she is resisting."

"But you can't marry one of our . . . !" the man began, then raised his shoulders. "Eh . . . well, it is in our contract. Any order. But, marriage? Did she . . . ask for this to be made an instruction?"

"You insult her," I said, spreading my wings out to their fullest extent. My skin turned a fearsome blue. "I am the one who asked!"

The male retreated slightly.

"Well, eh, then she has to obey," he said. "You hear that, Estela?"

"Yes, Vondyk, I do."

A small look of satisfaction spread on Estela's face. I saw that some of the unhappiness she had suffered here had been because of him. I did not read Terran expressions well yet, but I was learning.

"Do you mean it?" Vondyk asked me. I puffed myself up.

"I do. In fact, I insist," I said. "But I would rather have the lady agree. What do you say, Estela? Will you marry me?"

She studied me. The indecision in her eyes fled, to be replaced by the former warmth. The corners of her mouth turned upward. "You leave me no room but to agree, don't you, Ergal?"

"None at all, I hope," I said.

"Well, Estela?" the male said, fixing a look I knew was anger upon her.

I held out my wingtip to her. She came to take it. The shock resounded through me. I could tell that she felt it, as well. Her eyes were wide with wonder.

"This must all be done properly," my mother said, pushing through the crowd. "My second child is getting married, too! The stars are lucky for me today!"

"And for me," I said, as Estela came to press against me. My mother approved! I was relieved. All our friends and relatives gathered close, pushing the now red-faced male out of the circle. Aiechell stood at my side, and Ndera sidled up to support Estela.

Queen Denoa's eyes glowed with pleasure as she recited the marriage ceremony the second time. Her skin was yellow-green, but mine had dulled to a somber tone. This was a deep and sacred undertaking.

Then came the moment of life-sharing. It would be ceremonial, since Estela was not a Soteian. I brought my wings forward and gathered Estela to me. Our mouths joined with a passion I had never experienced before. I felt her body with all of mine, exploring and enjoying it as if she was an unknown galaxy. Her small hands caressed every centimeter of my flesh.

"I will always love you," Estela murmured. "Whatever time we have will be enough." I swore to myself that I would do right by Estela, for the years I had left. When at last we parted, I would make certain she was provided for. For now, we had years of exploring the stars and one another. I looked deep into her eyes. She beamed at me.

I felt the warmth coming from her infuse me again. To my astonishment, her face turned from gold to pale green. I saw my own skin fade to half its original hue. Impossible! Yet, when I let her go, the tone remained in her cheeks. It faded slowly, but I knew that she had changed, and so had I. My family let out exclamations of amazement.

"Could it be possible that we have life-shared?" I asked my mother.

Denoa gazed at us with delight. "It would seem so, my son."

"I told you she was meant for you!" my aunt cackled, poking me in the back with her wingtip.

"How long is a Terran life?" I asked Estela.

"Well," she said, her brown eyes impish. "Before, I would have said I could live another ninety years. But if you average out my one hundred twenty and your thirty, we could make seventy-five. Will that be enough?"

I put on a solemn expression.

"Never," I said, smiling at the surprised look on her face, "but it will have to do. We will treasure all those days together. Will you leave yourself open to the experience?"

"I look forward to it," she said.

We nestled together and I felt the pulse quicken in my veins, the beat to the dance of life.

FOR OLD TIMES' SAKE

Tim Waggoner

"**I** want you to tell me how I died."

I'd been a professional actor for over thirty years, but it still took all my training and experience to keep my expression relaxed as I looked up from my bitterroot ale.

"Hello, Preita." I smiled and then gave her a slight frown. "It *is* still Preita, isn't it? Or do you go by something else these days?"

"If you'd responded to any of my attempts to get in touch with you over the last two years, you wouldn't have to ask." Despite the words, her tone was warm, almost amused. I might've been charmed if I hadn't known her to be every bit the actor I was.

"So," she continued, "are you going to ask me to sit down, or am I going to have to be rude and just take a seat myself?"

I smiled again and gestured to the open seat on the other side of the booth.

"Please."

She accepted my invitation with a smile and a nod, but she was unable to completely cloak the cold anger in her gaze as she sat opposite me.

"Did you like my opening line?" she asked.

"Very dramatic. If we had an audience, they'd be sitting on the edges of their seats right now. Of course, as beautiful as you are, you wouldn't need a hook like that to capture an audience's attention. All you'd have to do is walk onstage."

I regretted it as soon as I said it, but I hadn't been able to help myself. She looked lovely. Artfully restrained use of cosmetics to bring out the best in her delicate features, blond hair cut short and professionally styled, trim figure accentuated by a sinfully expensive silkwraith gown that was currently the height of fashion on Amontillado, a couple tasteful accessories—phasegem earrings and a silvarium bracelet coiled around her left forearm. Everyone in the bar was either openly staring at her or pretending not to be staring, and I didn't blame them a bit. Preita was stunning. And it certainly didn't hurt that she appeared twenty years younger than when I last saw her . . . on the day I'd killed her.

"Flatterer," she said, mock-chiding me. "I can't take all the credit, though. A fresh reboot does wonders for the complexion."

"Well, it certainly agrees with you." I was saved from having to come up with something more to say when a server unit glided over to ask Preita if she wanted a drink. I wondered if she'd order her usual or something else—Cascadians weren't exactly the same person after a reboot, and her tastes might have changed—but she ordered a scotch and null-mist, as she usually did, and while I still had two-thirds of my bitterroot left, I ordered another. I had a feeling I was going to need it.

The server transmitted our order to the bar and then glided over to pick it up. Neither of us spoke while the server fetched our drinks. We sat and listened to the music vibrating forth from the walls—Vari cybersynth, which Preita had always found soothing but tends to grate on my nerves after a bit. A few moments later, the server returned and levitated our drinks off its tray and onto the table.

"Thank you," Preita said, and the server moved off to see to other customers. She looked at me and frowned. "Why are you smiling?"

"The server isn't sentient. There's no point in thanking it."

"Just because it isn't organic doesn't mean it isn't alive in its own way," she said, an edge in her voice. "It's narrow-minded and arrogant of us to think our definition of life is the only one that matters."

It was an old argument between us, and I found it oddly refreshing. I was tempted to get into it with her, just as we used to, for nostalgia's sake if nothing else, but I resisted. She hadn't come here to relive the past. At least, not that part of it.

"I caught the matinee today," she said, surprising me with the sudden shift in topic.

The idea that she'd been out in the audience watching me perform less than an hour ago both thrilled me and made me feel sick to my stomach. I took a drink of bitterroot and was pleased to see that my hand didn't shake.

I was currently trodding the boards at the Northern Grand, Amontillado's premier theatre, starring as Uncle Tuyet in a revival of *The Song of Ivory*. It was an old, tired play, and the reviews had been mixed at best, but it was septems in the bank, so I wasn't complaining. It hadn't taken a great feat of detection for Preita to find me. She knew me, in some ways, probably better than I knew myself. It was my custom to hang out in the nearest stage-door tavern between shows, and I usually drank alone. I don't like to socialize before I perform. I find it breaks my concentration.

"You were good," she said.

Preita was an excruciatingly honest critic, so I knew she wasn't lying. Then, as if to prove my point, she added, "Your energy flagged a bit in the middle of the second act, but you recovered nicely at the end."

"It's been a long run, and I'm a bit tired," I said, but I wasn't certain I was talking about the play. "How about you? What are you up to these days?"

"I've been working on Cascadia." She paused to take a sip of her scotch. "Teaching mostly, though I've done a couple small plays. New stuff. Nothing you've heard of."

I nodded as if I understood, and took another sip of my bitterroot. I knew Preita hadn't been able to afford that dress on an acting teacher's salary, but she'd had five lifetimes to amass wealth. One thing about Cascadian revivers—they're rarely poor.

"So . . ." she said, the word a study in practiced non-

chalance, "why didn't you return my calls? Is it disassociation? We talked about that before we married."

Talked was an understatement. We'd gone through
a month of counseling on Cascadia before the Assem-
blage granted our marriage petition. I'm an ordinary,
garden-variety human, with no enhancements beyond
the basic treatments given in the womb to promote
good health and long life. My kind is a minority in the
systems of the Seventh Tier, which in addition to the
Cascadian revivers is home to the telepaths of Unanim-
ity, the cybernetic Vari, the genetically enhanced Ascendants, and those who eschew physical life and prefer to
dwell in the virtual realm of Idyll. We're all descended
from the basic human stock that originated on old Earth
before our ancestors left their homeworld and moved
out into the galaxy a millennia ago. Since then, humanity
has developed along separate lines—not just here in the
Seventh Tier but throughout the Eternalliance—to the
point where we've almost become separate species. Not
genetically, perhaps, but certainly culturally, and Preita
had been determined that I understood what I was getting into by marrying a reviver. Hence the four weeks of
counseling.

The Cascadians have found a way to, if not defeat
Death outright, then at least cheat the bastard. When
their current body dies—whether from old age, natural
causes, or accidental death—a fresh one is cloned from
stored genetic material, brought to adult maturity in
a matter of months, and the individual's personality is
downloaded into its new home. Revivers save back-up
copies of their minds, memories included, every few

months, so when it's time for a reboot, the downloaded memories will be as current and complete as possible. I'd first met Preita when we were both cast in supporting roles in a small avant-garde play outside Amontillado's capitol city. She'd been just starting her fifth life then, and she'd looked the same as she did now—a beautiful woman in her mid-twenties who carried herself with a maturity far beyond her years. I'd become enamored with her the first time we ran lines together, and by the end of the play's run, I was hopelessly in love. Preita took a little longer to warm up to me. Appearances aside, she was far older than I and not given to jumping into relationships impulsively. But eventually, she agreed to go out on a date with me and a few years later, we were married. And we'd remained so for fifteen years.

Because a rebooted reviver isn't technically the same person but rather a duplicate, often their friends and relatives—especially the non-Cascadian ones—experience an emotional distancing from a reviver after a rebirth. As a counselor once explained it to me, for some people, seeing their loved one resurrected from the dead is like being haunted by a living ghost. With time, some people are able to adjust to the presence of their revived loved one on their own while others need therapy. But some, no matter how hard they try, simply can't adjust and choose to sever all ties with the revived individual. But that wasn't my problem.

"It's not that," I said. Though for the last two years, I'd been hoping she'd think that. It would've made things easier.

"This isn't my first reboot, you know," she said. "I'd

understand if you *did* feel disassociated from me. But if it's not disassociation, then what *is* it? We were married for fifteen years, Darach. I loved you, and I thought you loved me."

"Of course I loved you." I almost added, *I still do.* But how could I love this, this *ghost* made flesh? It was eerie to be sitting across the table from the image of the woman who'd been my wife. I remembered kissing those lips, making love to that body . . . except this was a duplicate. A clone with copies of my wife's memories. I'd never touched this body, no matter what my own memories were telling me.

"Then do me the courtesy of telling me why you don't want to be with me anymore. Did you grow tired of me? Did you miss being able to sample all the adoring young things lining up outside your dressing room?" She forced a smile, but it didn't mask the hurt in her eyes. "Please talk to me. For the sake of what we once had, if nothing else."

I took another sip of bitterroot to give me time to think. I'd imagined this moment many times over the last two years. Preita was strong-willed, and I knew that while it was the custom for revivers to eventually leave disassociated friends and relatives alone if they no longer desired contact, she would eventually track me down and demand to know why I didn't want to pick up where we left off. But no matter how many scenarios I'd run through in my mind, all the lines I'd imagined myself saying, now that were finally meeting, I found myself at a loss for words. But I shouldn't have been surprised. An actor is lost without a script to follow.

I put my glass down and decided to start with the question Preita had asked when she'd first approached my table.

"You want to know how you died."

"Well, I know the general details. We'd just finished an inter-system tour with the Wanderlust Theatre Company—as the headliners, of course—and we were headed back from Maelstrom when our barque was attacked by a group of Ng needlers. You managed to reach an escape pod, but I was killed in the battle and never made it off the ship. At least, that's what they told me at the revival center on Cascadia when I awoke. I have no direct memories of the event since the last back-up I'd made before my death was four months before the Ng attack, when our troupe performed on Cascadia. When I woke up after my reboot, I expected you to be there to fill me in the gap in my memory. That's what family and friends do on my world. They try to ease the transition from one life to another. But you weren't there." She said this last in an accusatory tone, and for a moment I thought she would continue berating me for having abandoned her—and I wouldn't have blamed her if she had. But she paused to take another sip of her scotch, and when she was finished, she said, almost too casually, "So . . . tell me what happened."

I could've lied to her, I suppose. God knows I wanted to. But I took a deep breath and told her the truth.

"What do you think about the captain?"

Our cabin was somewhat cramped, but luxurious by starship standards: queen-sized bed, bathroom and vibrashower, and enough space that we didn't have to crawl over the bed to get from one side of the room to the other. I hadn't seen the *Dragonwing*'s crew quarters, but I'd been on enough ships to know the guest rooms were usually much nicer, and since we were the troupe's stars, we'd gotten the best of the best. I doubted the captain's room was any larger.

Preita and I had just returned from dinner—where we'd sat at the captain's table, of course—and we were both still in formalwear. I was sitting on the bed, loosening the drawstrings on my vest—which, as Preita had pointed out several times during our tour, had become a bit snug on me—and she was standing at the bathroom sink, still in her dress, though she'd kicked off her shoes the moment we'd entered the room. She'd taken off her earrings as well, but not the silvarium bracelet she wore around her left forearm. She'd purchased the bracelet during a shopping spree on Twixt several years before, and she never took it off, not even to shower. It was a pretty enough piece of jewelry, I supposed, though rather plain compared to what Preita usually fancied, and I didn't understand why she was so fond of it. She was leaning over the counter and gazing into the mirror as she removed her makeup, the bathroom door left open so we could talk.

"He seems competent enough," I said. "A bit stuffy and humorless, but then that comes with the job, doesn't it? I mean, when was the last time we ran into a jolly, frivolous starship captain?"

"There was that trader who gave us a lift when we were stranded on the outer ring of the Indria system, remember? He was a delight." Preita spoke louder than usual to be heard over the hum of her makeup neutralizer. She passed it slowly over her face, and I loved watching the graceful, precise way she moved.

"I remember. He was drunk most of the time, and he nearly scattered our atoms throughout the Seventh Tier when he pushed his ship's engines too hard and the alluvion drive went critical."

Prieta laughed. "That's right. I'd forgotten that part!" Her expression grew serious again. "You're right about our captain being typical. He's nothing more than another closed-minded military man who'd prefer to shoot first and ask questions later. Or as far as he's concerned, not ask any questions at all."

I knew where this was headed, and I suppressed a sigh. "Need I remind you we're on a barque, dear? It's hardly a military vessel."

"The captain might be working commercial transport now, but he's a retired fleet officer," she said. "You couldn't have missed that little tidbit of information. After all, he spent the better part of the meal regaling us with tales of his *glorious* battles against the Ng on Backwater. Or have you finally mastered the art of sleeping with your eyes open and miss the whole thing?"

"I wish," I said. When it came to the subject of the Ng, Preita could get so worked up that what began as a discussion of differing viewpoints usually devolved into a shouting match. I'd been holding my breath throughout dinner, afraid she was going to get into it with the captain, and I'd been relieved when she'd made it through the meal without blowing up at him. Actors are, by our very nature, highly emotional people, and we're often drawn to support causes of various sorts. Some actors are merely dilettantes, though, feigning dedication to a cause for appearance's sake, but Preita was deeply and sincerely passionate in her belief that the citizens of the Seventh Tier unfairly viewed the Ng as monsters and treated them as such.

"If the captain had had any idea how you felt, I'm sure he would've chosen a different topic of conversation. I thought you demonstrated magnificent self-restraint tonight," I said, half-teasing, half-serious.

"It wasn't easy, believe me. The way he spoke about destroying that Ng installation on the southern continent was positively ghoulish. And the enthusiasm with which he related the gory details . . ." She shook her head in disgust. "It was like he was a vorball player reliving a favorite match. Or more like a hunter discussing a particularly exciting kill." She was agitated now and getting sloppy with the neutralizer, leaving dots of makeup beneath her skin. "People like him make me sick. They have no respect for life."

"The residents of Backwater probably have a different view," I said. "Seeing as how it was their world the Ng occupied."

Preita went on as if she hadn't heard me.

"I understand that there are conflicts between our species, but there are better ways to settle them than with warfare. If we could just learn to *understand* the Ng . . ."

"I don't think there's much chance of that, my dear. We've been contending with the Ng for centuries now, and if anything, we seem to understand them less and less as time goes by. They're just too different from us."

The Ng aren't aliens, exactly. They're a race of artificial intelligences descended from the AI's that operated unmanned probes in the first days of faster-than-light travel, when alluvian drive was deadly to humans. A number of the AI's that departed Earth never returned, and it was assumed their craft were lost or destroyed due to imperfections in the early alluvian drive engines. The truth was that the AI's decided to set off on their own, and a thousand years later when humans were able to fly faster-than-light starcraft safely and began moving out into the galaxy, they discovered the AI's—now calling themselves the Ng—waiting for them.

Preita walked into the bedroom, stopped at the foot of the bed, and regarded me, hands on hips, anger smoldering in her gaze.

"Why are they too different? Because they aren't organic? Because their minds are made of datastreams instead of meat? In case you've forgotten, you're married to a reviver. Our minds are stored as data and downloaded into cloned bodies. Does that make me too different from you? Does that make *me* a monster to be hunted?"

Whenever Preita was on the verge of being this upset, there was only one thing I could say that wouldn't make the situation worse.

"I love you."

She looked at me for a moment and then smiled.

"You damned well better."

If I'd had any doubt it had been the right thing to say, I was reassured when Preita began to remove her dress.

Later, when we were lying next to each other in the dark, Preita said, "Do you think he was serious or just trying to impress us?"

She had a habit of picking up the thread of a conversation hours, sometimes days, after we'd left it, and it took me a moment to realize she was talking about the captain again.

"You mean about his exploits on Backwater?"

"No, about the special cargo he claimed to be carrying."

She really had lost me now. I hadn't spent the entire dinner listening to the captain. A lawyer from Seigehold had been seated on the other side of me, a specialist in privacy laws for the telepaths that lived on her world, and she was a much more engaging speaker than the captain.

"I'm afraid I didn't catch that."

Preita *hrumpfed*. "Too busy ogling that lawyer, I suppose."

I wisely made no comment.

"He didn't come out and say so directly, but he hinted that the ship's carrying some sort of weapon built by the scientists on Maelstrom. A weapon designed to be used against the Ng. And not just any weapon, but *the* weapon—the one that will finally give humanity the edge."

Maelstrom was home to the Ascendants, the most genetically advanced humans in the galaxy. Scientists throughout the Seventh Tier had long been searching for a weapon that would allow us to defeat the Ng. We humans do have powerful weapons—warships equipped with energy lances, singularity charges, graviton mass drivers and more—but all of our great technology has only managed to allow us to fight a holding action against the Ng. I've always found Ascendants to be arrogant bastards, but there was no denying their intelligence, and if anyone could create the ultimate weapon to use against the Ng, it would be them. And the *Dragonwing* had departed Maelstrom only a couple days ago . . .

"I suppose it's possible," I allowed. "Did he say where we were taking the weapon?"

"He gave the impression that we were ferrying it to Amontillado for further testing. But it seems like a lot of trouble to go to. Why not just transmit the plans to Amontillado and let the scientists there build one? And if for some reason you did want to physically transport a prototype, why do it on a barque? A warship would be safer."

"Transmissions can be intercepted," I said. "And a warship might draw the Ng's attention. A barque's the perfect ship to use if you want to slip past an Ng patrol unnoticed. Assuming there really *is* a weapon on board."

"You sound doubtful."

"You said yourself that the captain's an ex-military man who likes to relive his glory days. The *Dragonwing's* cargo hold may be full, but I don't think there are any super weapons on board. The captain was likely amusing himself by telling a few lies to a beautiful woman."

"Maybe."

Our conversation ended there and we both drifted off. I don't know how long we slept—minutes or hours— but we were awakened by a loud sonorous chiming issuing from the walls around us. We sat up, and I ordered the room to turn on the lights. Neither of us spoke. We were both veteran space travelers, Preita more so than me due to her greater years, and we knew what to do in an emergency. While we swiftly dressed in comfortable clothes, I asked the room's computer to tell us what was happening.

"We are currently under attack by a squadron of Ng needlers," the computer said in a pleasantly bland voice. "Passengers are ordered to remain in their cabins while evasive maneuvers—"

A deep boom sounded from somewhere, and I felt the floor vibrate beneath our feet. The artificial gravity went wonky for a moment, and I felt a dozen pounds lighter. Preita and I grabbed hold of each other to steady ourselves, but we needn't have bothered. An instant later the ship's systems compensated, and the gravity returned to normal. I didn't have to ask what the boom meant: the Ng were firing on us.

"New orders," the computer said, sounding almost chipper this time. "All passengers are to head for the nearest escape pod and prepare to evacuate the ship." A pause. "Darach and Preita Cai, to locate the closest escape pod to your current location, exit your room, turn left, and follow the directional holos bearing your name. Thank you for choosing *Dragonwing,* and good luck."

We didn't bother grabbing any of our personal belongings, not that we had a lot with us. Actors learn early in their careers to travel light. I took hold of Preita's hand and together we ran out of the room and into the corridor, where we were almost knocked down by a panicking crowd of our fellow passengers in their mad dash to reach the escape pods. Considering that we were under attack by the Ng, I understood exactly how they felt.

The walls were crawling with holographically projected words spelling passengers' last names. I quickly located *Cai* on the wall next to our cabin door, and the moment my gaze fell upon it, the word began sliding along the wall, guiding us toward the escape pod the ship's main computer had assigned us to. We ignored the people around us, focused our attention on our name, and followed it, moving down the corridor at a run. Another boom sounded, this one louder than the first, and this time the gravity increased, drawing us down toward the floor. The fluctuation lasted a full thirty seconds before the gravity reset and the passengers were able to start running again, many of them now crying and wailing with fear. If it hadn't been for the steady way the names flowed along the walls, regulating the crowds' speed, I believe people would've run blindly down the corridors, like terrified animals fleeing a raging fire.

Preita and I were just as scared as anyone else, but we were actors, and we handled our fear as we always did: by performing. Only this time we were our own audience.

"Do you remember the courtroom scene from *Seeking Higher Ground*?" Preita gasped out as we ran.

In that production I'd played a corrupt prosecuting attorney and Preita, a peace officer falsely accused of murdering her partner.

"Shall we take it from the top?" I gasped back, and we continued running, keeping an eye on our guiding name as we launched into the scene. If the performance we gave didn't do the playwright's material justice, it kept our minds from succumbing completely to fear, and by the time we reached our assigned escape pod, we were actually laughing, though our merriment had more than an edge of hysteria to it.

"Won't this make a grand story to tell our friends when we get back to Amontillado?" Preita said.

"We'll be able to dine out on it for months!" I agreed.

Cai winked out as a section of corridor wall dilated open to reveal the entrance to the escape pod. I urged Preita to enter before me, and as I climbed inside a third impact shook the ship, this one much stronger than the other two, and I slipped and cracked my head on the plasteel of the pod's curved inner surface. My vision grayed, and I felt sudden nausea grip my gut. Preita helped me to sit beside her, buckled me in, and then the pod door sealed shut and its systems activated.

A fourth impact rocked the *Dragonwing*, and for a moment I thought the Ng had managed to destroy the ship before our pod could launch. But then I experienced a moment of vertigo, and I realized our pod was away. The pod was strictly a no-frills craft—dim lighting, basic artificial gravity, minimal inertial dampeners— but it had full life support, as well as simple protective shielding, and it was already transmitting a distress signal on all Tieran frequencies. I imagined hundreds of identical pods filled with passengers streaking away from the *Dragonwing*, and I wondered how the ship was faring against the Ng. There were no windows and no monitor screen, and when I asked the computer to give us a status report, there was no reply. It seemed the on-board computer wasn't very sophisticated either.

I thought of the captain we'd dined with earlier that evening, and I wondered if right now the man was wishing he hadn't been quite so eager to relive his military adventures. Though not without its defenses, the *Dragonwing* was only a barque, a commercial transport ship. It didn't carry the heavy armaments that a destrier or sun-runner did, and against the Ng it could do little more than put up a token fight. I wondered if the battle was already over, Ng nanobots flooding the ship, the crew dead or dying as the malleable machines flowed swiftly through the corridors of the *Dragonwing* like rivers of liquid metal, killing with ruthless efficiency as they went, the artificial intelligences driving them utterly pitiless and without remorse.

"How's your head?" Preita asked. She tried to get a closer look, but I turned away.

"It's fine. Just a bump."

She ignored me, unbuckled herself, and ordered the computer to show us the pod's supplies. The computer made no verbal reply, but a floor panel slid open to reveal a stash of nutrition bars and water tabs, along with a small medical kit. Preita grabbed the latter and began rummaging through it, and it was only when I saw the first drops of blood spatter onto my leg that I realized my head wound was bleeding. But I didn't care about that right then. My attention was focused on the plasteel hand weapon lying in the supply hold. I unbuckled and reached down to pick up the weapon, while Preita fussed over me, cleaning my wound with a disinfectant and then applying a patch of Nu-Skin.

"What's that?" she said, nodding toward the weapon I was now holding.

"I think it's a separator." I'd never seen one up close before, let alone held one, and I wasn't sure. They're devastating weapons, emitting short-range energy bursts that loosen the molecular bonds in objects. Organic, inorganic . . . a separator will turn them both into gray sludge.

Preita finished playing nurse, closed the medical kit, and replaced it in the supply hold. "It is," she said, and I wondered if she'd ever had occasion to use one in her long life. It wouldn't have surprised me. Even after fifteen years of marriage, there were still things I didn't know about her. "The question is, why would they put a weapon in here?" she added.

"As a precaution, I imagine. In case a pod has to make planetfall, and the occupants need to defend themselves." I gazed down at the gun in my hand. I felt a little sick holding that much destructive power. A separator is powerful enough to even affect the Ng. Too bad the scientists have never been able to get the weapons to work on a large scale.

"You can put that down," Preita said. "I doubt the Ng will try to board our pod. They're only interested in the weapon the *Dragonwing* is carrying."

I hadn't thought about the Ng trying to get into our pod, not consciously at least, but now that Preita had put the notion into my mind, I was reluctant to let go of the separator.

"I think I'll hold onto it a little while. Just in case."

Preita looked at me for a moment and then nodded. "If it makes you feel better."

We sat in silence for several moments as our pod drifted in space. The trauma of the evacuation was beginning to hit me and I found myself having trouble focusing my thoughts. Preita had said something . . . something that bothered me, but I couldn't quite put my finger on what it was.

After a time, Preita starting speaking again, her voice soft. So much so I could barely hear her at first. "They have a right to defend themselves, you know. That's all they're doing. A weapon that powerful . . . they had no choice but to attack the *Dragonwing*."

It took me another moment to register what was bothering me about Preita's words. I turned to look at her, and without meaning to, I gripped the separator more tightly.

"You sound as if you know what the Ng are thinking."

"No, but I can guess, Darach. I can empathize." She reached up to stroke the silvarium bracelet wrapped around her left arm. She looked at me then and gave me a weak smile. "That's what actors do, right? We need a high degree of empathy in order to portray different characters."

I looked more closely at her bracelet. I'd gotten so used to seeing her wear the thing that I never paid much attention to it. She'd told me it was made of silvarium, and it *looked* like silvarium, but in the pod's dim interior lighting, the metal seemed to take on a darker cast. Silver tinged with blue. Just like the Ng in the holos I'd seen.

I looked into Preita's eyes, and I thought she would lie to me, but she said, "They just wanted some of us to be their eyes and ears, that's all. They chose people who were sympathetic to their situation, people who understood that they were more than just machines, that they have just as much right to exist as we do."

I wasn't sure of all the details, but I understood the gist of it. The bracelet was made of Ng nanobots, and Preita had worn it to dinner where they'd heard the captain bragging about the new weapon he was transporting to Amontillado. They'd sent a signal to the rest of the Ng, and several hours later, a fleet of needlers arrived to attack the *Dragonwing*.

I couldn't believe what I was hearing. I'd known she was passionate about the Ng, but *this* . . .

"How many people were aboard the barque when the Ng attacked?" I asked her. "Five hundred? More? How many of them are dead, do you think? All because of your goddamned *empathy*?"

And that's when the bracelet uncoiled from around Preita's forearm and flowed toward me, quick as a striking serpent.

"What happened after that?" Preita said softly.

"I aimed the separator at the Ng and pulled the trigger. The safety sensors detected the presence of the Ng, activated the gun, locked on to the target, and fired. The Ng was destroyed."

"But the bracelet hadn't unwrapped completely from my arm, so the separator's energy affected me too."

I nodded, trying desperately not to picture the image of my wife's body collapsing into a pile of grayish muck, and failing. I'd sat there watching the viscous mess slowly disintegrate for nineteen hours until a rescue ship finally arrived, and by then no trace of the Ng or my wife remained.

"You lied about my death," Preita said. "You told the authorities that I'd died on the ship. Why?"

"Because I loved you and didn't want to soil your memory. Not just for our friends and relatives, but for all the people you'd entertained during your career. And because I didn't want your new self to get in trouble."

"You needn't have worried about that. By Cascadian law, a reviver can't be held liable for actions a previous incarnation undertook if the personality back-up was made before any wrongdoing was committed. As is the case with me."

"I knew that. But I also knew the military would question your new self to learn when and how you'd been contacted by the Ng, and to force you to name any other 'eyes and ears' you might know. And they'd be very interested to see if your new self had picked up where your previous self had left off." I nodded to the bracelet this version of Preita wore. "I suppose I should've told the truth to the authorities. Hell, I probably committed an act of treason by keeping my mouth shut, but . . ."

"You loved me," Preita finished.

"Yes."

"Past tense," she added sadly.

My voice was thick with emotion as I answered. "Given what you did ... Three hundred and thirty-six people died in the attack on the *Dragonwing*. And as bad as that is, do you know what's worse? Once I returned to Amontillado I started asking questions. It took me a while to find the right people to talk to, and I had to raid my retirement fund to bribe them in order to get them to talk, but guess what I learned? There was no super weapon on board the *Dragonwing*. I'd been right. The captain had made the story up just to impress a beautiful actress who was a passenger on his ship. The men and women who died during the Ng attack died for no reason other than you wore a certain piece of jewelry to dinner one night."

Preita looked stunned, but she quickly recovered. We actors are good at rolling with punches. "I understand how you feel, Darach, but *I* didn't do that. My previous incarnation did."

"Maybe. But can you tell me that's a real silvarium bracelet this time?"

Preita opened her mouth to reply, but she said nothing, and after a moment she closed it again.

"Now that you know I know—and more importantly, *they* do—" I nodded toward her bracelet, "—I guess I'm officially a threat to the Ng. I know they won't try anything here. Too many witnesses. But I imagine it won't take them long to get around to doing something about me. You may serve as their eyes and ears, but I'm sure they have other agents willing to serve as their hands as well." I wondered how long it would be before I received a visit from one.

I drank the last of my bitterroot before getting out of the booth. "Time for me to leave. I need to get ready for tonight's show." I managed a smile. "Who knows? It may turn out to be my farewell performance."

I left then, and I didn't look back. I was tired, in so many ways, and I wasn't looking forward to stepping onto the stage tonight, but you know the old adage: the show must go on.

Even when you no longer have the heart for it.

DRINKING GAMES

Kristine Kathryn Rusch

Hands fumbling, fingers shaking, head aching, Rikki leaned one shoulder against the wall, blocking the view of the airlock controls from the corridor. Elio Testrail leaned against the wall at her feet. She hoped he looked drunk.

Things hadn't gone as planned. Things never went as planned—she should have learned that a long time ago. But she kept thinking she'd get better with each job.

She completed each job. That was a victory, or at least, that felt like one right now.

Her heart pounded, her breath came in short gasps. If she couldn't get a deep lungful of air, her fingers would keep shaking, not that it made any difference.

Why weren't spaceships built to a universal standard? Why couldn't she just follow the same moves with every piece of equipment that had the same name? Instead, she had to study old specs, which were always wrong, and then she had to improvise, which was always dicey, and then she had to worry that somehow, with one little flick of a fingernail, she'd touch the wrong piece, which would set off an alarm, which would bring the security guards running.

High-end ships like this one always had security guards, and the damn guards always thought they were some kind of cop which, she supposed, in the vast emptiness that was space, they were.

Someone had fused the alarm to the computer control for the airlock doors, which meant that unless she could figure out a way to unfuse, this stupid airlock was useless to her. Which meant she had to haul Testrail to yet another airlock on a different deck, one that wouldn't be as private as this one, and it would be just her luck that the airlock controls one deck up (or one deck down) would be just as screwy as the controls on this deck.

She cursed. Next spaceport—the big kind with every damn thing in the universe plus a dozen other damn things she hadn't even thought of—she would sign up for some kind of maintenance course, one that specialized in space cruisers, since she found herself on so many of them, or maybe even some university course in mechanics or design or systems analysis, so that she wouldn't waste precious minutes trying to pry open something that didn't want to get pried.

She cursed again, and then a third time for good measure, but the words weren't helping. She poked at that little fused bit inside the control, and felt her fingernail rip, which caused her to suck in a breath—no curse words for that kind of pain, sharp and tiny, the kind that could cause her (if she were a little less cautious) to pull back and stick the offending nail inside her mouth.

She'd done that once, set off a timer for an explosive device she'd been working on, just managed to dive behind the blast shield (she estimated) fifteen seconds before the damn thing blew.

So she had her little reflexes under control.

It was the big reflexes that worried her.

"Need help?" Male voice. Deep. Authoritative.

She didn't jump. She didn't even flinch. But she did freeze in place for a half second, which she knew was a give-away, one of those moments like little kids had when they got caught doing something wrong.

"I'm fine, thanks," she said without turning around. No sense in letting him see her face.

"Your friend doesn't look fine." He had just a bit of an accent, something that told her Standard wasn't his native language.

"He's drunk," she said.

"Looks dead to me," he said.

She turned, assessing her options as she did. One knife. (People were afraid of knives, but knives were messy; hard to clean up the blood.) Two laser pistols. (One tiny, against her ankle, hard to reach. The other on her hip, obvious, but lasers in a corridor—dangerous. They'd bounce off the walls, might hit her.) Fists. (Might break something, hands already shaking. Didn't need the additional risk.)

Then stopped assessing when she saw him.

He wasn't what she expected. Tall, white blond hair, the kind that got noticed (funny, she hadn't noticed him, but then there were 2,000 passengers on this damn ship).

Broad shoulders, strong bones—not a spacer then. Blue eyes with long lashes, like a girl's almost, but he didn't look girly, not with that aquiline nose and those high cheekbones. Thin lips twisted into a slight smile, a *knowing* smile, as if he knew what she was doing.

He wore gray pants and an ivory shirt without a single stain on it. No rings, no tattoos, no visible scars—and no uniform.

Not security, then. Or at least, not security that happened to be on duty.

"He's drunk," she said again, hoping Testrail's face was turned slightly. She'd managed to close his eyes, but he had that pallor the newly dead sometimes acquired. Blood wasn't flowing; it was pooling, and that leached all the color from his skin.

"So he's drunk, and you're messing with the airlock controls, because you want to get him, what? Some fresh air?" The man's eyes twinkled.

He was disgustingly handsome, and he knew it. She hated men like that, and thought longingly of her knife. One slash across the cheek. That would teach him.

"Guess I've had a little too much to drink myself," she said.

"Oh, for godssake," the man said as he approached her.

She reached for the knife, but he caught her wrist with one hand. He smelled faintly of sandalwood, and that, for some reason, made her breath catch.

He slammed the airlock controls with his free fist, and that made the damn alarm go off and the first of the double doors open.

"What the hell?" she snapped.

He sighed, as if she were the dumbest person he had ever met, then let her go. She did reach for the knife as he bent at the waist and picked up Testrail with one easy move.

She knew that move wasn't easy. She'd used an over-the-shoulder carry to get the bastard down here, after having rigged the corridor cameras to show footage from two hours before. Not that that did any good now, now that this asshole had set off the alarm.

He tossed Testrail into the airlock itself, then reached inside, and triggered the outer door. He barely got his hand back into the corridor before the inner door closed, protecting them from the vacuum of space.

"What the hell?" she asked again.

The man gave her a withering glance. "He was dead, you were going to toss him out, and then you were going to go about your business as is nothing happened. I just helped you along a little."

"And now every security agent on the ship will come down here," she snapped.

"Yeah," he said. "But it won't be a problem."

"It won't be a problem?" she asked.

But he already had his arm tightly around her shoulder, and he pulled her along. "C'mon," he said. "Stagger a little."

"What?" she asked, letting him pull her along. Her hand was still on her knife, but she didn't close her fist around the hilt. Not yet.

"Do you know any drinking songs?" he asked.

"Know any . . . what?"

"*Stagger*," he said, and she did without much effort, since he was pulling her alongside him, not allowing her feet to find a rhythm.

They stepped onto the between-decks platform, which she loathed because it was open, not a true elevator at all, and he said, "Down," and the stupid thing jerked before it went down, and suddenly she was on corridor cameras.

"Do you know any drinking songs?" he asked again.

"No," she said, ready with an answer this time. "I don't drink."

"No wonder you lack creativity," he said, and added, "Stop," as they passed their third deck. He dragged her down the corridor to the airlock, and slammed it with his fist.

Another alarm went off as the inner door opened, and he reached inside, triggering the outer door.

"What the hell are you doing?" she asked again.

"Is that the only question you know?" he asked.

"Just answer me," she said as he turned her around and headed back toward the between-decks platform.

"Weren't you ever a teenager?" he asked.

"Of course I was," she said.

"Then you should know what I'm doing," he said.

"Well color me clueless," she said, "because I don't."

His eyebrows went up as he looked at her. "Color you clueless? What kind of phrase is that?"

"The kind of phrase you say when someone won't tell you what the hell they're doing."

"Watch and learn, babe," he said. "Watch and learn."

He took them to the platform again, and as it lurched downward, he pulled her toward him using just his arm and the hand clutching her shoulder. A practiced move, and a strong one, considering how much resistance she was putting up.

He held her in a viselike grip, and then, before she could move away, kissed her. She was so startled, she didn't pull back.

At least, that was what she told herself when he did let go and she realized that her lips were bruised, her hand had fallen away from the hilt of her knife, her heart was pounding rapidly.

"Yum," he said, as if she had been particularly tasty, and then he grinned. He was unbelievably handsome when he smiled, and she didn't like that either, but before her addled brain figured out what to do, he added, "Stop," as they reached one of the lowest decks.

He propelled her forward with that mighty arm of his, and she tripped stepping from the platform into the corridor, which was a good thing, since a male passenger stood near the platform, looking confused.

The passenger, middle-aged, overweight, tired, like most everyone else on week three of an interstellar cruise, peered at them.

The man beside her grinned, said, "Is this the way to the lounge?" and then kept going.

The male passenger said, "What lounge?" but they were already too far away to answer him.

They reached yet another airlock and the man hit the controls with his fist, setting off yet another alarm and doing his little trick with the doors.

This time he kept going straight, swaying a little, knocking her off balance.

"Too bad you don't know any drinking songs," he said. "But then, you don't smell like booze. Enhancer, maybe? Too many mood elevators? No, that doesn't work. You're not smiling."

They rounded a corner, and came face to face with three terrified security guards, standing in three-point formation, laser rifles drawn.

"Stop!" one of them, a man as middle-aged and heavyset as that passenger, yelled. He didn't sound nearly as in control as Rikki's companion had when he told the platforms to stop. In fact this guy, this so-called guard, sounded dangerously close to panicked.

Rikki stopped, but the man didn't and neither did his arm, so he nearly shoved her forward, but she'd faced laser rifles before, and had even been shot with one, and she'd never forget how the damn thing burned, and she wasn't going to get shot again.

"Ah, jeez, Rik," the man said, and she jolted. The bastard knew her name. Not the name she was using on this cruise. Her real name. "Let's go."

"I said stop," the guard repeated.

"*You*," the man said, turning to the guard, "are too tense. C'mon with us. We're heading to the lounge."

"What lounge?" the only female guard asked. Not only was she the sole female, but she was the only one in what Rikki would consider regulation shape. Trim, sharp, but terrified too. Her rifle vibrated, probably because she wasn't bracing it right.

Amateurs.

"I dunno what lounge," the man holding Rikki said. "The *closest* lounge."

He grinned as if he had discovered some kind of prize, and if she didn't know better, she would've thought he was on something.

"You've gotta be kidding me," the third guard said. "Is that what this is all about?"

"I dunno," the man said, "but you sure got a lotta doors leading to nothing around here. Where's the damn lounge? I paid good money to have a lounge on each floor and I been to—what, hon? Three floors? Four—"

He looked at Rikki as he said that and pinched the nerve on her outer arm at the same time. She squeaked and hopped just a little as he continued,

"—and we ain't found no damn lounge anywhere. I wanna drink. I wanna enhancer. I wanna burger. Real meat. You got real meat on this crappy ship?"

The first security guard sighed, then lowered his rifle. The other man did the same, but the woman didn't.

"Oh for god's sake," the female security guard said to the guard in front. "You gonna let them get away with this just because they're drunk?"

"I'm not drunk," Rikki said, and the man pulled her close again so that she had to put a hand against his waist to steady herself.

He tried to kiss her again, but she moved her face away. "She's not drunk," he said, rather grumpily, "because we can't find the damn lounge."

The front guard shook his head.

"They opened three airlocks," the female guard said.

"They're passengers," the male guard hissed at her.

"Reckless ones," the female guard said.

"What's your room?" the guard asked.

"Um . . ." the man said, his hand so tight around Rikki's upper arm that he was cutting off circulation. "B Deck, Something-something, 15A?"

"If you're on B-Deck, it would be 15B," the female guard said.

The man extended his free hand. "'S on here," he said, and to Rikki's surprise, let them scan the back of his hand to get the code upscale passengers had embedded into the skin so they didn't have to carry identification.

"B Deck," the female guard said to the others, "Section 690 15B."

"Suite," the male guard hissed again. "Expensive."

Rikki tried not to raise her own eyebrows. She had a cabin, K Deck, without a view. Cheap.

"We'll take you to a lounge," the male guard said to the man holding Rikki, "but we're going to have to fine you."

"For taking me to a lounge?" He sounded indignant. "Jus' tell me where to go."

"I'd love to," the female guard said.

"No," the male guard said. "We'll fine you for the airlocks."

"Not interested in a damn airlock," the man said. "Wanna lounge."

The second male guard shook his head. "I need a new job," he said softly to the woman.

"Good luck with that," she said back to him.

"I've got your information," the male guard said to

the man holding Rikki. "I'll be adding 6,000 credits to your account. Two for each airlock you opened."

"Didn't open no damn airlock," the man said.

"We'll talk about it when you're sober," the male guard said.

"Don't plan to be sober any more this entire trip. Too damn dull." The man glared at him. "You said lounge. Where's the damn lounge?"

"This way," the guard said, and headed off down the corridor.

The man holding Rikki lurched after him, dragging Rikki along. She tripped again, this time because her toe caught the man's heel. He was doing that on purpose, but she didn't argue. She was slightly breathless from the strangeness of it all, and from the way he held her.

The other two guards followed a good distance behind, clearly arguing.

The first guard led them to an actual elevator, in the main section of the ship. Four other passengers stood inside, three women, one man, all older than Rikki, all better dressed. They eyed her as if she lowered their net worth by factors of ten.

The man holding her grinned at them. It was a silly, sloppy grin, and it made him seem harmless. "You goin' to the lounge too?" he asked.

She realized as he slurred his words, all trace of that accent was gone.

The four passengers leaned against the walls, and looked away, wanting nothing to do with him.

They got off on the main level, but the guard led

Rikki and the man to B Deck and took them to the B-Deck-Only lounge.

"It's exclusive," he said to the man. "Just touch the door with your fist, like you did with the airlocks."

She stiffened. The man holding her had ID embedded in his hand. They had known who he was from the moment he hit the first airlock.

That was why she stayed below decks. Cheaper. No identification required.

He grinned at the guard and gave him a mock salute. "You need a favor, friend, I'm there for you," he said, then slapped his palm against the door to the B-Deck lounge.

The guard nodded, almost smiling himself. "You won't say that tomorrow when you look at your accounts."

"Hell, I got enough. Should tip you, really," the man said.

"No, you shouldn't." The guard was smiling now. "Enjoy your evening, sir."

The guard stepped back as the door slid open. The man staggered inside, pulling Rikki along. The noise startled her—conversation and music, live music, and a view. The entire wall was clear, showing the exterior of the ship, darkness, pinpoints of light, patterns she didn't recognize.

Full tables, filled with overdressed passengers, laughing, talking, a few waving drinks. Some people at a roulette wheel to the left, others at a card table to the right, some sitting on couches, leaning against each other, listening to the music.

No one noticed as Rikki and the man holding her entered.

"Thanks," Rikki said, starting to pull away, but he held her tighter.

"Not yet, babe," he said as if he had the right to call her "babe." He pulled her to the bar, slammed his fist on it as if it were an airlock control, and said, "Two cervezas, por favor," and the accent was back, thick, and wrong. He clearly didn't speak Spanish either, at least not like a native, so he wasn't from Earth, not that Earthers were common this far out.

The bartender—a real person, male, wearing a blousy shirt with tight sleeves, matching pants and some kind of decorative apron—poured two amber-colored beers with an expression of distaste. The foam flowed down the side of both glasses.

Rikki fumbled for her credit slip, but the man caught her hand. "On me, sweets," he said.

Then he grabbed his beer, still holding her, and started for a table, stopping suddenly, and nearly spilling.

"You need your drink," he said with the mock seriousness only the really drunk seemed to have.

He backed up, but didn't turn around, so she had to move slightly to grab her beer. The glass was cool and wet beneath her fingers, the foam yeasty, like real beer, not the stuff they served below decks.

His grip on her wasn't as strong, and she knew she could shake him off. But she wasn't quite ready to now.

She let him lead her to an empty love seat near the

clear wall. The material between her and space itself looked thin and unreliable, even though she knew it wasn't. It made her dizzy, especially when she realized she could see herself reflected against the view.

She did look out of it, hair messed, shirt askew, pants stained along one thigh. Shadows under her eyes, cheeks hollow, too thin by half, but muscled. Hard to miss the muscles, even with the shirt twisted.

He kept his arm around her shoulder until they reached the love seat. Then he slid his hand up to her clavicle, and shoved hard, so that she either toppled sideways or sat down.

She sat, without spilling a drop. Apparently, her shaking had left her long ago.

"Do you always manhandle people you've just met?" she asked as he sat beside her.

His smile was different now, slightly feral, revealing a perfect row of teeth. "How do you know we just met?"

Her pulse increased. She studied him again. White blond, blue eyed, naturally pale skin, not the pasty stuff that came from living in space. Mid-thirties, maybe younger, stronger than she was, which was saying something, and—oh, yeah—he knew her name.

"What was all that?" she asked.

"Just me, saving your ass," he said.

"I don't need saving," she said softly.

"Oh, honey, yes you do." He sipped the beer, made a satisfied sound, and leaned back on the love seat.

"Well," she said, and set her glass down, resisting the urge to wipe her soggy hand on her pants. "Let me thank you for the beer and the grand adventure, but—"

"No," he said, catching her arm. "You're not leaving."

"Why?"

"Because the entire crew of this ship thinks we're here to drink, so we're going to drink. We're going to get roaring drunk. We're going to dance and laugh, and come close to screwing right here in the lounge. Someone'll tell us to go to our room, which we'll do, and then we'll look mighty sick when we come out, twenty-four hours later. Hung-over, queasy, because we forgot to take something before we decided to get drunk. Might help if you can puke on cue. Can you puke on cue?"

"Are you kidding?" she asked.

"Just hoping," he said, and sipped his beer again. "So drink up, milady. It's gonna be a long night."

He wouldn't talk to her any more, at least about important stuff. He drank more than she'd ever seen anyone drink, and he glared at her if she didn't keep up.

She wouldn't have to pretend queasy, she was getting queasy. He ordered food and told her to eat some, and it helped the queasy, but not the sickly swirly feeling in her head.

She never drank on the job. She never drank off the job. She hated enhancers, hated this out-of-control feeling but, she had to admit, she'd had the out-of-control feeling since she met the son of a bitch who, she realized halfway through the evening, hadn't told her his name.

They were on the dance floor when she mentioned it, whispered it actually, in his right ear, and he pulled her even closer, then he slid his hands down to her ass, and kissed her. Kissed her as hard as he had earlier, maybe even harder, kissed her so hard that she couldn't breathe, and wasn't sure she wanted to.

Still, she tried to pull away, but he brought one hand up and placed it on the back of her head. "Not so fast," he whispered in his not-drunk voice. "Information has a price. You want my name? You buy it, one kiss at a time."

Then he kissed her again, and she didn't fight, she really didn't want to fight if she told herself the truth. He was a good kisser, the best she'd ever kissed on the job or off, and she decided it wouldn't be a hardship to back him against the wall, peel off his clothes, and take him right here in the lounge, the *exclusive* lounge, here on B-Deck.

But part of her brain told her—the rational, always in-control part—she really was drunk or at least tipsy (hell, no, drunk) and the desire to screw him brainless probably came from the alcohol. Still, he was handsome, he tasted good, he smelled good, and he was as aroused as she was, so she reached inside his shirt, and he said,

"Room. Need to go to the room."

And the voice sounded drunk again. He'd been sober before, telling her—what? Something about information. He put his hand around her again, only this time reached inside her shirt, and tweaked her nipple and it felt damn good, and someone said something about leaving and he said they were and could they have one for the road? And the bartender gave them an amber bottle.

They staggered out into the corridor—and she really was staggering this time—and the door closed, the air was cooler, smelling fresher, and she felt—oh, still dizzy, but she didn't care—and he took her hand, pulling her along, *much better this way*, she thought, not being forced to move with him, but moving because she wanted to, through all the corridors down to the end of the hall and big double doors that opened as he approached into one of the largest suites she'd ever seen. The living room alone was four times the size of her room.

The doors closed, he held up a hand, and took out something—some kind of zapit that disrupted audio— and set it down, then said something about names.

She didn't give a good goddamn about names and said so, muttered, "Bed," and he laughed, taking her up a curving flight of stairs (stairs! On a ship!) into a room with a bed the size of her first apartment, and she was the one who pulled him on it, she was the one who tore off his clothes, she was the one who was finally, finally in control.

She woke up the next morning, sprawled, naked and sore, on the bed of a man she didn't know, in a room that had to cost as much as she earned in an entire year.

He wasn't in bed next to her, although the sheets were mussed. He was standing near the door, wearing pants, a shirt half buttoned, barefoot, holding a glass of something foamy, which reminded her of the beer, and made her stomach lurch.

"Misha," he said.

"What?" Her head ached too. God, how much had she had to drink? Her mouth tasted like dirty socks.

"My name," he said. "It's Misha. I figured you earned that much."

Earned it. She didn't like the idea of earned, as if she'd paid for it with sex. A lot of sex. Damn. How many times had they—

"And yes, we met," he said, "but I doubt you remember."

It was as if they were having a conversation she didn't remember either. Her head hurt, and she brought a hand to her eyes. They felt gummy and sore. Everything was sore. And she had bruises on her wrist. Had he done that?

She could remember parts, but not all of it.

What she remembered confirmed why her inner thighs felt sticky.

"Here," he said, and handed her the foamy liquid. "Drink it fast and try not to taste it."

She glanced at him through her splayed fingers. He looked serious, and younger than she remembered. Hadn't she thought him mid-thirties? His body was mid-thirties—flat abdomen, visible muscles, and at least half a dozen scars—but his face was maybe fifteen, at least at the moment, without the feral smile. He had shadows under his eyes, and his mouth turned downward, as if a frown were his natural expression.

She had no idea who he was. Misha? She didn't remember a Misha, even though he said they had met before.

She shouldn't take the drink. But if he were going to hurt her, he would have done it last night, while she slept.

She sat up, the sheet falling away. Bruising on her skin—finger marks, love bites. She even remembered some of them, and the memories aroused her all over again, despite the headache and queasy stomach.

He leaned forward, handing her the glass as if he didn't want their fingers to touch. She took it, and following instructions, downed it.

It tasted like carbonated bile with a touch of dog hair, but she managed to swallow it all without getting sick.

Her stomach settled the minute the crap touched it, and slowly her headache eased.

"What was that?" she asked.

"A couple of alcohol antidotes mixed with an emergency scrubber that I always carry," he said. "Works, even if it tastes like day-old vomit."

She grimaced, then wiped her mouth with the back of her hand. She no longer felt hung-over, although she did feel wrung out.

"What happened last night?" she asked.

He smiled and looked pointedly at her breasts. "If you don't remember—"

"I mean," she said, not wanting him to continue. "What were you doing, following me?"

"Of course I was following you," he said.

She sat rigidly, her fingers still cupped around the glass. Her heart rate increased.

"Who trained you?" he asked.

"What do you mean?" she said, trying to keep her voice calm.

"C'mon," he said. "We're past games. You've been killing your way through this part of the sector, and you've managed to eliminate some primo targets. Somehow."

A sarcastic emphasis on the word "somehow" made her glare.

"Someone trained you," he said. "I'm just wondering who."

"No one trained me," she said, and couldn't quite keep the pride out of her voice. She had stumbled into this profession, literally. She'd accidentally killed a man in a bar, and another man handed her a small fortune in thanks. Then asked her if she'd do it again, if he protected her from the consequences.

She liked to think she had qualms about it, but she didn't. Not really. She quickly figured out that people who had a price on their head deserved that price, and sometimes deserved a much larger one.

"No one trained you." Misha's mobile mouth pursed for a brief second. "That explains a lot."

"What the hell does that mean?" she asked.

He stared at her, his expression flat. Now he looked ageless, maybe twenty, maybe fifty. But deadly.

She was, for the first time, truly conscious of her nakedness, and how vulnerable it made her. But she also knew better than to draw attention to it by getting up and getting dressed. She'd do that, but slowly, and not as a reaction to his expression, no matter how hard her heart was pounding.

"It means," he said, "you get noticed."

"I do not." She used that bit of sharpness to throw the covers back, step out of bed. He didn't stop her. She grabbed her blouse. It was ripped on one side. Dammit. "No one is looking for me."

"True enough," he said. "But your deaths look like kills. They don't look natural."

"So?"

"So, the authorities know someone's operating in their territories," he said.

She slipped the blouse on, and picked up her pants. The stain down one leg was brown. She didn't want to think about that.

He grabbed a package from the chair beside the bed. "Here," he said. "Try these." And tossed the package at her.

She caught it. It was soft. She opened it. Tan pants, a faded pink blouse, underclothes. Took her a minute to realize they were all hers.

"Where'd you get this?"

"Your room," he said.

"I thought we weren't going to leave this room," she said, remembering that much of their conversation the night before.

"No one knows I left," he said, and for the first time, she believed him.

She took off the ruined blouse, left the stained pants crumpled on the floor, and carried the package toward the bathroom. Clean clothes meant she needed a clean body.

He followed.

"Privacy," she said.

"No," he said. "Besides, we're not done talking."

"I am," she said.

He caught her arm, fingers tight around her elbow.

She had the stray thought that he could twist his hand slightly and break her arm.

"You're bungling your way through my territory," he said.

"*Your* territory?" she asked.

"My territory," he said. "Because of you, I've been questioned and arrested and denied passage on more than one ship."

"So they know who you are and they don't know me." She shrugged. "Guess I'm more successful."

He pulled her close, that flat look in his eyes still there. Her heart rate increased again, and she knew he felt it.

"They know me because I'm registered."

"How quaint," she said. "I didn't know anyone registered any more."

He was so close that his arm brushed against her stomach. "My mother was legal," he said. "She worked for a variety of governments, then went out on her own. She trained me."

"Goody for you," Rikki said.

He pulled her against him, her skin against his shirtless torso. His skin was hot. He slid his free hand on her buttocks and it took everything she had not to lean in closer.

"Three times I've had to prove I have nothing to do with you," he said, "and that's three times too many."

"So?"

"So I could have shoved you through that airlock last night, claiming I was saving Testrail. I didn't. I saved you."

She froze. He not only knew her name; he knew Testrail's too. "What is this?"

"This is me, improvising," he said.

"Improvising what?" she asked.

"I hired you," he said.

"You did?"

"How better to get you on board this ship?" he said. "I've been following you too long, cleaning up after you, getting blamed for you. I figured I'd watch Testrail until you came for him, and then I'd get you."

Her eyes narrowed. Her breathing was rapid, even though she didn't want it to be. "I thought that was a legitimate job."

"There's money in your account," he said.

"Why would you want Testrail dead?" she asked. What little she knew of the man—and she knew very little, preferring to keep her victims as anonymous as possible—was that he was some kind of corporate mucky-muck whose mismanagement had cost billions, and sent entire communities into financial disarray, with all that entailed, resulting in heart attacks, suicides, and a few murders, none of which could be pinned on him, and all caused by him.

His death didn't solve anything, but it made the other victims feel better. She had always liked those jobs. She felt constructive then.

"I wanted Testrail dead because I was hired to kill him," Misha said.

"So you had me do your dirty work," she said.

He shook his head. "I would have made sure he died in a way that threw suspicion on no one."

"How would that satisfy the client?" she asked.

"I *am* the client," he said.

"I mean your client," she said.

He gave her a sideways look. "I'd've let him know in advance that on this date at that time, Testrail would commit suicide. Then Testrail, for all intents and purposes, would have committed suicide at that instant. My client and I would know he had help dying, but no one else would."

"Aren't you efficient?" Rikki said.

"I am," Misha said. "That's why I get hired."

"But this wasn't the kind of job a registered assassin would do," she said.

"How do you know what a registered assassin would do?" he asked.

"I know what they won't do," she said. "That's why I get hired. Is that why you hired me?"

"No," he said. "I take off-the-books jobs. Most of us do."

He moved his hand up to her lower back, then rubbed his thumb in a small circle just above the base of her spine. Who knew that was an erogenous zone?

She tried to ignore it.

"I hired you," he said, "so I could track you."

"If you were good, you should have tracked me before."

He let her go and stepped back. She felt the physical loss, but she didn't move.

"I was going to kill you," he said. "In the act."

"The hero defense," she said. "Why didn't you?"

His gaze met hers, and something flickered through his blue eyes, something she didn't quite recognize. Desire? Anger? She couldn't quite tell.

"Because you were amusing," he said.

Whatever she had expected, it hadn't been that. "Amusing?"

"You did everything out of order. You seduce him—which, I must say, was effective—and then you break his neck. Then you realize you need to dispose of the body, so you get him down to the airlock—"

"I planned that," she said.

He smiled. "Sort of," he said. "You planned it sort of. You wanted to screw him in the hallway, but he was a prude. He wouldn't go. If he'd gone down there with you, then you could have broken his neck and shoved him out before he knew what hit him. But he wouldn't go, and you got disgusted by him—"

"I did not," she said.

"I saw that look on your face when he had his arms around you. You looked like you'd stuck your hand in a pile of garbage."

She had felt that way too. So he had been watching—from somewhere. "I'm not a prostitute," she said.

"Obviously," he said, and she felt a slight sting in his words. He must have noticed her expression—again—and his smile grew. "I meant, with him. With me, you seemed genuine enough."

She *had* been genuine. For godssake, this man attracted her, and he knew it. But she didn't tell him that.

He was arrogant enough.

"The man had no adventure in his soul, and no amount of cajoling was going to change him, so you got frustrated and snapped his neck."

She had. Dammit.

"Then you had to get him to the airlock. Nice work that. I'm amazed no one saw you. First you dragged him, and then when you knew the cameras were disabled, you carried him. You're stronger than you look."

He tucked a strand of hair behind her ear, then cupped her chin. "But it was the airlock itself that I found most appealing." He let his hand fall away. "Why didn't you study the specs?"

"I did," she said, "but they changed them."

"Hmm," he said as if he didn't believe her. "You were trying to avoid the alarm, which was the least of your problems."

"Oh?"

"Standing in the corridor with a dead man, that was your biggest problem," he said.

"I was trying to solve that," she snapped.

"Not well," he said. "So I stepped in."

"You stepped in because I couldn't open an airlock?" she asked.

"No," he said, grinning. "Because you made me laugh."

She bristled. "It wasn't funny."

"It was ridiculous. No one who had training would have done any of the things you did."

"But it worked. He's dead."

"And gone," Misha said. "But here's the rub, Rikki. Two thousand passengers boarded this ship. One thousand nine hundred and ninety nine will disembark. Someone will eventually notice the discrepancy and want to know why. Then they'll look for someone like me."

"Yes, well, they shouldn't have trouble finding you, since you're hiding so well," she said indulging in her own bit of sarcasm.

"I don't have to hide," he said. "This is my job. It's people like you that screw me up."

She glared at him. "So you want to train me so that you don't get arrested."

"Yes," he said.

She rolled her eyes and continued to the suite's bathroom. He followed.

"I'm not going to train so you can feel better," she said as she went through the clear door.

He caught it before she could close it. "It's not so that I feel better," he said. "Some day, you'll screw up so badly that someone will kill you."

"What does that matter to you?" she asked. "You were going to kill me until you realized I made you laugh."

He studied her for a moment. "You don't remember how we met, do you?"

"No," she said flatly.

His gaze met hers. That look again, the one she couldn't quite read, passed through his eyes.

"I'm the one who dragged you out of that burning room," he said softly. "The night my mother killed your father. The night you realized that sometimes the universe is a better place without certain people in it."

Her chest ached suddenly, like it had that night, the house burning around her. The boy—he wasn't much older than she was—arm around her shoulder, pulling her forward, like he had done in the corridor just the night before, pulling her, keeping her on her feet, getting her out.

It'll be all right, he said. *He won't hurt you any more.*

Misha had all the scars, on his chest and his back, scars from a dozen different wounds. She'd had hers removed, but they remained, just like his. None of his scars were burns.

None of hers were either.

And none of hers were inflicted after her father died. In that fire, or so everyone believed.

She never said a word about the woman who had come into the living room of their modest house or the blond boy who had stood silently behind her, watching her work.

Rikki's father had begged. He had always told Rikki that begging got you nowhere, and he had been right. It had gotten him nowhere.

The woman had killed him as easily as Rikki had killed Testrail. One sudden movement, the snap of a neck, and the fire, so easily set in barracks houses.

Later, they said it was for the good that her father had died. He'd been selling governmental secrets. He would have been indicted, things would have come out. Better that it all ended.

And someone—the woman at the hospital who had led her away from the boy, who had put Rikki into state custody—had said, *Sometimes it's better not to say what you saw*, as if she had known.

She had known. Rikki became convinced of that much later. Much later.

"When did you know who I was?" she asked. "When you hired me?"

He shook his head. "When you registered on the ship. You used your own name."

"Why not?" she said. "I'm not wanted."

"Not yet," he said. "Maybe not ever if you let me train you."

"Why would you do that?" she asked. "Because you saved my life once?"

For a half second, she thought he was going to nod. Then half of his mouth turned up in a smile, as if the thought bemused him.

"Because," he said with that trace of an accent, "when I tucked you under my arm in that corridor last night, I wanted to kiss you. I haven't wanted to kiss anyone in very long time."

She had felt that too. That pull toward him. She still felt it.

Dammit.

"So you kissed me," she said. "Was it worth the risk?"

His grin reached his eyes. He was unbelievably handsome when he smiled. When he really smiled, and his eyes twinkled, and his entire face engaged.

"Only if," he said, "you let me kiss you again."

"Will that be part of the training?" she asked.

"I think that would be one of the benefits of training," he said, pulling her close.

"For whom?" she asked.

"For me," he said as he leaned in to kiss her. "Definitely for me."

She slipped her hands around him, feeling those scars on his skin. The kisses would be worthwhile for her as well.

But she wasn't going to tell him.

She wasn't going to tell him anything—not how relieved she was to get help nor how aroused she was whenever he got too close.

Although, she had a hunch he already knew that.

Or could guess.

After all, he was not a dumb man.

And she, for all her ineptness, was not a dumb woman. Just an untrained one.

Except in one area.

She looped her fingers around the waistband of his pants and pulled him into the bathroom.

"We're not supposed to leave for twenty-four hours," she said. "We'll need to keep busy."

"Doing what?" he asked.

"Let me show you," she said, and kicked the door shut.

ABOUT THE AUTHORS

In addition to writing stories in the science fiction, fantasy, horror, thriller, and comedy genres for anthologies like, *Steampunk'd, Timeshares, Zombie Raccoons & Killer Bunnies, Imaginary Friends, The Dimension Next Door, Front Lines*, and *Fellowship Fantastic*, Donald J. Bingle is the author of *Forced Conversion* and *GREENSWORD: A Tale of Extreme Global Warming*. Also check out his webpage at www.donaldjbingle.com for complete writing information and an update on his most recent novel, a spy thriller. He is a member of the Science Fiction and Fantasy Writers of America, the International Thriller Writers, the International Association of Media Tie-In Writers, the GenCon Writer's Symposium, and the St. Charles Writers Group.

Lois McMaster Bujold was born in Columbus, Ohio, in 1949; she now lives in Minneapolis. She began reading SF at age nine. Romances came later, when she discovered

Georgette Heyer in her early twenties. She started writing for professional publication in 1982, a goal achieved in 1986 with her first three SF novels, *Shards of Honor, The Warrior's Apprentice*, and *Ethan of Athos*. Bujold went on to write the Nebula-winning *Falling Free* and many other books featuring her popular character Miles Naismith Vorkosigan, his family, friends, and enemies. The series includes three Hugo Award-winning novels; readers interested in learning more about the far-flung Vorkosigan clan are encouraged to start with the omnibus *Cordelia's Honor*. Her books have appeared on numerous bestsellers lists, and have been translated into seventeen languages. A fan-run website devoted to her work, The Bujold Nexus, may be found at www.dendarii .com.

After starting out in science fiction and fantasy, Lillian Stewart Carl is now writing contemporary novels blending mystery, romace, and fantasy, along with short mystery and fantasy stories. Among many other novels, such as the romantic fantasy *Blackness Tower* and the spiritual thriller *Lucifer's Crown,* Lillian is the author of the Jean Fairbain/Alasdair Cameron cross-genre mystery series—America's exile and Scotland's finest on the trail of all-too-living legends—which concludes with *The Blue Hackle*. Her second short story collection, *The Muse and Other Stories of History, Mystery, and Myth*, appeared in 2007. She has lived for many years in North Texas, in a book-lined cloister cleverly disguised as a tract house. Her web site is *http://www. lillianstewartcarl.com*

Brenda Cooper has published fiction in, *Nature*, *Analog*, *Oceans of the Mind*, *Strange Horizons*, in the anthologies, *Sun in Glory*, *Maiden, Matron, Crone, Time After Time*, and more. Brenda's collaborative fiction with Larry Niven has appeared in *Analog* and *Asimov's*. She and Larry have a collaborative novel, *Building Harlequin's Moon*, available now in bookstores. Her solo novel, *The Silver Ship and the Sea*, was released in 2007. Brenda lives in Bellevue, Washington, with her partner Toni, Toni's daughter, Katie, a border collie, and a golden retriever. By day, she is the City of Kirkland's CIO, and at night and in early morning hours, she's a futurist and writer. So she's trying to both save and entertain the world, with sometimes comical results as the two activities collide, and sometimes, blend. Neither, of course, is entirely possible.

Anita Ensal has always been intrigued by possibilities inherent in myths and legends. She likes to find both the fantastical element in the mundane and the ordinary component within the incredible. She writes in all areas of speculative fiction and is honored to be a part of this anthology. Her stories have also appeared in Eposic's, *The Book of Exodi,* and at Raphael's Village (www.raphaelsvillage.com), as well as in *Boondocks Fantasy*. You can read more from her at her blog, Fantastical Fiction, at www.anitaensal.blogspot.com.

Nina Kiriki Hoffman has been writing science fiction and fantasy for almost thirty years and has sold more than two hundred fifty stories, plus novels and juvenile and media tie-in books. Her works have been finalists for the World Fantasy, Philip K. Dick, Sturgeon, and Endeavour awards. Her first novel, *The Thread That Binds the Bones*, won a Bram Stoker Award, and her short story, "Trophy Wives," won a Nebula. Her middle school fantasy novel, *Thresholds*, came out in 2010. Nina does production work for *The Magazine of Fantasy & Science Fiction,* and teaches short story writing through her local community college. She also works with teen writers. She lives in Eugene, Oregon, with several cats, a mannequin, and many strange toys.

Sylvia Kelso lives in North Queensland, Australia, and writes fantasy and science fiction, usually set in analogue or outright Australian landscapes. She has a Creative Writing MA built around one SF Novel using alternate North Queenslands. Her short stories have appeared in *Antipodes: A North American Journal of Australian and New Zealand Literature*, and in US and Australian anthologies. Two of her five novels have been finalists for best fantasy novel in the Aurealis Australian genre fiction awards. A collection of Sylvia Kelso's essays entitled, *Three Observations and a Dialogue Round and About SF*, was released in 2009. Her most recent fantasy novel, *Source*, was released in 2010.

Jay Lake lives in Portland, Oregon, where he works on numerous writing and editing projects. His 2010 books are: *Pinion The Specific Gravity of Grief, The Baby Killers,* and *The Sky That Wraps*. His short fiction appears regularly in literary and genre markets worldwide. Jay is a winner of the John W. Campbell Award for Best New Writer, and a multiple nominee for the Hugo and World Fantasy Awards.

Jody Lynn Nye lists her main career activity as "spoiling cats." She lives northwest of Chicago with two of the above and her husband, author and packager, Bill Fawcett. She has published more than thirty-five books, including six contemporary fantasies, four SF novels, four novels in collaboration with Anne McCaffrey, including, *The Ship Who Won*; edited a humorous anthology about mothers, *Don't Forget Your Spacesuit, Dear!*; and written over a hundred short stories. Her latest books are, *An Unexpected Apprentice*, and *Myth-Chief*, co-written with Robert Asprin.

Shannon Page was born on Halloween night and spent her early years on a commune in northern California's backwoods. A childhood without television gave her a great love of books and the worlds she found in them. She wrote her first book, an adventure story starring her cat, at the age of seven. Sadly, that work is currently out of print, but her short fiction has appeared in *Clarkesworld*, *Interzone*, and *Fantasy* (with Jay Lake), *Black Static*, and several independent press anthologies. Shannon is a longtime practitioner of Ashtanga yoga, has no tattoos, and lives in Portland, Oregon, with nineteen orchids and an awful lot of books.

Kristine Kathryn Rusch is a bestselling, award-winning author who has written under a variety of names in fantasy, science fiction, mystery and romance. Her latest novel *Diving into the Wreck* is based on the award-winning novellas first published in *Asimov's SF Magazine*.

Steven H Silver is the publisher of ISFiC Press. He has edited anthologies for DAW (*Wondrous Beginnings, Magical Beginnings,* and *horrible Beginnings*) and two collections of Lester del Rey's work for NESFA Press (*War and Space* and *Robots and Magic*). His short fiction has appeared in *Helix SF* and *Zombie Raccoons and Killer Bunnies*. The founder of the Sidewise Award for Alternate History. He has been nominated for the Hugo Award in fan categories twelve times.

Dean Wesley Smith has been an editor, a publisher, and is the bestselling author of more than eighty books and more than one hundred short stories. Over the years he has won a World Fantasy Award, a Locus Award and others, and has been nominated for every major award in science fiction and fantasy. Over the past decade, Dean has worked a great deal in the *Star Trek™* universe, and still edits an annual anthology called *Star Trek: Strange New Worlds,* where he helps new writers and fans join into the fun of writing *Star Trek™*. As a former publisher, editor, and now full-time writer, Dean understands both sides of the business, and over the past decade has worked with just about every major publisher in New York.

Kelly Swails is a clinical microbiologist by day and a writer by night. Her short fiction has appeared in several anthologies, including *Boondocks Fantasy* and *Pando-*

ra's Closet. When she's not working or writing, she and her husband wrangle a houseful of cats. You can find her on the web at www.kellyswails.com.

Tim Waggoner's novels include *Pandora Drive*, *Thieves of Blood*, the *Godfire* duology: *Like Death* and *Nekropolis*. He's published more than eighty short stories, some of them collected in *All Too Surreal.* His articles on writing have appeared in *Writer's Digest*, *Writers Journal*, and other publications. He teaches creative writing at Sinclair Community College in Dayton, Ohio. Visit him on the web at www.timwaggoner.com.

ABOUT THE EDITORS

Martin H. Greenberg is the CEP of Tekno Books and its predecessor companies, now the largest book developer of commercial fiction and non-fiction in the world, with over 2,100 published books that have been translated into thirty-three languages. He is the recipient of an unprecedented four Lifetime Achievement Awards in the Science Fiction, Mystery, and Supernatural Horror genres—the Milford Award in Science Fiction, the Bram Stoker Award in Horror, the Ellery Queen Award in Mystery, and most recently, the Solstice Award for his work in science fiction—the only person in publishing history to have received all four awards.

Kerrie Hughes lives in Wisconsin after traveling throughout the states and seeing a bit of the world, but has a list of more travels to accomplish. She has a marvelous husband in John Helfers, four perfect cats, and a grown son who is beginning to suspect that his main purpose in life is to watch said cats and house while his parental units waste his inheritance on travel. Thank you, Justin. She has written seven short stories: "Judgment" in *Haunted Holidays*, "Geiko" in *Women of War*, "Doorways" in *Furry Fantastic*, "A Traveler's Guide to Valdemar" in *The Valdemar Companion*. And with John Helfers: "Between a Bank and a Hard Place" in *Texas Rangers*, "The Last Ride of the Colton Gang" in *Boot Hill*, and "The Tombstone Run" in *Lost Trails*. She has also written nonfiction, including the article "Bog Bodies" in *Haunted Museums*, and has edited two concordances: *The Vorkosigan Companion* and *The Valdemar Companion*. *Love and Rockets* is her ninth co-edited anthology, along with *Maiden Matron Crone, Children of Magic, Fellowship Fantastic, The Dimension Next Door, Gamer Fantastic, Zombie Raccoons and Killer Bunnies, Chicks Kick Ass,* and *The Girl's Guide to Guns and Monsters*.

Gini Koch

The Alien *Novels*

"This delightful romp has many interesting twists and turns as it glances at racism, politics, and religion en route. Darned amusing." —*Booklist* (starred review)

"Kitty's evolution from marketing manager to member of a secret government unit is amusing and interesting ...a hilarious romp in the vein of 'Men in Black' or 'Ghostbusters'." —*Voya*

ALIEN TANGO
978-0-7564-0632-5

TOUCHED BY AN ALIEN
978-0-7564-0600-4

To Order Call: 1-800-788-6262
www.dawbooks.com

Laura Resnick
Doppelgangster

"Resnick introduces a colorful cast of gangsters and their associates as she spins a witty, fast-paced mystery around her convincingly self-absorbed chorus-girl heroine. Sexy interludes raise the tension as she juggles magical assailants, her perennially distracted agent, her meddling mother, and wiseguys both friendly and threatening in a well-crafted, rollicking mystery."—*Publishers Weekly*

"Esther Diamond is the Stephanie Plum of urban fantasy! Unplug the phone and settle down for a fast and funny read!"—Mary Jo Putney

"*Dopplegangster* is a joy from start to finish, with a sexy hero, a smart heroine, a fascinating plot, and a troop of supporting characters both lovable and otherwise. It's a wonderful blend of comedy and surprising suspense. If you haven't met Esther Diamond yet, then you're missing out on a lot of fun."
—Linda Howard

978-0-7564-0595-3

To Order Call: 1-800-788-6262
www.dawbooks.com

DAW 145

Seanan McGuire

The October Daye *Novels*

"...will surely appeal to readers who enjoy my books, or those of Patrica Briggs." —*Charlaine Harris*

"Well researched, sharply told, highly atmospheric and as brutal as any pulp detective tale, this promising start to a new urban fantasy series is sure to appeal to fans of Jim Butcher or Kim Harrison."—*Publishers Weekly*

ROSEMARY AND RUE
978-0-7564-0571-7
A LOCAL HABITATION
978-0-7564-0596-0
AN ARTIFICIAL NIGHT
978-0-7564-0626-4

To Order Call: 1-800-788-6262
www.dawbooks.com

DAW 142